D0107544

New England Mysteries

Book #1 - *A Cold Morning in MAINE,*
published in October, 2014.
ISBN 978-0-9962397-0-7

Book #2 - *A Quiet Evening in CONNECTICUT,*
published in April, 2015.
ISBN 978-0-9962397-1-4

Book #3 - *A Bad Night in NEW HAMPSHIRE,*
published in November, 2015.
ISBN 978-0-9962397-2-1

Book #4 - *a PIZZA NIGHT in the BAHAMAS,*
published in November, 2016.
ISBN 978-0-9962397-3-8

Bookstores, kindle and amazon – audio books
available from audible.com and iTunes.

www.nemysteries.com

A Hot Afternoon in

MASSACHUSETTS

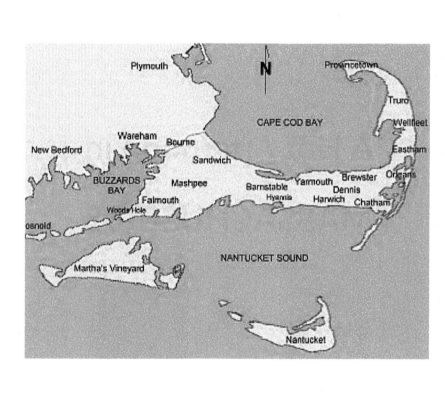

A Hot Afternoon in

MASSACHUSETTS

Terry Boone

ISBN 978-0-9962397-4-5

First Paperback Edition: May 2017
10 9 8 7 6 5 4 3 2 1

Published by
THREE RIVERS GROUP

Cover photo by the author.

A Hot Afternoon in

MASSACHUSETTS

This is a work of fiction. Names, places, events, timelines, distances and other information have been adapted or created entirely by the author. While some aspects of the story were inspired by career experience as a broadcaster, far and away much of what you will read in this book is made-up. Any similarity to real people and real events is *mostly* coincidental.

Published by **THREE RIVERS GROUP**

Contact: threeriversgroupvt@gmail.com

A Hot Afternoon in MASSACHUSETTS - All rights reserved. In accordance with the US Copyright Act of 1976, the scanning, uploading and electronic sharing of any part of this book without the permission of the author is unlawful piracy and theft of the author's intellectual property. If you would like to use material from this book (other than for review purposes), prior written permission must be obtained by contacting the publisher.

Thank you for your support and the author's rights.

Dedicated to the memory of

Ulysses J. 'Tony' Lupien
1917 – 2004

and

Donald A. Thurston
1930 – 2009

Bay State native sons who loved Vermont.

One

The train of thought kept chugging back to the same stop; a roster of individuals I'd known who had had up close, first-hand experience with personal tragedy. Some were just amazing in their ability to cope with grief, help others who struggled with it, and eventually move on.

Bonnie's father struck me as being the very model for that kind of person.

I walked at the edge of the water. Rocco was walking backward and bouncing around, his tail wagging like a metronome at its fastest tempo, eyes on me for any sign that I would raise my arm. I threw the ball as far as I could. He was off kicking up sand and sprinting away. My arm was tired. We'd been here for nearly an hour, covering pretty much the same stretch of the Town Beach on the bay in Sandwich, MA, a small town right at the beginning of Cape Cod.

If Rocco had any sense that Bonnie was not coming back, you couldn't tell it. But then again, he'd been with me now for almost a full month. He'd stayed with me previously, so what was the big deal? Get the leash and let's go.

"Let's take a break here, champ," I said. He dropped the ball at my feet. "I'll give you a bonus." He'd learned this good word from me and knew that it meant a biscuit, a piece of bread, maybe ice cream, just about anything that I happened to be eating at the moment. He cocked his head and sat. I clipped the leash to his collar, picked up the ball and walked toward a bench thirty yards ahead.

The drive from Vermont had taken just over three hours. I'd missed the heaviest traffic around Boston and it was a surprisingly easy run south on I-93 to the Sagamore Bridge, then another ten minutes to Sandwich. The GPS allowed me to make the correct turns without mistake.

My watch showed that it was twenty after six – THU 25. I gave Rocco a piece of a bacon treat from the bag in my backpack, then sat on the bench and took a long pull from my water bottle. After he ate the treat, he turned around a couple of times, then curled up next to the bench. He was panting, feet covered with sand and he smelled like one wet dog.

The sun was behind us now, two hours from setting and the temperature had dropped considerably. When we had arrived, it was still in the low-80s, down from a high of 90, according to a man I'd spoken with when we got here. Now it was just me and Rocco at this end of the beach.

It had been just over a week since the memorial service. I was having periodic conversations with Bonnie. At my breakfast counter, in the car, now walking on the beach. Some of the conversations were silent, sometimes I

4

talked out loud. Sometimes I cried.

But what was going to take a long time to absorb was hearing the report on the radio: a plane crash short of the runway at the Cincinnati airport. The flight had originated in Los Angeles and was enroute to Pittsburgh. The plane's departure had been delayed for nearly an hour because of an equipment malfunction. Then it crashed. Seventy people died, ten passengers and two crew members survived.

When I'd heard the report, I pulled over to look at my phone. The last text I'd received from Bonnie said that her flight was scheduled to arrive in Pittsburgh at 2:40, then onto Burlington, VT. She had said nothing about a stop in Cincinnati. She had mentioned the delay from LA because of some minor equipment malfunction and that they thought they would have to switch planes, but then it was fixed and they were getting ready to taxi.

The news clip on the radio that caused me to go numb included the reference to the flight's delayed departure because of an equipment issue. Over the next twenty-four hours, the shock and numbness that I'd felt had changed to incomprehension, then total disbelief. It would take several zombie-like days, mostly going through the motions of my normal routine, before the sense of grief inched forward enough to allow me to call up some of the best memories. Bonnie's father, Hugh, helped me get started.

Sitting on the bench, looking across the bay, I closed my eyes and replayed a conversation with the Reverend Mackin. It was the day after the crash and shortly after positive ID had been established for the deceased victims from the passenger list. He'd called me at home.

"Michael, we got a call from an airline spokesman. She's gone."

I'd taken a deep breath before responding,

"Hugh, I am so sorry." Empty words that confirmed what we'd feared from the moment I'd shown up at his door the day before with news of the crash. I thought about Bonnie's boyfriend, soon to be fiancé, still in California. I suspected the Mackins had already spoken with him.

There was a silence on the phone, followed by a choke in Hugh's voice before he spoke again.

"It will be at least two days before they can send her home," he'd said. "Helen and I will start thinking about a service."

"If there is anything that I can do, *anything at all*, please tell me," I responded.

"Thank you. I will." A silence, then he added, "Maybe we can talk again tomorrow."

"Yes. I'm here. Just call."

We ended the conversation and my numbness wavered enough to signal the beginning of heartache. Over the hours and days that followed that phone call, I tried to comprehend the pain and sorrow that Bonnie's family would take on.

Two

A trip to Cape Cod was Ragsdale's idea. He'd suggested the very spot where I was staying, one of three efficiency units owned by an elderly widow. They were basic, small, no frills bunk houses. The clientele for Jean McKearney was mostly fishermen and budget conscious vacationers. The location was just a two-minute drive or short walk to the beach.

Louie Ragsdale, a walking, talking pop music oldies encyclopedia, often a provocateur, undercover drug cop and a friend. Never one to miss a chance to offer advice, he'd encouraged me to take the time, make the drive, get a handle on processing the death of a close friend and former lover.

"Trust me, Hanlon, she's going to be with you for a long time," he'd said.

'She' was Bonnie Mackin, dead at the age of 34. Hanlon, Michael Perry Casey, 50, that would be me. *Private Investigation/Background Security Services*, as in, "Whatd'ya need?"

Bonnie and I had been together as a couple for just a

little more than a year. But it was, as some say, pretty intense. She was smart, funny, thoughtful, considerate and a very nice person. During the time we were together, she had nursed me through the recovery from a serious gunshot wound, doing all my shopping and errands, my laundry, checking on me every day, prodding me to be disciplined with the physical therapy exercises. And she'd regularly egged me on to "expand" my musical interests.

After the break-up, over a year ago and at her initiative, we'd remained good friends. She and her California boyfriend, Billy, had come to my house for dinner. I'd helped her father with some PR work for his church just a couple of months back. And Rocco, Bonnie's golden retriever not yet three years old, stayed with me anytime that Bonnie went out of town.

Now Rocco, at the urging of Bonnie's father, was most likely going to be my companion on a permanent basis.

Hugh Clarkson Mackin – US Navy Viet Nam vet, devoted husband, proud father and United Methodist minister for nearly forty years. The man reminded me of a sturdy, aged, post and beam barn just over the hill from my house; every time I saw it I felt inspiration, as I did when I saw Hugh.

Even in his darkest days of wrestling with the cruel, sudden loss of his daughter, he was able to give strength and comfort to all those around him, family, friends and parishioners.

For a man of the cloth, or at least my perception of same, his sense of humor must be a carry-over from his days in the Navy. Bonnie would often wince at his ribald comments and off-color jokes. But her dad and I hit it off immediately, which came as a bit of surprise to me as I am not a religious person, not in any stretch of whatever definition of that term might be. My conversations with Hughie, as his family calls him, were always uplifting, insightful and refreshing.

Watching and listening to him in the days immediately after Bonnie's death, especially during the family reception following her funeral, I began to think about that word *inspiration*. It didn't take very long for me to conclude that it was the example he set by his actions more than the words he spoke. Anyone who knew him knew all about his hospital visitations to people of all faiths, his engagement with the citizens, town government officials and numerous civic organizations. And for a guy his age, a surprising penchant for participating in numerous youth sports activities. According to family lore, Hughie was quite the athlete when he was younger. At 70, he was still fit, standing six feet tall and weighing 195.

Now, pulling the car into the driveway, I switched off the engine and sat for a moment. My thoughts seemed to be settling a bit from the past two weeks of roller coaster twists, turns and loops. I recalled one of Hughie's comments a year or so back when he observed that life sometimes is much like a pinball machine, that we ricochet from one circumstance to the next.

I didn't kid myself that the Reverend Mackin was likely to convince me to attend church anytime soon, but he certainly was setting a high standard for helping the rest of us cope.

I gave Rocco some dry food and a bowl of fresh water, then headed for the shower. Later we'd go get some clams and any other seafood that might be featured this evening at Seafood Sam's, just down the street. Pick up some beer and come back and listen to the ballgame. Go to bed early, get up in the morning, head out to see more of The Cape.

The Sox were at home against the Texas Rangers and were leading 2-0 in the fifth inning. I was nodding off and jerked awake at the sound of my own snoring, so I turned off the radio, took Mister High Energy out for a final pee, came back in and was asleep two minutes later.

Three

Friday morning, 6:15. The highway sign read Bourne Bridge, 11 miles. The driver knew that the town of Bourne was the first exit off the bridge once he crossed the Cape Cod Canal.

He'd been driving all night, more than twelve hours since he left the 'Motor City'. Across the Mass Pike, down 495 southeast to Route 25 and the bridge. Get some coffee, take a piss, back in the van. This would be his first stop of the day, then on to Hyannis, the preferred 'drop' for this bundle.

Donnie Richards was a good driver. No accidents, no speeding tickets, no complaints. He couldn't remember the last time that he went more than five miles an hour over the speed limit, *any* speed limit – school zone or a long stretch on the interstate. Pickups and deliveries, that's what he did. Haul a body 850 miles from Detroit, stop in Atlantic City on the return trip, no problem.

Donnie didn't have the CDL required for commercial drivers. He did not work with mortuaries or the county morgue. And Donnie didn't advertise his availability. He knew the major highways in the US as well as any long-haul driver. He knew the bad spots in the cities, where *not* to go. He was prompt, efficient, completely professional and expensive. But he'd never heard of a complaint.

A number of unsavory, will-not-win a good citizen award characters knew about Donnie. They knew him by his first name. There was a chance that a few knew his last name, at least the last name that he'd been using for more than twenty years. But to reach Donnie, you had to go through his agent. And just about every mob boss and violent thug east of the Mississippi knew Donnie's agent, 'Slim' Sal Hurley.

However, no matter how long you'd known Donnie, or no matter how many deals you might have done with him, if you wanted his services, you still needed to book him through Sal. On the darker side of life associated with activities that most people never encounter, something Sal and Donnie had once discussed at length, Sal was indeed very much like some well-known sports agents.

Much like sports agents, Sal had more than one client. He didn't have the same overhead – insurance, classy office space, marketing expenses and a budget devoted to schmoozing with the media and status seekers – yet he still took a healthy cut of every "trip" that he booked for Donnie. It was unlikely that all of Hurley's "fees" would show up in his tax returns. W-9s, 1099s and other tax forms were *not* part of his transactions.

Donnie knew all of this. He and Sal had grown up in the same tough section of Youngstown, Ohio half-alifetime ago. Each had pursued other careers and interests far from the Mahoning Valley of northeastern Ohio, but they reconnected at a high school reunion and in very short order, formed an alliance. It had been good from the get-go. The money got better fast and they had formed a bond. So far, it had never failed either of them. That's why Donnie really didn't give a shit about Sal's other clients. Not one time in twenty years had there been an issue.

Coming off the bridge, Donnie watched the signs as he approached the traffic rotary. He slowed, flipped the signal indicator and watched his outside mirrors.

Aside from the so-called higher level of knowledge, skills and experience required for those who actually obtain a Commercial Driver's License, there was common sense that applied regardless of the size of the vehicle you were driving. One basic consideration in that common sense had to do with how your vehicle was loaded and avoiding a cargo shift in transit. Even without the license, Donnie was meticulous on this particular point. Only *he* loaded and unloaded the cargo.

Carefully packed, strapped and iced in the cargo bay behind him, were double-wrapped blue tarps that looked very much like a roll of carpeting. That was one of the techniques used for all runs, make 'the bundle' appear to be plausible. He'd done it literally hundreds of times and for the past five years, every bundle looked like a roll of carpet. The blue tarps were always new and he'd even printed phony labels that he attached just in case of an interior inspection.

Exiting the roundabout onto Route 6A and travelling along the canal towards Sandwich, Donnie was confident that his cargo had not moved.

A brief stop at a McDonalds took care of the biological and caffeine needs that he'd felt over the past couple of hours. Back at the van, he swapped over to phony Mass plates, just as good and just as believable as the phony plates that he removed and stowed in a custom-made box inside the van.

Among other items, the interior two foot by four-foot panel-mounted box, held faux license plates for twenty-six states, including thirteen that required front and back. Privately manufactured and adapted each year, the plates came with the required stickers. And he didn't bother with the states west of the Mississippi.

Matching, phony state inspection stickers – carefully slipped into transparent sleeves – were easily switched on the windshield when he made a plate swap. Of course, if he ever *was* stopped and had to fool some cop, things could become problematic. Better to be a careful driver and reduce the risks of a pull over.

The little three-minute change over task was done and he headed east to pick up Route 6 in Sandwich.

Four

A map spread across the table in front of me, half of my second mug of coffee getting cold, I scrolled through one of the articles I'd found online.

Cape Cod, fifteen towns all in one county, Barnstable, with a combined population of 215,000. A historical map from 1890 illustrated the hook-like shape of what the locals refer to as the Upper Cape, Mid Cape, Lower Cape and Outer Cape. The oldest town, right where I was at the moment, is Sandwich, founded in 1637. Reputed by some as the second oldest town in the US, Sandwich now has a year-round population of just over 20,000, but gets a big bump with summer tourism, mostly in July and August.

At the far end, the very tip of the Outer Cape, is Provincetown, known by most as P-town, population of approximately 3,000 until summer rolls in, then it can hit 60,000. Long known for its status as a vacation spot for the LGBT community, P-town is just over an hour's drive from Sandwich. Perhaps on Sunday. My interest today was for a shorter drive, maybe down to Falmouth to check out the Woods Hole Oceanographic Institution.

The lengthy online article referred to the Cape as *conterminous*. There you go, not a word one hears every day. Most likely cartographers and civil engineers use it all the time. Reaching for my phone I typed the word into Google. OK, *common boundary*. Back to the article. A little farther down in the online historical overview was the insertion of the Sandwich town motto, *Post tot Naufracia Portus*.

"Where's our old Dartmouth Prof when we need him?" I said to Rocco. Google would have to bail me out again. Translation: *After So Many Shipwrecks, A Haven.*

Shutting down the laptop and placing the phone on the chair, I walked to the sink. My former wife's voice scolded me, "Education shows, friend." Yep. Dumping the rest of the coffee and rinsing the mug, I tried to recall if my high school even offered Latin. If they did, somebody forgot to tell me about it.

I placed the mug beside its twin next to the small coffeemaker. This was a housekeeping unit; fresh linens and towels, yes. Clean up the dishes, you can handle it.

"Let's go, Rocket Man," He was up and ready before I got my sandals on. Our wake-up priority had dictated that we'd gone for a short walk and that he had had his breakfast shortly after I got out of bed. I would get a breakfast sandwich somewhere on the way.

We loaded into the car and a minute later were heading west on 6-A.

Louie Ragsdale looked at the text message on his phone. '90 yesterday, maybe hotter today. Heading to Falmouth. Thanks for Mrs. McKearney's contact.'

After a long winter and too many days and nights away from home, Ragsdale had wrangled a summer schedule that was really a transition to retirement. At least that's what he told himself. And his wife. Some of his colleagues at the Northeast Counter Drug Task Force had other ideas. Louie was too good at his work and too valuable to the task force to leave it altogether. His superiors, a small group of senior law enforcement officials representing all of the New England states and part of eastern New York, would find some way to keep him involved. Most likely, that would end up as Louie training new officers in some of the finer points of undercover work.

In any event, he'd negotiated to have the entire month of June off, and future assignments closer to home on a 'four days on/three days off' schedule for the rest of the year. In another eight months, he would hit his thirtieth anniversary in police work, with ten of those years as part of the team now working to find and apprehend drug dealers all over the Northeast.

Ragsdale sent a text back to Hanlon. 'See what's going on w/stripers. Might join you next wk.'

When he'd encouraged Hanlon to take some time for himself, he'd suggested the possibility of striped bass fishing, reminding Hanlon that fishing could be a great way to get "other concerns" out of your mind. He *didn't* mention that he was feeling a touch of guilt about the days when he'd taunted Hanlon because of his age difference with Bonnie Mackin. And still later when Ragsdale had razzed Hanlon about Bonnie being smart enough to find a companion closer to her own age.

Louie had expressed the guilt feelings to his wife, Becky, after they had attended the funeral for Bonnie. It had been an overflow crowd at her father's church. The Ragsdales' hadn't known anyone as they lived in a different part of the state, so they had not attended the reception after the service. It had been during the drive back home to northeastern Vermont when Louie regretted his dumb guy humor and the frequent, tactless comments to Hanlon. Now Bonnie was gone. And Hanlon was rattled.

Fast forward to this warm morning, driving to a small town in southwestern Vermont where he would spend the next few days doing more undercover drug surveillance, Ragsdale began thinking of a plan: persuade Becky that they should visit her brother and his wife in Massachusetts, then maybe go spend a few days on the Cape. Why not?

I went through another roundabout and took Route 28 for fifteen miles directly down to Falmouth. Rocco was stretched across the back seat looking pretty comfortable.

I'd seen a sign indicating the direction of the Oceanographic Institute, so I took a right onto Woods Hole Road. The Woods Hole Oceanographic Institution, WHOI, and the Woods Hole Research Center, according to what I'd seen online, were in the same part of town. It was five after ten and I hoped to make it before the next tour advertised to start at 10:30.

I passed the Research Center on the right and a short distance along, in the village, spotted a cluster of three storey red brick buildings that I presumed to be part of WHOI. I looked for a place to park.

Five

What I discovered about two minutes after arriving at the Woods Hole Oceanographic Institution was that the public tours were in July and August only. Unless you had a school group of ten or more and had scheduled in advance. Bummer.

What the hell? We would just take a stroll, see what we could see, maybe come back another time. Rocco would be happier to get out and there were lots of other sites. I glanced at my watch; ten-twenty-five.

We walked around a small waterfront park for a few minutes, returned to the car and drove back towards the center of Falmouth. I could stop at the Woods Hole Research Center just up the road and see what they were all about. Or not. Planning is a good thing, Hanlon. You should do it more often. That sentiment came courtesy of whichever voice was directing me at the moment.

"Oh-h-h, Bonnie," I said out loud. Rocco sat up. I watched him in the mirror.

"It's OK, kid." He cocked his head, then turned to look out the side window. I hit the button to lower it even more

21

so that he could stick his nose out. He loves the smells.

When we got there, a man at the Research Center set me straight; the real Visitors Office for WHOI was in a small building on Water Street, back in the village.

Becky Ragsdale was eager for her husband to have the entire month of vacation. They had been together for a long time and she knew that there was a high probability that Louie would twitch his way into something other than just taking it easy.

She didn't really think of him as a fidgety. About the only time that he showed much animation was when he was spoofing someone. Like Michael Hanlon.

So, the earlier phone call from Louie suggesting that they "take a run down to Massachusetts next week" did not come as a surprise. She was aware that Hanlon was already on Cape Cod and that even if they spent one night with her brother and sister-in-law, Louie was sure to suggest a trip to the ocean. That was fine with her. She liked Michael, knew that he and Louie had a real friendship and, since the incredible tragedy of Bonnie Mackin's death two weeks ago, she also suspected that Michael could use a little support.

Becky had watched Michael at the conclusion of Bonnie's funeral service. He'd been able to keep his composure, but when they embraced outside the church, Michael hadn't said anything to her, just shaking his head

22

slowly, tears in his eyes and he hugged Becky again. She'd patted his arm and did not say another word. She and Louie went home and even though Louie had gone back to Quechee two days later to visit Michael, she hadn't spoken with him since the service.

Becky recalled losing a very close friend in a car accident, a woman she'd known all her life. At times the grief was simply overwhelming. People need support, it's as simple as that. Conversation, *no* conversation, just a short visit, a note, flowers, figure it out. When you think that you know someone and you know that they are hurting, try to *do something*.

Yes, they would go to Massachusetts. Yes, they would go to the Cape. No, she would not permit Louie to fall in to his "Hoo-ah" mode and offer as therapy "Let's go fishing." Unless, of course, Michael really wanted to do that.

Opening a cupboard door above the sink Becky looked at the calendar. The only thing written was a note on Friday, June 9th about "Bucky, vet?" a reference to their black Lab. And June 1st was next Thursday.

She went to the phone to call her sister-in-law in Massachusetts.

Six

Donnie pulled in behind a Shaw's Supermarket and cranked the AC. Pretty fucking hot for the end of May. What the hell did these people do in July and August?

What Donnie had no way of knowing was that record high temperatures would be set in numerous towns and cities throughout New England on this day. He was also unaware of the fact that, normally, most towns on Cape Cod benefit from a nice breeze on hot days. *Any* hot day; May, July, August – it rarely mattered, the breeze usually made it bearable. That wouldn't be the case today.

Something that Donnie did know was that he was about to fall back to Plan B. Instructions for delivering this specific bundle offered *two* locations; Hyannis was the first choice. If not there, Sandwich. Subject to any security cameras, police presence, pedestrians, or any reason not to unload the cargo in a preferred spot, it was Donnie's call. The understanding was always made clear by Slim Sal in setting up arrangements. It was Donnie's ass, so he was adamant; no comebacks on Donnie or the van.

Of course, *water drops* - as in rivers, lakes and ponds,

one time a swamp in Georgia - those were the easiest. But that was not the situation on this trip. Nearly six hours repeatedly circling through Hyannis, to the outskirts of town and all through the neighborhoods and he knew that it was a no go.

Donnie was careful to scout any town with his circular driving routine before making a drop. But once he'd picked his spot, he had to move quickly without being seen and without drawing attention to the van. A bit trickier to pull off in daylight.

At the age of 49, Donnie could easily pass for being ten years younger. If someone happened to encounter him sitting there in his van, they might think that he was an off-duty UPS driver, an electrician, or maybe a plumber. The van was indistinguishable, a darker gray going to blue, three years old, in good repair. And no company markings. In preparation for trips, he would keep the exterior on the dirty side, no recent drive-thru car washes and nothing shiny.

If Donnie stepped out of the van and encountered someone else, that person would see a man of five-foot-nine, one hundred-seventy pounds, dark work-like pants and a non-descript, tan short-sleeved shirt. He had short black hair becoming gray at the edges and handled himself with an easy manner, no hurry about anything. How ya' doin?

But Donnie was still inside his van and no one was stopping by to talk to him. Just looking at the exterior back wall of the supermarket, out of the way from any deliveries that could arrive, he continued to study the map on the screen of his phone and confirmed that the best route back to Sandwich would be to hang a left out of the parking lot, take Ocean Street north to the traffic rotary next to the airport and back onto the Mid-Cape Highway.

Take it slow, stop for something to eat, no rush. He chuckled to himself; maybe a sandwich in Sandwich? Probably a joke that had been around for more than 250 years. Donnie had a vague recollection from his school days that the word sandwich reportedly came from a story about some late-night hours in England during the mid-eighteenth century. It was said that the Fourth Earl of Sandwich was too busy gambling to stop for a meal. Donnie's high school history teacher said the Earl's valet brought him some pieces of meat packed between slices of bread. Nobody seems to have reported how the Earl did that night with the gambling.

A quick glance at his watch: 1:18. He put the van into gear and eased away from the building.

Seven

How was it that Robert B. Parker paraphrased George Bernard Shaw's witty quotation? "Youth, like caffeine, is wasted on the young?" Maybe.

In any event, after ninety minutes of walking around the Oceanographic Institution with young Emma St. Jean, a college student from Nova Scotia, I was stoked-up on envy and wishing that I was twenty-years-old again. It is unlikely that I would have mustered her curiosity, focus and self-discipline at that age, but what an opportunity. And she clearly enjoyed being there.

Despite the "No Tours until July" info I had previously discovered, my well timed arrival at the Visitors Center allowed me to tag along with Emma and a retired WHOI research biologist by the name of Carl Wirtz. He was providing her with an orientation and I got the benefit of a VIP tour.

I chalked it up to the only woman in the office feeling sorry for me. Perhaps I looked a bit forlorn. Joanne was on her name tag and she was generous with her time and patient with my questions. It was a quiet morning and we'd talked for several minutes. Then in came Carl and his student and off we went.

As a staff member of more than 30 years, he knew the place inside out. The highlight of the tour was 30 minutes on the brand-new exploration ship, the 238 foot *RV Neil Armstrong*. Carl took us top to bottom. The ship was scheduled to leave port in another week.

After leaving WHOI, I made a brief stop at the Nobska Lighthouse on the way out of town. The original light was constructed in 1828, looking out to Vineyard Sound. In 1690, the Indian name for the settlement, Suckanesset, was changed to Falmouth. I took one of the brochures for a non-profit organization, Friends of Nobska Light.

Crab cakes, coleslaw and a beer for lunch at the Quicks Hole Tavern, a short walk for Rocco and we were headed back to Sandwich by two o'clock.

The temp on my dashboard now showed that it was 86F. I decided to go back to the beach in Sandwich for another walk out across the boardwalk and head in the opposite direction of where we'd gone yesterday. Throw the ball, get some exercise and the breeze. It seemed as though I couldn't get enough time talking to myself and to Bonnie. The walking helped. I would shower and clean up later, maybe a drive this evening out to see Chatham Lighthouse.

As I pulled into the parking area, only one other

vehicle was in the lot, a dark van parked near the bench I'd sat on during our previous visit. I parked two spaces over from the van. Rocco sat up and sensed that we were about to get out again. He didn't seem to care how hot it was. How long does this young dog energy last?

I got a bottle of water from the cooler in the back, took off my sandals, snapped on the leash and got the tennis ball. We approached the boardwalk and I could see a man way off to the east, near where we had walked yesterday. We went west in the opposite direction towards the Cape Cod Canal.

Eight

Out across the bay, Donnie wasn't sure if he was looking at Provincetown. He was familiar with the way the land hooked around, at least as he'd seen it on the map.

The idea of driving out there had gone through his mind when he was in Hyannis. But not now. Unload the bundle, take a quick photo and head up to Boston, then on to Atlantic City. No fuckin' around. He turned and started walking back to the van.

When he was back at the parking lot, another vehicle had arrived. A Honda CR-V with Vermont plates. Donnie stood next to the van and looked in all directions; nobody in sight. He hit the button to unlock the van and looked at his watch – 3:08. Moving to the back, he opened the doors and stepped up into the van.

The bundle was secured with yellow nylon straps in three places. It hadn't moved since he'd packed it in twenty-four hours earlier. He slipped on a pair of work gloves, loosened each strap and rolled the bundle away from the side panel. The plastic bags of ice were mostly water at this point, but still cold. He pushed the bags aside and pulled the bundle toward the open doors.

Stepping back onto the hot asphalt of the parking lot, he took his time looking around again. The van was parked right up to the edge of the sand, close to a bench and a trash receptacle. He'd been careful to park there earlier in a manner that would block any view from houses on the far side of the road that led back to Main Street.

With one quick pull, he had the near end of the bundle resting on the bumper. Another step back, a quick scan of the houses and he pulled the bundle completely out. He positioned it on the sand behind the bench, removed the gloves, took his phone from the case on his belt, snapped a couple of photos and was behind the wheel and pulling away ten seconds later.

Slowly driving back to Route 6A, he stopped only long enough to snap a shot of the sign that read, ENTERING SANDWICH – Inc. 1637. But Donnie was *leaving* Sandwich. And his vehicle was now approximately 150 pounds lighter.

Cross the canal and follow Route 3 to I-93, then north to Boston and he should reach Logan Airport in under two hours. Not quite 60 miles, but hard to know what the traffic was going to be.

At ten after four we got back to the boardwalk leading to the parking lot. I threw the ball one more time in the direction of the car. Rocco was showing some exhaustion. He dutifully trotted after the ball but sidetracked to stop

31

and sniff a large blue-tarp bundle on the ground next to the bench.

"Leave it," I yelled. Right! He was not about to leave it, whatever he was smelling.

Ragsdale had suggested that the Rocket Boy would be a good bird dog, except that I'm not a hunter. Many times when he got a good scent, or a smell that he liked, he wouldn't let it go. That's what he was doing now, moving back and forth along the tarp and sniffing at spots every few inches, the top, the sides, the ends.

"Rocco, come," I yelled with as much authority as I could get into my voice. Nope. Tail up like a hyper alert squirrel, he continued moving quickly back and forth.

As I got closer, I thought about the obedience classes that Bonnie had taken him to when he was only a few months old. I remembered that most of the commands had seemed to work for *her* and I felt a little guilty that I was not as attentive when he was with me. That would have to change.

"Rocco!" I shouted again, ready to reattach the leash.

Now he had his head down, tail up and nose buried at the end of the tarp taking in repeated sniffs. Maybe not really 'on point', but focused. I got the leash snapped and pulled him away, but he resisted. I was stronger but he was more determined. At near 70-pounds, he gives a surprisingly tough tug of war.

"Let's go," I said, pulling harder. I was walking backward and so was he, short steps and then an attempt

32

to move forward. "Now," I added.

When I got him into the back seat and lowered the windows, he immediately stuck his head out the side in the direction of the bench and the rolled-up blue tarp. I started the engine and would let it run for a minute before closing the windows and turning the AC to max.

I sat and looked out at the tarp. Just over six feet in length, not quite two feet in diameter, rolled tightly, cinched with white cord at each end and in the center. A bundle of house painter's materials, construction tarps? A roll of carpeting?

"What is it, kid?" I said. Rocco didn't respond and didn't even give me the courtesy of a look. He was too curious about *it* and not me.

Nine

"**Sandwich Police 9-1-1 recorded line**, what is your emergency?" a woman's voice answered. I had the phone on speaker as I generally do when calling from the car.

"Not sure it's an emergency, but can you connect me to the Sandwich PD?" I replied.

"Sir, what is your location?"

"I'm in my car, parking lot at the Sandwich Town Beach."

"What is the nature of your call?"

Too bad you can't bring up a photo of the person at the other end, perhaps like Skype. She certainly was being professional, but I thought that I detected a slight edge to her tone.

"My name is Michael Hanlon. I'm in my *car*. There is a large *bundle*. It is wrapped in a blue *tarp*, next to the beach. My dog got the scent of something and he didn't want to let it go." I heard myself being just a little bit asshole, so I backed off.

"I don't know, may be nothing. But I think the police need to make that determination."

"Which beach?" she asked.

"Where the boardwalk is. I'm pretty sure this area is part of the town beach."

"Please hold for a minute."

I'd closed the windows and the AC was doing its job. Rocco was still standing on the seat behind me, nose about two inches from the window. I reached back and scratched him just above his tail. Still no look for me. Thanks, anyway. The 9-1-1 operator came back on.

"A patrol car is on the way. Can you wait there?"

"Yes. I'm the only car here in the lot. Silver Honda CR-V. Vermont plates."

"Thank you. An officer will be there very shortly." She ended the call.

Crossing the Sagamore Bridge, Donnie watched for a sign for fuel or food. He would pull over long enough to swap the plates, changing to the blue, white and gold single Pennsylvania registration.

He preferred gas stations that featured coin-operated, high-powered vacuum service which allowed him to go through the motions of cleaning the cargo interior of the van. Regardless of where he stopped, he had the routine down to under two minutes; keep both rear doors open to obstruct the view, switch the plate, done. When it required two plates, he would turn the van around to block a line of sight, then pretend as though he was checking something under the front bumper.

There was a plaza on the right and he could see signs of a Friendly's Restaurant as well as a SHELL station. Moderate northbound traffic for a Friday afternoon, but heavy traffic coming in the other direction, weekenders heading for the Cape. He put his blinker on and moved to the right lane.

It was 3:46 when he backed the van into a spot in the far corner of the Friendly's parking area, away from other cars. He sat with the engine running and watched the entrance to the restaurant.

Satisfied that he could do the drill in the usual manner, he climbed out, walked to the rear of the van and opened both doors. Once he had the PA plate on, he used a short-handled broom and did a quick sweeping of the cargo area. He dumped water from the melted ice bags and balled them together for disposal, then got back behind the wheel to turn the van around. He left the engine running as he dropped first to one knee, then rolled onto his left side to get under the front bumper.

With the front license plate removed, he laid it on the floor between the front seats and put the empty, wet plastic bags on top. He would stow the plate back in the box later when he stopped for gas. He locked the van and headed for the restaurant to use the men's room.

At 4:05, Donnie pulled out of the Friendly's lot. On to

Logan International Airport for a brief stop, then back across the Mass Pike and south through Connecticut. He came up the entrance ramp to Route 3 north, watched his outside mirror and merged into traffic. No reason that he couldn't make Atlantic City by midnight.

Ten

The Ford SUV patrol car came into the lot within two minutes of the end of my call to 9-1-1. Only one cop in the car that I could see and he headed straight for my car. I opened the door to get out.

The officer inside the black and white cracked the driver's door while at the same time talking into a hand mic attached to his shirt, I presumed to his dispatcher. He put the mic aside and got out. Dark blue uniform, short-sleeved shirt, name tag read J. Brutelli. He stood maybe six feet, a hundred-eighty-plus. Short dark hair, wrap-around sunglasses. I guessed him to be mid-thirties.

The cop gave me a nod, made a quick glance at the bench and the blue tarp.

"Afternoon," he said.

"Hot one, huh?" I replied. Michael Hanlon, aka *Your Local Weatherman.*

"Yeah. We're having an early heat wave, it seems," J. Brutelli said. He jerked his head in the direction of the blue bundle behind the bench. "What time did you get here?"

I looked at my watch. "Ah-h, just about an hour ago."

"Any other vehicles here?"

"There was a van when we arrived," I said. "I took my dog for a walk down that way," I pointed away from the parking lot in the direction of the canal. "When we came back, the van was gone and the bundle was there." Brutelli again looked over at the tarp, then back to me.

"You see the driver of the van?"

I shook my head and pointed down the beach to the east, away from where Rocco and I had gone.

"There was a man way down there. No idea if he was the driver," I said.

Brutelli walked over to the window where Rocco had his head out. He held his hand out for Rocco to give him a sniff, then scratched the dog's left ear.

"Good lookin' dog. What's his name?"

"Rocco."

He laughed, leaned closer to the dog and said, "You don't *look* like a Rocco." He looked at me and said, "Can you wait here for a few minutes?"

"Sure."

He walked over and stood in front of the bench just looking around. He stepped onto the sand and squatted close to the blue tarp but didn't touch it. I could see him inhale through his nose, two deliberate, deep breaths. He rubbed his right hand back and forth across his mouth like he was puzzling over something.

Brutelli stood up and stepped back onto the blacktop. He put his left hand up to the shoulder mic, cocked his head and said something that I couldn't hear. I heard another voice come back at him and then he said something else.

I looked back at Rocco. His tongue was hanging and he was panting. He needed a drink. I went around to the other side of the car, opened the door and got out his dish and a bottle of water. I filled the bowl halfway before I reattached the leash and let him get out. He first looked in the direction of the tarp, then began lapping up the water.

The cop was coming back toward us. Rocco stopped drinking, head up, tail wagging, he watched as Brutelli approached.

"How old is he?" he said, giving Rocco a couple of pats.

"Almost three, but more like going on six months" I said. "He's really full of it."

Brutelli looked at the plates on my car. "Where in Vermont?"

"A little village called Quechee," I said. "It's in the town of Hartford. But most people think of it as White River Junction."

"The Quechee Gorge," he said.

"Right."

"I was there a couple years ago. My wife's cousin has a place at a golf community," he said.

"Quechee Lakes. Two great golf courses, I'm told. But just one very small lake."

"But there's a river," he said. "Anyway, her cousin

goes for the skiing."

"Yeah, the Ottauquechee. Flows more than forty miles from over at Killington. That's it running down through the gorge, dumps into the Connecticut."

We talked for a couple of minutes about Quechee, about Bernie Sanders, the Vermont Institute of Natural Science Raptor Center, where Brutelli had taken his kids, and about Vermont's craft breweries.

"How about that Heady Topper?" Brutelli said. "Pretty nice beer."

"Indeed. Tough to get a hold of. Although they have a new brewery. Don't know if that's helping meet demand or not. But there are quite a few others around."

Another patrol car came into the lot. Two cops in front and what appeared to be a dog in the back seat. I gave Rocco's leash another wrap around my hand.

The traffic picked up as he got closer to Boston. Donnie watched the signs directing him to Logan Airport, the exit coming up in three miles.

If the other car was where it should be, Level 4 of the Central Parking Garage, he could retrieve the parcel and be out of there in a matter of minutes. Sal had assured him that it should be an easy run. They had exchanged text messages just before Donnie headed north. Sal had followed-up with another text about the guy who would be at Logan looking for Donnie, ETA 5:30 pm.

41

The pick-up was cash. How much, he didn't know, but no question a substantial amount. It was not his first run as a 'courier of convenience' for Sal. And it was Donnie's impression that whoever was orchestrating this particular fetch, Sal had previously done some work for them. In all likelihood, Donnie had worked on their behalf.

5:09 on his watch. He signaled and moved right.

Brutelli, the two other cops and the dog had been next to the blue tarp for maybe twenty minutes. One of the other cops had gone back to his patrol car and talked to someone on the two way. They had taken several photos and now the guy who appeared to be the senior officer, or at least the one giving all the directions, was squatting on his ankles at one end of the tarp. He wore latex gloves and was beginning to untie the white cord closest to him. He used a small pocket knife to loosen the knot.

Working his way along, he untied the middle cord and then the last one at the other end. He stood and with the help of Brutelli, rolled the bundle away from the bench onto the sand. There was another tarp, this one appeared to be wrapped with some kind of shiny tape, similar to duct tape but bright and metallic looking. The police dog was a little hyper, but the other officer kept him back.

With his knife, the cop slit under the tape in five spots along the bundle. It no longer looked to me like carpet, but showed bumps and indentations along its length. One end of the second tarp fell away from the bundle. The cop went to that spot, looked up at Brutelli and motioned that they should roll it again.

"Ahh, shit," I heard the in-charge cop say. He looked up at Brutelli.

Eleven

Once it was apparent that they were dealing with a body, the three cops stood talking and the dog sat at full-on alert. The heat was only slightly relieved by a weak breeze.

I'd taken Rocco over to encourage a pee at the other end of the parking lot. He really wanted to meet the police dog. Nothing doing, champ. Back in the car. Now I walked across the lot to one of two porta-toilets and didn't need much encouragement to relieve myself.

When I came out, a man and a woman were coming down the street toward the beach, each holding the leash of tan colored dogs. The one the guy restrained was slightly larger and maybe older, both of a breed that I didn't recognize; long ears, shaggy mustache and beard, muscular hind legs. The dog the woman was connected to was definitely younger.

I looked over at the car to see if Rocco had spotted them. No sign, so he must be lying down. The couple was headed for the boardwalk and the beach. Both of their dogs caught sight, probably scent first, of the police dog. Here we go, I thought.

The cop attached to the police dog stepped away and tightened the leash. His dog appeared to be as social as any, but he kept it back. When the cop in charge saw the couple, he said something to Brutelli who went over to them. He appeared to know them, they talked for a minute and then the couple reversed course heading back in the direction of the street.

I caught up with the man and woman and asked about the dogs.

"Italian Spinone," the man said.

"Are they related?"

"No. The same breeder, though. He's five," the man pointed at the larger dog, "and this one will be a year old in July."

"Sweet lookin' guys, I said.

"They're a lot of fun," the woman responded. The couple kept walking back toward the neighborhood from whence they came.

Officer J. Brutelli and I stood next to his patrol car. He'd asked me to answer some questions about when I had arrived, exactly what I'd seen, how long I'd been out on the beach with Rocco before coming back, was there anything that I could recall about the man I'd seen on the beach?

"Nah, he was really way down there," I pointed again.

"Alone?"

"I didn't see anyone else."

"Tell me about the van," he said.

"Dark blue, I think. Coulda' been gray, I guess."

"Plates?"

I thought for a second, then shook my head. "Boy, I don't know. We parked right there," I pointed at the Honda, "then walked out across the sand toward the boardwalk. I really didn't pay much attention to the van. Sorry."

Two more cops had arrived and the police dog was back inside the second patrol car, engine running for the air conditioning. I knew what to expect next, the arrival of a Medical Examiner. They wouldn't move the body before that.

"Can you stick around for a while longer? I wanna' be sure the Sergeant doesn't have more questions for you?" Brutelli said.

"I'm good," I replied.

He went back to the group and a minute later, two of them were putting out the yellow tape, stretching it all the way to the entrance of the boardwalk that crossed the stream separating the parking lot from the beach. Any evening strollers were going to have to find an alternate route.

Twelve

A black Tesla Model S with red wheels moved slowly between rows of parked cars on Level 4 of the Logan Airport Central Parking Garage. The driver braked, looked back over his left shoulder, then into the outside mirror. There was the van, driver behind the wheel.

Donnie watched the Tesla. He laughed at a sticker on the rear bumper; *Roger Goodell Sucks* in bright, popsicle blue letters. It also included a doctored photo of the NFL Commissioner wearing a New York Yankees cap. The Tesla had a vanity license plate GAMEOVR, issued by the state of Rhode Island.

The guy was backing up. The car stopped directly in front of him and the driver's tinted window went down. A man with a small gold earring in his left ear looked directly at him. Donnie gave a thumbs-up. As pre-arranged by Sal, once the drivers acknowledged each other, they would proceed to the top parking level and find spaces close together. Donnie eased the van out and followed the Tesla.

It was 5:43 PM.

In Detroit, Michigan it was also 5:43, one state shy of the Central Time Zone. In his office, only a five-minute walk from Cadillac Tower in one direction, Comerica Park in another, Sal Hurley was about to call it a day. He would wait for one more text to confirm the pick-up and that Donnie was on his way to Atlantic City.

Drinks and dinner at Vicente's, then drive across the border into Canada and win some more cash at Caesars Windsor. Some of his best contacts were regulars there. Never so much business to ignore being seen. And on top of that, Sal was the kind of guy who *liked* to be seen.

His phone beeped. New message. Sal picked up the phone and looked at the screen.

"Good to go – The Donald." Fucking clown. He was the same way in school. Sal laughed anyway. One of the things that he liked about Donnie was that his wisecracks and humor always leaned to the boastful side, self-promotion without being self-important. Donnie never took swipes at others, even the assholes who deserved it. And he never called Sal "Slim". That moniker was pasted on him from his early days in Detroit. A few of the mob guys who, for the most part, liked Sal, but were always quick to let a guy know exactly where he stood in the pecking order. Especially guys from Ohio.

Now twenty years later, no small number of those same mobsters frequently turned to Sal to arrange for 'activities outside their jurisdiction.' Sal was always amused when he saw a photo in the newspapers –

business and social pages – of one of his clients. Through civic and charitable activities, they manipulated public perception the same way a studio created hype for a new film, or a new star. In fact, Sal knew a couple of these bums had publicists on their payroll. Hey. What the hell? It's all business, right?

Sal kept his car in a garage just around the corner from Vicente's. That's how he originally discovered the Cuban restaurant. Once he'd had the Paella, he became a regular. Lobster, shrimp, calamari, scallops, Spanish sausage, chicken, clams, mussels, vegetables and Spanish saffron rice, all prepared Cuban style, was their number one dish.

It was Friday night, so the place would be packed. But he would be gone before the Salsa dancing got underway. He would get his entertainment at Caesars' Super 4 Progressive Blackjack Table. Since the game had been introduced, Sal was up more than twenty grand. And he was a *cautious* better.

Walking to the restaurant, he ran through a mental checklist on Donnie's current assignment: the bundle delivered, photo confirmation; parcel accepted in Boston; courier service to the Atlantic City International Airport, confirmation there when accepted; return to Detroit. He should be back late tomorrow. Are the Tigers at home Sunday afternoon?

Sal thought about the pick-up in Boston. This was on behalf of a client who had been trying to stay under the

49

radar since one of his legit businesses, a chain of self-storage units around Detroit, had been charged with prematurely selling off some personal items belonging to customers who were delinquent on monthly rental fees. Sal was certain that Donnie's pick-up in Boston was cash.

Like all the contracts that Sal worked, flat fee. He never went for percentage stuff, too iffy. Donnie could be retrieving millions, not his concern. Get it, deliver it. That's it. And always photo confirmation. The same for 'bundle' extraction and deliveries. Flat fee, calculated on difficulty, distance and the number of bundles to be handled, maximum of four with any one contract.

None of the contracts were in writing. But Sal kept a boilerplate checklist that he always used when making the arrangement. It was how he stayed on top of things, avoided 'misunderstandings', and quickly reigned-in new clients. Spell it out upfront; this is how it works. They always accepted the terms.

And while most deliveries were to *one* specified location, it was not unusual that they could be made to a choice of drops. The ultimate location was always Donnie's call. Not once had there been any blowback from the choices Donnie made.

As soon as he opened the door to Vicente's, the aroma was right there.

"Está volao," Sal whispered to himself.

Thirteen

By the time they were clearing the beach I knew that my evening plans were about to change. Walking back to the car to check on Rocco, I told the short cop where I was going and that I would return.

The Sandwich Police Chief had arrived. His guys on the scene had been there for nearly an hour. It was obvious that I would have to go through the story again. Maybe I should start carrying my little digital recorder with me all the time.

Wait, Hanlon. Breakthrough! People actually use their smartphones to record everything these days. Reflexively patting the pocket on my shorts holding the phone, I kept walking and didn't take the phone out.

The sun was dropping and it was starting to cool down, but I'd left all the windows in the car half open anyway and Rocco was fine. After all the running, he seemed to be happy to be resting in the shade of the back seat. He raised his head to look at me, but made no move to get up. I would give him more water and his supper when we got to the bunk house.

Back at the edge of the parking area, I watched the Chief talking to one of the officers, the same one who had told me his name was Brutelli. They were standing just below the boardwalk, maybe fifteen feet from the body. I leaned against the car and waited.

As I expected, the Chief turned and looked at me, said something to Brutelli and then began walking in my direction. I stood up and took a couple steps forward.

"Peter Whalen," he said, almost as informal as though we were a couple guys meeting at a ball game or a grocery store. Whalen was a solid-built, clean-cut guy, maybe 50-years-old.

"Michael Hanlon." We shook hands. He pointed at one of the benches away from the body. We walked over and sat.

Also as anticipated, he had me go through pretty much the same questions that Brutelli had asked earlier. But Whalen stayed on the description of the van, hoping that he could jog more detail.

"So you *didn't* see the plates, or for that matter, that it had a *front* plate?" I shook my head.

"You said dark blue, possibly gray."

"The glare from the sun was pretty intense. Even with glasses, really bright." I pointed out to the sand away from the boardwalk. "We started that way first, then turned around and went across the stream. The van was behind me." Whalen nodded.

"You guys must have some cameras around town.

Where could the van go?" I said.

"Oh, we'll see it soon enough," he replied. "Be quicker if we knew the plates."

Whalen stood up. I stood up. He looked at his men on the beach. A woman from the state medical examiner's local satellite office had joined the group. She was now by herself, examining the body.

"How long you here?" he asked.

"A few days. Just going to check out some places."

"First time on the Cape?"

"Believe it or not, yeah. Been to Boston a lot. Never came down here."

He gave me his card and extended his hand again.

"Jeff got your contact info, yes?"

"Officer Brutelli? Yeah. He said that I would need to come by the station to sign his report when he got it written up."

"Thanks for your help. Much appreciated." He turned and went back to the other cops.

I looked at my watch; twenty after six.

Rocco sat up when I got in the car. He gave me the brown eyes 'I'm your friend' look that you get from some dogs. It damn near made me choke-up.

Body back there, bodies from a plane crash. Jesus. No end to it. Bodies *somewhere* all the time.

On the short drive back, I could feel the heaves working their way up through my chest. Was I about to have a resurgence of the nearly uncontrollable crying that came unannounced in the days immediately following Bonnie's death?

I put the front windows all the way down. Even hot air might help.

After a shower and a beer, I fed Rocco and got him back in the car. Poor guy was probably wondering how he got assigned to *this* relaxing drill: drive here, drive there, Hey! Let's do that again.

It was still light and I drove east on Route 6A to the Mid Cape Highway. I wanted to go somewhere and see the ocean, not back to any of the beaches in Sandwich. My stomach was a little queasy and I had no appetite. I kept the windows open.

Forty-five minutes later I pulled into a parking spot at Nauset Beach in Orleans. We sat in the car for a minute and I watched the breakers out in the Atlantic. Where do the continental banks end and the ocean canyons begin?

Walking for nearly an hour, we were now back at the car and Rocco was wet and sandy. He jumped up to the back seat, I got behind the wheel and started the drive back. Twenty minutes later I got off the highway and followed 6A through Yarmouth and Barnstable. Not much traffic on a Friday night. I did see a diner that I thought I might try tomorrow.

The whole incident at the beach with the body was too much. Trying to move along with the grieving process of Bonnie's death had just come to a roadblock. I needed a phone shrink.

"**Michael, are you OK?**" Becky Ragsdale asked. It was 10:45pm when the phone rang, Louie was in bed and had been asleep since 10 o'clock.

"Eh-h, not so great," I said, taking a deep breath and blowing it out through my mouth.

"What's wrong? Are you still on the Cape?"

"Yep. Pretty hot here. Thermometer hit *90* for a second day in a row." I laughed before adding, "I didn't expect temperatures like this."

"The weather channel said the heatwave is all along the Northeast, from Delaware and Maryland all the way up through the Massachusetts coast. It's breaking records for this early in the summer," Becky said.

"I can believe it. Even Rocco is showing some signs of slowing down."

"Louie's asleep. But you knew that."

"Yeah, that's why I called on the landline. Hope you don't mind."

"You're not calling about the weather. Did something happen?" she asked.

"Howd'ya guess?"

"I hear it in your voice. You're thinking about Bonnie."

"I've been thinking about Bonnie for most of the last two weeks. I was convinced that I was making some

55

progress. But I'm still having out of the blue conversations with her. And that helps. Up until a few hours ago, I thought that I'd turned the corner."

Becky was quiet and let me rattle on.

"I was starting to laugh at some of the dumb things that we'd said and done together. Even with the age difference, we really did have a lot of fun. Bonnie was a thoughtful, considerate person." I stopped talking.

"Michael, you know about the five stages of grief," Becky said.

"Yeah, yeah. Denial, then anger, what, followed by bargaining? A lot of depression, then acceptance, right?"

"Yes. And it doesn't happen at the same pace for everyone. Some people have a really hard time getting past the anger." As soon as she said this, I knew that was *not* my issue. Hugh Mackin had helped me move past the anger almost immediately.

"I think that I am stalled at stop number four. The depression is really starting to settle in."

Becky listened without interruption. I wasn't sure of everything that I was telling her and if I was repeating myself. Then I got to the clincher.

"So, this afternoon, after we came back from Woods Hole, I took Rocket Boy back to the beach to throw the ball. Whadda' we find on our way back? A body."

"WHAT?" Becky said in a muffled scream.

"Yeah. Someone, *somewhere*, wrapped a body in a couple of tarps and dropped it at one of the beaches here in Sandwich. We're on our way back to the car when Rocco goes all bloodhound on me."

"*You* found it?"

"That would be a yes. I didn't know what it was, looked like a rolled carpet. But I called it in. Took the cops about two minutes to figure out what they had."

"Michael, that's just *horrible*. No wonder you're feeling depressed. I'm so sorry," she said.

"The medical examiner was still there when I left, around 6:30. But one of the cops I spoke with indicated that it's a woman's body."

"Oh, Michael."

"Yeah. Put me a little closer to the edge."

"Listen, Louie was going to call you anyway. We're driving down to my brother's tomorrow. You met John?"

"Yeah. He lives out near Greenfield, right?"

"Yes. And we're going to drive out to the Cape." I laughed when she said this.

"Hot dog, Ragsdale goes on tour. Your husband might be getting out of control."

"I wish," she said. "No, we've been thinking about it since Louie was able to arrange for a whole month off. John really believes that he can get Louie to play golf," she laughed. "Try to picture *that*."

"Kinda' like watching Moe, Curly and Larry out on the links," I said.

"And you can bet, as soon as we get anywhere near the water, Louie's plan will be to fish."

"No doubt. Listen, Becky, thank you for letting me talk." I didn't tell her that she was number two on my list. A call ten minutes earlier to my sister in California went to voicemail and no call back.

"Of course. I'll have Louie call you in the morning."

"Sorry that I called so late."

"Michael, that is not a problem. Get some rest," she added, then ended the call.

Fourteen

Saturday morning, after *not* getting much rest, I decided to go back and check out the diner in Barnstable. How could you pass up a throwback to the '50s with a sign sporting a silhouette of a '59 Chevy Impala above the words *Diner Shore*?

The colorful neon sign that had caught my attention last night, had one arrow pointing toward the diner entrance, and another arrow under the word Shore, which pointed to the east.

Inside, a counter with eight vinyl-covered stools and only four booths, two on either side. The color scheme was heavy on different shades of blue. The place sported a lot of US Navy memorabilia, along with some civilian sailing posters and photos. All along the wall above the counter were black and white photos of different types of ships, large and small, including some stock news photos of landing craft and soldiers that were part of the D-Day invasion in Normandy.

Only a few people in the place; three guys in one of the booths and two older men at the counter near the door. I walked past them and took a stool two seats over. As I picked up a laminated menu, another older man came from the kitchen area and sat at the end of the counter. There was a coffee mug and a newspaper in front of his spot. He gave me glance.

"Morning," he said, then picked up the paper and folded it over.

"Good morning," I replied and went back to the menu. All three men at the counter had at least twenty-five years on me, perhaps forty. The guys in the booth were younger.

A young man - early-twenties, maybe - behind the counter, asked if I would like coffee.

"Please. Cream on the side."

He slid a heavy porcelain mug in front of me, filled it with coffee and placed a couple of plastic creamers on the counter next to the mug.

"Thanks," I said.

The two to my right were talking about calibrating barometers. In actuality, one guy was doing all the talking, the other guy was chewing slowly and nodding.

I ordered one egg over easy, hash browns and an English muffin. The counter guy wrote it on a pad and went to the kitchen window to post it. The old guy to my left lowered his newspaper. He hollered to the cook, I presumed.

"Brandon, one cluck up, spuds, French connection."

The young counter guy just shook his head and went

to check on the men in the booth. I looked at the old guy next to me.

"OK, got it. One cluck up, egg sunny side up. Spuds. But *French connection*?" I said. He gave a little snicker, then turned the page of the newspaper.

"Just hoping I can teach Phil and Don here the ropes," he said. He looked up and made a motion with his head to the kitchen. "These boys here are my grandsons," he said. "Think they might catch on if I stick around for another ten years or so."

"This is your place?" I said. He raised his head and looked right at me.

"Your first time here?" Now I was getting the local eyeball treatment, checking out the stranger.

"Yeah. Saw your sign last night and made a *special trip* this morning just to get breakfast," I said.

His tone and manner reminded me of an old Select board fellow I'd known many years ago. Gruff and a bit dismissive. When these guys hit the ball at you, you had to hit it right back at them.

"Grampa Willie, give it a rest," the counter guy said walking back behind us. The old man laughed.

Local color. I drank my coffee, studied the photos and memorabilia and waited for my breakfast.

Becky told Louie about the phone call from Hanlon. He listened without comment, but raised his eyebrows at the information about a body being discovered at the beach.

"In Sandwich?" he said.

"That's what it sounded like," she replied. "Michael said that he'd been out throwing the ball with Rocco. When they got back to the parking lot, Rocco wouldn't stay away from a tarp, apparently rolled up near a bench. So, he called 9-1-1." Louie listened, then took a sip of coffee

"Have you ever heard me mention the name Peter Whalen?" he said. Becky shook her head.

"We were at UMass at the same time. I didn't really know him then, but got to know him briefly a few years back. He was with the Mass State Police." He took another swig of the coffee.

"Now," he added, "he is the Chief of Police ..." he paused for effect, "in Sandwich."

Becky looked at him. "Small world," she said.

Louie didn't reply, but clustered the fingers of his left hand, pursed his lips and repeatedly patted his Van Dyke, a routine that Becky had seen a thousand times. It would end with a little gesture that gave him the appearance of someone about to blow a kiss. Only Louie never blew kisses.

"You need to call Michael," she said. "We were on the phone for *fifteen minutes* last night. He's having a hard time."

Louie shook his head. "Guilt," he said.

"You honestly think so?"

"Yes. Bonnie really loved him, wanted to have *kids*. He wouldn't commit. She chose to move on. Now's she's dead."

They stared at each other. Finally, Becky stood up, picked up both of their cups and started for the kitchen counter.

"Do you want more coffee?" she asked.

"Not now. Don't dump it, I'll have more later."

"Call Michael."

Fifteen

Donnie was ticked. This had only happened once before, a "no show." No reply yet from Sal, even though he'd sent a second text earlier in the morning.

Taking advantage of the continental breakfast at the Ramada West, he took a second raspberry muffin and another cup of coffee back to his room on the top floor. Checkout was at Noon. Donnie had no intention of being in Atlantic City for a second night. But, he sure as shit wasn't going back to Boston either. Or, at least he'd told himself that he wasn't.

C'mon, Sal. Let's get this fucking show on the road. He didn't text that. Instead, he simply typed, 'What now?' What Donnie *hoped* was 'now' was that Sal, back in Detroit, was working it out. Surely someone would make the connection this morning. He really didn't give a shit if was not the same man who failed to show last night.

The airport was ten minutes away. The boardwalk and all of the tourism activity at the casinos was only five minutes away. If it came to that, and he had to stay over, worse things could happen. He just wanted to get home. He looked at his watch; 9:40. Where the fuck was Sal?

The gunmetal gray, polycarbonate rolling suit case, Samsonite, no less, was on the floor next to the bed. It was heavy, more than fifty pounds. He had no idea how much cash could be in there. And he was pretty certain that it was cash. Maybe bearer bonds, not jewelry. The combination lock was of no concern to him. The case was solid and secure. Donnie just wanted the case to be in someone else's possession. Sooner rather than later.

9:42. Let's go, Sal.

"We're looking into it," the man said to Sal. "Nobody is happy about this. Nobody."

"How long's my guy gonna' have to wait?" Sal said. He switched the phone to his other hand.

"I can't tell you that yet. There's a guy in Philly, who has to *talk* to a guy in Atlantic City, who has to make it happen. Maybe a coupla' hours."

"He can do that. But you'll stay on top of this? It's a priority, yes?"

"No, Sal, it's not important to us that this happened. We don't care about our guy goes missing in Atlantic City. Of course it is a *fucking priority*!"

"Hey," Sal interjected, "Just trying to hold up our end here."

"Thank you. I wouldn't expect less. Now please tell

your boy Donnie to just sit fucking tight. *We're on it*, OK?"

The call ended. They hadn't discussed the 'bundle' drop on Cape Cod. That was done. If there was going to be any fallout, not Sal's issue. Any connection to the pick-up at Logan Airport had never been brought to his attention, so Sal was happy to assume that they were unrelated. As far as he was concerned, transporting a valuable case from Point A to Point B was the only thing active. So, let's just finish it up.

Sal typed into his phone. 'Late night, sorry. I'm on it. Back to you ASAP.'

Sixteen

Walking out of Diner Shore my phone started with the opening to *Here Comes the Sun*. I looked at the screen; Ragsdale.

"Your wife says that you're going to spend the month of June trying to qualify for next year's Vermont Open Golf Tournament," I said by way of answering.

"Twenty-five years of marital bliss but she still tells *way* too many lies," Louie said. "And John Hill is going to get me on a golf course about the same time that *you* take up fencing."

"Only trying to encourage some camaraderie between you and the brother-in-law."

"Thanks for being so thoughtful," he said.

"So, are you actually coming down to the Cape?"

"Do big Striped bass eat Mackerel? Of course we're coming."

I wasn't sure that I could muster much interest in fishing, so I let the comment go. And I hadn't brought any gear. The trip was simply to get away for a short spell, take it easy, let each day play out.

"Hanlon, I know you're having a hard time," Louie said. "Becky told me about the call last night."

"Yes. I was just a little out of it. She was kind to let me bend her ear. She told you about the body?"

"It friggin' never ends, no matter where you go."

"Yeah, I was sort of coming to the same conclusion," I replied. "Blowing up night clubs, shooting people at an airport. A body in a lake there, a body on the beach here."

"Makes you want to get some hand grenades and hide in the basement."

I laughed at this, not because I thought it was funny, but because of the World War II guys back inside the diner; tattoos, short hair and old war stories. Good for them.

"So, I'm leaving this neat diner where I just had breakfast," I said. "Some old Salt giving everybody a hard time. Non-stop comedian."

"Willie's. In Barnstable?" Louie gave a chuckle.

"Diner Shore. How did you know that?"

"Place is a landmark," he said. "Willie Ridell has been insulting customers, probably since before the Kennedy administration. I first went there with my uncle when I was in high school. Guy is a real *hoot*."

"He has his twin grandsons here running it now. Apparently, he hangs out all the time making sure they don't mess it up."

"Bet that's just a real treat," Louie replied. "They'll probably have him committed. Are you taking care of that dog?" he added.

"In fact, I'm standing here looking at him. Gotta' let him out for leak. But Rocco is having a grand time." As I was talking, I scratched his muzzle. "Don't think that he's put it together that he will be staying with me from now on." As soon as I said this, I had a recall image of the first time that Bonnie brought him to my house when he was a pup.

"You're a dog guy," I added. "How do you know when they figure out that somebody's *not* coming back?"

"They're all different. Some dogs sulk, but eventually get over it. Other breeds don't miss a beat. Hard to say."

I reached in and scratched behind his ears. It hadn't start to heat up yet, but I still wanted to get him out of the car.

"When do you think that you're going to get here? And by the way, you'll probably have to find another place to stay. Jean McKearney is full-up. Both of the other units are occupied I think all next week."

"Becky's brother and his wife will handle it. They'll find some rooms. Stay tuned, I'll get back to you on that," he said.

"Well, I have nothing going on back home. But if this heat hangs on, I may run up to Maine."

"It's gonna' break. I looked at Weather Underground this morning. The Cape should be back down to normal temperatures starting tomorrow."

"OK, let me know how the plan shapes up."

"Check. And one other thing," Louie said.

"Yeah?"

"Assuage your guilt. It's just *not* going to help you get through this."

"Right. I'll work on it."

"Please do that."

Sandwich Police Chief Peter Whalen spent much of the early morning on the telephone, not his favorite use of time. It was bad enough during a normal week, but with a yet-to-be-identified body showing up on one of the town beaches, Whalen and his department would be part of the media dance until the case was solved.

The Medical Examiner's office would call the next tune. The body was a female, most likely dead for 'a few days' when it was dropped here. So, if and when the ID came, then *where* did the body come from? That would become the immediate focus.

Whalen was skeptical, based on a gut feeling, that the body was local. Might have come from somewhere else on the Cape, could have come up from Providence or down from Boston. Or, from any number of other cities and towns. Dumped bodies were, unfortunately, not a new phenomenon. In his days with the state police, dozens of bodies each year were processed by the Chief Medical Examiner's office then through the Department of Transitional Assistance in arranging burials.

But it would likely be days, possibly weeks, before any burial of this particular body. On the last, hot Saturday of May, a holiday weekend, Chief Whalen was devoting his time to rounding-up reports from digital traffic videos in search of a dark-colored van, and consulting with former colleagues at the Mass State Police headquarters on recent reports of Missing Persons/Female.

Whalen would join with the Cape & Islands District Attorney for a briefing to reporters. Once the basic info was out to the media, that's when questions and updates on the investigation would shift to the DA's office.

Seventeen

Back at the efficiency unit, I told Jean McKearney that I was planning to stay at least through the end of the coming week. She was fine with that. I had already paid for the first four nights, so I gave her another $300 and we agreed to settle up when I was ready to leave.

My plan was to hit the road for short day trips and act like any other tourist on a first visit to this historic vacation spot. If nothing else, I could do one the things that I most enjoy; drive. Maybe that would help shift my mind to things other than dead people.

Pretty good chance that it was going to be another hot one, so before it got too warm, I did some stretching and five minutes of exercises. Rocco's favorite was sit-ups. He tried to bite my elbows each time I came up. A quick shower, fresh shirt and shorts and we were back in the car.

Since I'd already been down to Woods Hole, then out to Nauset Beach last night, I decided to stay on the inner Cape to start, follow 6A and some of the side roads. Just drive and see what looked interesting.

On the trip from Vermont earlier, listening to music CDs had triggered a lot of memories involving Bonnie and me. At some point I was going to have to get beyond that. But music on the radio, generally, is one of the pleasures of a road trip. Maybe I could just drive in silence for a while and see how I did with that. For the moment, I went to 107.5 FM for classical, WFCC out of Chatham. The signal was strong, so I set the volume low for background.

Going through Yarmouth I was tempted to stop, but resisted, at the Edward Gorey Home and Museum. Driving without the AC felt good. Every time I slowed down or stopped at a light or intersection, if any pedestrians were around, Rocco got a wave and a smile. I knew that he looked pretty handsome and liked the attention with his head out the rear passenger side window.

Not much traffic on this state highway for a Saturday morning. But it was only the 27th of May and from all that I had read, the pace wouldn't pick up for about a month. Dennis, Brewster, then I was in Orleans again, where 6A merged with the Mid Cape Highway. I decided instead to follow some side streets that wound through marshes leading to streams that fed into the bay.

At five after twelve, I was on Herring Brook Road and, according to a sign, apparently close to Great Pond, one of the fresh water ponds that Ragsdale had mentioned when he was pushing for me to come down here.

OK, let's take a right turn.

The body brought in the previous evening was that of a woman. Caucasian, the age range of 40 to 50, dead most likely for at least 72 hours. Cause of death undetermined; no visible wounds or marks on the body. At first glance, the woman appeared to be fit and in good health before she died. But even that remained to be confirmed.

Dr. Katherine Lofgren marked boxes on the standard work sheet form. Her routine was to checkoff easy things first before performing an autopsy and completing a preliminary report. Assigned to this office just a few months earlier, it would be her fifth autopsy at the ME's lab on Cape Cod. However, she was a forensic veteran who had conducted or assisted with more than 100 autopsies.

Like those who taught her and with whom she still consulted, Lofgren was keenly aware that she could be called to testify if and when certain deaths wound up in court. That possibility was simply a reinforcement of the always present need to be thorough. Unlike a fixed amount of time that a doctor might allocate for visiting with a patient in an office setting, Lofgren would take all the time that she needed here. Get it right the first time.

She clicked the ballpoint pen, attached it to the clipboard holding the form and got ready to scrub for the post mortem exam.

Eighteen

One downside of being your own guy is that when anything at all goes off the tracks, *you* are responsible for handling same. In Sal's enterprises, that normally required putting other activities aside.

Triage was not a word that Sal often used. He was, however, familiar with the term. There had been a few occasions in recent years when he had been so absorbed in a particular activity that he would briefly consider trying to find an assistant. This was one of those times.

When they initially connected after a trip back to Ohio and the old haunts of his youth, Sal was flattered by Donnie's frequent comparison of what Sal did, with the work done by successful sports agents. It fed his ego. And Donnie was always cool about it, too. He knew the names of all the big-time agents and which athletes they represented. He would egg Sal on by saying things like, 'You won't have any of the arrogant owners or players' unions to mess with you.'

But Sal also knew that he would not seriously recruit

someone, even as an assistant. Nor would he ask around, or poach somebody from his network of clients and associates. It was this little mental masturbation exercise that he did and it always brought to a halt the idea of expanding. Moving out beyond the Great Lakes region was tempting, the thought of becoming a bigger player, of having more. It continued to be just one very entertaining thought, unlikely to be acted upon.

Running more people like Donnie Richards, his most productive, most reliable and most trusted guy on the road, was one thing. He could - and would - send Donnie anywhere. Not the same with the half-dozen locals he used at any given time within Detroit. All the mobsters knew them and they knew the mobsters. *Loyalty* was like the winds coming down from Lake Huron or up from Lake Erie, as in; Stay alert, they change every day.

What Sal also knew about himself was that he really had come to like gambling, especially at the casinos. For him, it had recently become the most lucrative aspect of his work. And he did it solo, no fucking fooling around with bookies or anyone else. This really was all part of the same psychological mix that had driven him since he left Youngstown more than twenty-five years back. It boiled down to trust. The people he *trusted* could be counted on one hand, even if he counted twice.

Three hours had passed and still no word on a new contact in Atlantic City. Sal picked up his phone to call Donnie, a text message wouldn't do. They would discuss 'what now?' and talk through the possibilities while Sal waited to hear new information.

Donnie eventually found a cable TV channel called retro TV, programming old classic shows that, as far as he could tell, ranged from the 50s through the 70s. There was something on from the BBC called *Doctor Who*, a show that he'd heard about but had never actually seen. Looked pretty low budget.

His phone whistled at him. He hit the mute button on the TV remote and picked up the phone. It was 12:17 according to the clock on his phone screen. The call was from Sal.

"Please tell me there's *someone* at the airport right this minute waiting for me," Donnie said. He got up from the bed, walked to the window and opened the draperies.

"Listen," Sal said, "let's give 'em until 5 o'clock. If we don't have a new guy and drop scheduled by then, it's their loss."

Donnie looked down at the hotel swimming pool, the parking lot and out at some lake not a hundred yards away. He could hear highway traffic from the other end of the building. He took a deep breath. Now he would have to tell the front desk that he was keeping the room.

"And if we don't hear from them?" Donnie said.

"We shift to our plan?"

"And the shift would be?"

"That's why I'm *calling* you," Sal said, a slight wisp of exasperation in his voice. "We need to talk about this." No reason to get in a big yank with Donnie. He was not the problem.

"These guys are good clients. I've known them since almost the first week I was in Detroit. Long time. They've always been smart, no fuckin' around. Now they're adding more jobs that need outside help. Like us."

Donnie could detect Sal's defensiveness, so he let him go on.

"You said the case weighs over fifty pounds?" Sal said. "That's a lot of cash. They're not gonna' dick around with this. I think they're a little anxious about their Atlantic City guy disappearing."

As Sal was talking, Donnie rolled the suitcase from the closet and gave it a heft. Maybe 80 pounds, like one of those deceptive looking bags of cement mix that you get at Home Depot.

"Why didn't they just have the Boston guy bring it down here?" Donnie said.

"I don't ask those questions. They want me to know something they will tell me. *But*, I can speculate." Donnie waited for more.

"Somebody in this group, a guy back east, has been charged with fraud, some internet investment scam. And there's a relative involved up in Boston. Might be that *my guys* are scrambling to extricate themselves before *they* wind up in front of a Grand Jury."

"So, my missing Jersey guy here is the cut-off man?" Donnie asked.

"Maybe. That doesn't matter to us. He's either gonna' show or not. Or, we're gonna' have a new contact. Let's go past 5 'clock today."

"OK. Our plan. Whaddya' have in mind?" Now Sal was quiet.

Donnie watched people down at the swimming pool. He knew from seeing the weather on TV earlier that all along the New Jersey coast they were expecting to have temperatures again in the 90s.

"If I don't hear from him by 5 o'clock," Sal said, "I will call and tell him that you need to be in Chicago tomorrow night. That when we set this up, the Boston to Atlantic City leg, we were expecting you to get back here by Sunday morning. That's less than 24 hours away and it puts us in a bind."

"And when you call him, if he says, 'Sal. Keep your man right there?' you will tell him what?"

"I will tell him that you and the pick-up case are headed home," Sal replied.

"They don't have a new guy here by then, you think he's going to be OK with that?"

"Probably not. But it will push the ball to their side of the field and maybe move things along. I'll tell him the Chicago run has been locked down for weeks and we can't blow it off."

Donnie watched the guy on TV, the one he'd figured

out was Doctor Who, stepping inside an old blue police box. What the hell's that about?

"You're the man, Sal. I'm right here. Call when you know what I'm doing"

"How quick can you get back to the airport?"

"More traffic than there was last night. Maybe ten minutes." Donnie said.

"Then could be that he wants the suitcase somewhere else. Might not *be* the airport," Sal said. "You said you're close to the parkway?"

"Yeah. Guess what the name of the road is?"

"Let me think," Sal answered. "How about The Donald Trump Boulevard of Losers?"

"Black Horse Pike. Gotta' have some local historical significance, don't ya think?"

"They probably renamed the highway after his casino went under."

Nineteen

After Back and forth phone calls with her brother and sister-in-law, Becky Ragsdale was ready to leave by 1:30. Louie had both dogs and their duffel bags in the truck. He'd been ready for half an hour.

The plan was to spend the night at the in-laws, then Louie and his brother-in-law, John, would head out first thing Sunday morning for the Cape. Bucky, an older black Lab, and a young rescue mutt, Chico, would stay with their niece. Becky and her sister-in-law Angie would drive to the Cape on Monday. John had found a guest cottage that could accommodate up to four people near Corn Hill Beach in Truro.

The drive from Vermont to Orange, MA would take three hours. When they took trips like this, it was their habit to have relaxed, rambling conversations, often about things going on not just in their life but in the lives of family and friends. Occasionally they rehashed gossip about the small town where they lived in the Northeast Kingdom.

A minute after they got on the highway, Becky offered

up the first topic.

"Can I go back to what we were talking about this morning?" Louie gave her a sideways glance.

"Michael," she added. "How he is coping with Bonnie's death."

"Sure."

She tugged on her seatbelt so that she could shift enough to be facing Louie. Gone were the days when a passenger could turn sideways and pull up her feet onto the seat. Unless you were stupid. Maybe you could squirm around sideways and still keep your belt fastened?

"You know him very well," she began. "I have listened to the two of you *countless* times ragging each other. I know it's a guy thing, all of you do it. I get that."

She waited for a response. Nothing. Louie kept his eyes on the driving. There might have been a quick, slight movement of his mouth.

"I just need to tell you that from *my perspective*, he is truly in grief." Now he turned again with a glance at his wife. But he remained silent.

Becky was measuring what and how she would say, what she needed to say next. She didn't want to sound as though she were badgering her husband, but she needed him to accept her interpretation of how she thought that Hanlon was coping.

"Do you remember how you were in the months after your mother died?" she said.

Louie made a little sound with his mouth, swallowed

and nodded his head.

"I don't mean to say that this is the same. It's not. But the way anyone reacts to someone's death, boy, there can be a lot of things going on." She spoke slowly and with more caring in her voice than in their usual conversations.

"Upbringing, religious views, life experiences. How they have encountered death before. Family dynamics," she went on. "Just a *lot* to contend with. And, yes, usually some form of guilt. Survivor's guilt at a minimum," she added.

"What I'm trying to say, Louie, is that I know Michael is important to you. Sometimes you two remind me of brothers. Including the teasing. And I know from some of the things that you have said over the years, that that kind of thing goes on all the time the army."

"Hanlon has never been in the military," Louie said.

"I know that. But the way he gives it back to you sometimes, you wouldn't know it." Louie smirked when she said this.

"Becky," Louie said, turning to her for quick eye contact, then back at the highway. "Hanlon is not some fragile flower, despite how he may act"

"No, he's certainly not. It's not what I'm suggesting." Shaking her head, she tapped her breastbone.

"OK. Just let me get this off my chest," she continued. "All of the times that you taunt Michael about his," she made air quotations with her fingers, 'lovelies' and 'how he let Bonnie slip away.' Don't you think that *that* is part of what he's thinking about now?"

"Of course," Louie said.

Neither of them said anything for a minute. Both dogs were asleep and might as well have been on a road trip to Alaska. Becky waited for another minute to finish, then made one final plea.

"Just promise me that you will go easy. That you will show him that you understand about grief."

After five seconds, both hands gripping the steering wheel, Louie nodded.

"I promise."

Twenty

A couple of hours driving around Great Pond, Jemima Pond and Depot Pond eventually got me to Eastham and Route 6. I continued cruising on neighborhood roads rather than getting back on the highway.

The turns onto residential streets were just to admire the houses, everything from small, maybe one bedroom homes to three storey, multi-dormer structures that had to come with hefty annual property tax bills. Most of the homes had weathered, gray shingle siding, or they had some cedar shingle component to the exterior along with shutters and white trim. It made me wonder when builders and real estate people first began using the term 'cape' in their marketing?

We wound up parking near the old Coast Guard Station and walking out to the ocean. A hot Saturday afternoon on Memorial Day weekend and there were a lot of people. Families, a few younger guys with surf boards, and several other dogs around. I kept Rocco on the leash until we got to the beach.

Not sure why it hadn't occurred to me, but I was surprised to see a prominent sign that included a warning to swimmers and waders; 'Great white sharks live in these waters. Avoid swimming near seals.' O-o-K, we can do that.

What didn't come as a surprise was Rocco getting all sniffy, sniffy with a good-looking Siberian Husky. The dog had beautiful markings. They did the little tail-up, nose to butt dance for a minute, then the husky took off back down the beach. A quick tug on the leash and Rocket Boy wanted to go play.

"Another time, kid," I said. "Stay." He half obeyed, only stretching the leash tight but not pulling me over.

Too many people and I wasn't in the mood to be sociable, so we turned and headed back to the car. Dope slap to the heart; I had another flashback. It was one of walking with Bonnie back from Popham Beach in Maine two summers ago. I'd been recovering from shoulder surgery. Rocco was only a few months old at the time and it was all that she could do to keep him under control then.

Now he was fully-grown at seventy-pounds. Even with my normal strength in both arms, he was a challenge. I tugged on the leash to get his attention, then knelt on the sand next to him. He gave me the full-on stare.

"Listen, champ," I said softly as I hugged him. "We're gonna' shape-up, get *more* training and maybe even get you your own TV show."

Something that amused Bonnie when I'd been around

86

and Rocco saw a dog on television, his ears would perk up and he would watch, then I would tell him, 'Those guys are getting *paid*, pooch. You need to work at it. They're not just gonna call you up out of the blue and invite you to come do a commercial.'

I stood up, Rocco held fast for a few more seconds, then we kept walking back to the car. It was almost three o'clock.

Coming back to the center of Eastham near a small park that had an old wind mill at its center and benches scattered around, I pulled behind a dark colored van with a Massachusetts plate. This van was a burgundy color, but a similar style to the one that had been parked near where the body had been dumped at the beach in Sandwich.

I stared at the plate. Blue letters, red numerals. *The Spirit of America* across the bottom under the numbers. Two small decals on the bumper, one yellow, the other one green. Couldn't make out what they were for.

The van turned right, I turned left onto Depot Road. Circling around to get back to the Mid Cape Highway, I watched the van in my rearview mirror until it was out of sight.

Did that dark gray van at the beach have Mass plates?

My memory tried to call up the image. We'd crossed the boardwalk and had started in the direction of the canal. I had bent down to pick up a shell. When I stood again, I'd looked in the direction of the parking lot and my car. I'd hit the key fob to be sure the doors were locked. The lights on my car had flashed. The van, a couple of spaces away from my car, had been parked near a bench, face out, backed-up to the sand.

It was the red numerals. I was now remembering, at a minimum, the plate had been white. And I was pretty sure that the numbers had been red.

I glanced at my watch; quarter after three. Probably an hour back to Sandwich if I stayed on 6.

"OK, Rocket. Let's go fess up," I said. He was settled on the back seat. Probably pissed off that I was such a lousy beach partner.

Twenty One

At 3:30, Donnie briefly considered going to the pool to take a good look at the women. It was mostly families and besides, he didn't have the clothes that would let him fit in. Unless he was OK with looking like the route salesman who had just stopped by to check the vending machines.

Instead, he rolled the suit case to the van and placed it in front on the passenger side. He got in and went off looking for an auto car wash that had vacuum service available. Clean out and rearrange the rear compartment. Now that the Cape Cod delivery was behind him, he would go through the car wash. Maybe a good time to change plates again, too.

Nothing to eat since the muffins at breakfast. Maybe get a burger. Or, a sub sandwich. What the hell did they call them back here, a *Blimpie*? Wasn't that an old cartoon character from Popeye? He thought about it. No, that was *Wimpy*. Whatever. Just find some food.

Donnie hoped that he would get another call from Sal before 5 'clock.

"Turns out that we got problems other than Atlantic City," the man on the phone said.

This was the first time that Sal could recall any hint of uncertainty from these guys. All the jobs in the past, 'go here, do that, we're done, thank you.' It was an example that Sal himself had emulated; know precisely what task is required, be organized and efficient, move on quickly when you're finished.

It was in 1997 when Sal had his first serious encounter with five men whom he began referring to, only to himself, as 'the Safari Boys,' a short-lived name he lifted from a professional indoor soccer team. It had been at one of that team's final games at the Palace of Auburn Hills when Sal got the opportunity to take his first 'big' assignment from the group. From that day forward, his contact was a man named Nick.

All phone calls, all of the fee transfers and all other arrangements went through Nick.

It was at a time when corporations and organizations everywhere were 'outsourcing,' a trend that trickled out to all sorts of enterprises. The first job that Sal had landed was a simple 'pick up and take away', which he'd done himself. That had led to other jobs, other clients, to these guys, and eventually leading Sal to the recruitment of his old Youngstown pal, Donnie. And here we are today.

But now, maybe a glitch. Sal knew that nothing good would be accomplished by throwing in the 'we have a previously booked, must attend' job in Chicago tomorrow night. At least he wouldn't trot that out until he heard the rest of what the man had to say about 'problems other than Atlantic City.'

So, he waited for the rest of the explanation about why Donnie's contact was MIA.

"Maybe coincidence, but we don't *think* so, that all of a sudden we have lost contact with our Boston friends. That includes the jamoke who gave your guy the suitcase." Sal wasn't hearing any humor in Nick's voice.

"And thanks for the photo of the Tesla with the fucking Goodell bumper sticker. Might come in handy in locating our lost friend," he added.

"Part of the service," Sal said. "Since smartphones, we get photo confirmation on all jobs."

"Good idea. Probably saves on a lot of bullshit later, huh? Like the cops and body cameras."

"Something like that," Sal replied, skirting the edge of sarcasm.

"What it's lookin' like at the moment," Nick continued, "is we're gonna ask your guy to just bring the fucking suitcase back here. The casino boys in Jersey will have to take care of their end."

While Sal frequently speculated about the motives for his clients' activities, he was not dumb enough to bring it up at his own initiative. Always better to listen. But right at that second, he did wonder about *why didn't we make this decision a few hours ago*?

"We're waiting for one more call. Last chance, you

might say. If that don't work, I'm asking you to bring your guy home with the suitcase."

"Good. That can work. Sooner is better."

"You know, and I'm sure that your driver knows, that suitcase is full of cash. Maybe five mil," Nick said.

"Hey. I don't ask. You give us the request, I tell you the fee, we have a deal," Sal interjected. "We don't scan anything, you don't have any forms to fill out, and we can get it there overnight, too."

"*Better* than FedEx, huh?" Nick cracked.

"Without question."

"I'll call back. Won't be long."

"Thank you," Sal replied. He tapped the end call button, then immediately tapped the redial to Donnie's phone.

Twenty Two

When I arrived at the Sandwich PD, there was just one other civilian car parked in front of the station, an ancient looking, apple green Datsun 210, long before they dropped the name and went with Nissan.

I parked in front of the Datsun, lowered the windows for Rocco, then went up the steps to the front door of the station. There was a small foyer with a glass display case. Inside the case were old police hats, badges, night sticks and some really old handcuffs. Also, a few sports trophies that I presumed had been awarded to members of the police department. I couldn't make out any of the names or teams listed on the trophies.

Four chairs were against the wall and there was a 24/7 Prescription Drug and Medication Drop Box. To my left was a security window that had a button and a small speaker mounted on the wall near where I was seated. After two minutes, I realized that the lights were off in the area behind the tinted window. No one had acknowledged my arrival and I didn't see anyone, so I pushed the button. A few seconds later, a voice came over the speaker.

"Can we help?" a man's voice said. I glanced around and saw a camera mounted at angle between the window and a steel door to my left. I guessed that the door led to offices and probably to an interview room and a holding cell.

"Yes. My name is Michael Hanlon. I was at the beach yesterday when the body was found," I said. "Wonder if I could speak with Chief Whalen?" I doubted that he would be there late on a Saturday afternoon, but figured whoever was on duty could connect me by phone.

"Just one minute, please," the unseen male voice said.

Maybe thirty seconds later, there was a buzzer sound and the door behind me was opening. I turned to see the Chief coming through the door.

"Mr. Hanlon," Whalen said, extending his right hand. He was wearing a navy polo shirt and khaki pants. The shirt was open at the neck and sported the Sandwich PD logo above his name.

"I didn't really expect that you would be here," I said. "But I wanted to tell you something else about the van."

He motioned to the door behind us. "Come on back," he said. I followed him through the door into a hallway that had doors to the left and the right. He turned left.

When we reached his office, he gestured to a chair and I sat. His desk had some papers on it, along with an open laptop and a plastic cup sporting a NY Yankees logo.

"Would you like something to drink – water, a soft

drink?" he asked.

"Thanks, no. I'm good."

He sat behind the desk and pulled the cover on the lap top toward him, not completely closed but out of the way as not to obstruct his line of sight.

"So, the van?" He was sitting almost at attention but leaned back slightly. He picked up a pen from his desk, rested his right elbow on the arm of the chair, tapped the pen a couple of times on his chin and left it there.

"I think it had Mass plates," I said. "I saw another van this afternoon that reminded me of it."

Whalen nodded. "OK. That helps," he said, reaching for the cup and taking a sip.

"What I remember is that I had turned around to click the locks for my car. Just after we left the parking lot. I saw the lights flash and I *think* that I recall seeing a white plate with red numerals on the back of the van."

Twenty Three

Becky and Louie Ragsdale were having dinner with John and Angie Hill on an enclosed porch at the Hills' residence in Orange, MA. John was starting to clear dishes from the table when Becky began talking about Hanlon.

"Bonnie was a *really* good partner for him," she said. "At least that's what I thought. She was a lot younger than Michael, but you really couldn't tell that that made much difference when you were around them." She looked at Louie. He nodded in agreement.

"I mean, she was fine with all of the things that he liked. Baseball, movies, cooking, politics, fishing. *Music!*" Louie snickered at his wife's reference to the music.

"Yeah. We were always dumping oldies on her, just about every time she was at his house. But I think that before they broke up, Hanlon was actually starting to learn about more recent music," Louie said. "Bonnie had given him some CDs. I think that she was making progress in getting him to load MP3s onto his phone." Now Becky nodded.

"Certainly some artists that *I've* never heard of," Louie added.

"How long had they been apart before the plane crash," Angie asked.

Becky looked at Louie, then said, "What, two years?"

"I think it was just before Christmas a year ago," Louie said. "So more like a year-and-a-half."

"But they were still, I think, good friends. Really from the day they broke up," Bonnie added.

"Isn't that why he has the dog," John asked, picking up flatware from the table and placing it on the dirty plates to go to the dishwasher.

"Yes," Becky said. "And thank God for that. If he didn't have Rocco with him right now, I think that he'd be a basket case."

"On the other hand," Louie chimed in, "you *know* that the dog is stirring up a lot of memories. I mean, he was just a pup when Bonnie and Hanlon first got together."

"That has to be hard," Angie said.

"It's *all* hard," Louie said. "Christ, one day you're on the phone with somebody across the country. The next day they're dead. Along with 70 some other people. No good byes. Just gone."

They were all silent for a minute, then Angie got up to help her husband. Becky reached over and took Louie's hand. Louie pursed his lips, inhaled through his nose and slowly shook his head.

The Red Sox game with the Mariners was on TV and almost over. Louie and John sat down to watch, while Becky and Angie took the dogs for a walk. There was still an hour or so of daylight left.

"You said that Bonnie was engaged to someone else when she died," Angie said. Becky shook her head.

"No, they hadn't announced it yet. But yes, they were planning to get married. Michael said she was going to announce the engagement at her parent's anniversary next month."

"Oh, that is just so sad," Angie said.

"Bonnie's father is a minister and to hear Michael tell it, they have a big get together for their anniversary every summer. Family, people from the church, others in the community. Michael went once. He said it was like an Old Home Day. Softball, badminton, horseshoes. Tons of food. Apparently a lot of stories and singing. And not all *hymns*," Becky laughed. "Reverend Mackin apparently has a real sense of humor. Michael said that some of the tales were pretty outrageous."

Becky stopped walking and took her sister-in-law by the arm. Angie looked at her.

"John told you about what happened yesterday?" Angie shook her head. Becky squeezed her arm.

"Michael was coming from the beach back to his car," she hesitated a beat, "and he discovered a woman's body that had been dumped next to the parking lot."

Angie put her hand to her mouth and said, "Oh my

God."

"That's the real reason we're going out to the Cape tomorrow instead of later in June. I was on the phone with Michael last night. Louie and I agree. He truly needs some friends right now."

The last phone call to come to Sal from his 'Safari Boys' contact, Nick, had set in motion a series of actions that threatened to get out of control fast.

It began with a request for Sal to arrange for a Skype call with his man in Atlantic City. Nick had told him that they were abandoning efforts to connect with anybody else on the East coast and that they wanted Sal to have his man bring the suitcase back to Detroit. But first, they wanted to confirm the contents of the case and wanted to do that by having it opened while they watched live in real time.

It was not difficult to set up. Sal and Donnie figured out how Donnie could do it in his hotel room, using his smartphone, and keeping his face off camera, which was important to both of them. Donnie would be given the combination to the lock via the phone call and would then proceed to open the suitcase. Nick had no issues with this and he told Sal to schedule the call for 8 PM.

The first problem popped up – live on camera – when Donnie used the combination given to him. He opened the case and pulled out a several packets of $100 bills. Then, a

99

bunch more of the same, and then a few more and then, far too many copies of recent issues of *The Boston Globe*. In fact, the bulk of the contents of the case appeared to be old newspapers.

Sal was connected to the call. As soon as he saw what was happening, his gut told him that this was not going to end well for someone. There sure as shit was *not* 'five mil' in that suitcase.

You could see Donnie's right hand pulling the rest of the newspapers from the case. They fell to the floor at his feet. When it looked like the suitcase was empty, there was a white envelope taped to the bottom of the liner. Donnie pulled it free and held it up to his phone so those at the other end could see the envelope.

Printed large, in a dark red block font, were the letters **ROI**. The letters were underlined twice.

"Open it," said a voice from the other end of the call. Sal had no idea who or how many others were listening and watching.

Donnie proceeded to lay the envelope face down on a table, fumbled the phone for a second, then slipped a small plastic coffee stirrer under the flap and slit the envelope open. He extracted one single sheet of paper, unfolded it and held it to the camera of his phone.

No one said anything for a couple of seconds. Sal brought his phone closer to see what was written on the page.

The note, also in block letters, read: SORRY. MARKET MISCALCULATION.

Then a deep voice at the other end offered a three-word assessment that clued Sal, and Donnie, into the fact that this was *not* what had been expected.

The voice, not Nick's, simply said, "That little prick."

Twenty Four

At 5:30 Sunday morning, Louie and John were on the road, Louie driving. It would take them just over two and a half hours to reach the Cape. The plan was to meet Hanlon at Diner Shore in Barnstable for breakfast.

In addition to the luggage for both couples, they had loaded two sets of golf clubs, for John and Angie, and Louie's fishing gear.

Following Route 2 east to 495, then down to 25, they hoped to be close to the Sagamore Bridge by 8 o'clock, assuming light traffic this early in the day. By the time they had reached Worcester, Louie couldn't take any more of ESPN radio on WEEI, so he tried WBZ-FM for a few minutes and wound up turning to Classic Rock on WZLX. John gave him a thumbs-up and Louie left it there. The highlight came with a three-song set by Bob Seger, ending with *Night Moves*, one of the tracks recorded with the Silver Bullet Band.

Both men drank coffee. They were comfortable with each other's company and, like other occasions when they

102

had gone somewhere together, they felt no need for a lot of conversation.

At 7:52 they were crossing the Cape Cod Canal.

Chief Peter Whalen often shifted to 'citizen' on Sunday mornings. One pursuit that he enjoyed was clamming, simply taking a clam rake, a basket and a pair of rubber gloves to dig quohogs. The local season ended in May. But on this particular Sunday morning he decided to pass on that and instead, to take one of his junior officers out for breakfast.

"Jeff, what's on your calendar this morning?" he said into the phone without introduction.

"Chief. What's up?" Brutelli replied.

"I'm going to take a run out to Willie's diner for breakfast. Care to join me?"

Brutelli almost laughed out loud. What was he going to say? 'No Chief, sorry. I have some other things to do here at home. Too busy.' He didn't say that.

"Ah, yeah, sure. What time?"

"Half-an-hour," Whalen said. "Say 9 o'clock?"

It was fortunate that Brutelli actually did not have other responsibilities on tap. An outing with his wife and kids was slated for later in the afternoon.

"I'll meet you there," Brutelli said.

"Good. Thanks."

Avoiding another trip back to Town Beach, I instead took Rocco for an early walk along a blacktop path just off Main Street. Jean McKearney had suggested it and a path that led to the state operated fish hatchery. Apparently, the place was one of the oldest hatcheries in the US and had been in operation for more than a hundred years.

We stopped along one of the raceways to watch trout swimming back and forth. Rocket Boy was certainly curious, ears perked and tail wagging. Fortunately, he didn't bark at the fish. He would save that for the seabirds along the beach.

I looked at my watch: eight-twenty. Louie had said that he and his brother-in-law should make it to the Diner Shore by 8:30, so we headed back to the car and made the short drive to Barnstable.

Guess that I shouldn't have been surprised when we got there and the parking lot was full, plus a couple of cars parked along Route 6A. Sunday morning, popular spot with very limited seating. Two couples were at the door waiting to be seated. Inside I spotted Louie in one of the booths. He saw me, waved and I excused myself past those standing in line.

All the seats at the counter were taken as well. The old guy who owned the place, Willie, was back in the kitchen helping one of his grandsons. The other twin was working the counter making sure food orders were right and that everyone had coffee.

As soon as I got to the booth, Louie moved over to let

me sit next to him. John Hill was across the table and we shook hands.

"Good to see you," John said.

"Thanks. Likewise."

Louie's trademark smirk seemed to be at half-mast. You never knew if he was going to pop some wiseass comment, or just smile to himself at something that he was thinking and not sharing with anyone else.

"Brother Ragsdale, I said. "Nice to see you as well." His wordless reply was a simple nod. Both men had coffee mugs in front of them on the table, but no food.

"How long have you been here?" I said to John. He looked at his watch.

"About ten minutes. We'd no more than walked in and half-a-dozen others came in right behind us." He turned and stretched his neck to look at the crowd.

"This is John's first visit, too," Louie said.

"To the Cape?" I said, a bit surprised. John shook his head.

"No, first time to this diner. Louie says that guy," he pointed at Willie back in the kitchen, "could have given Don Rickles a few pointers."

"Shoulda' heard him going yesterday," I said. "He was getting after two guys at the counter and they were giving it right back to him. They were talking about barometers and he tells them, 'That's just what we need. An Armenian and a paisan consulting on meteorology.'

"One of them laughs and replies, 'Willie, why don't

you get a cooking show on TV, like Emeril? You could show everyone how to cook this greasy food all you navy guys love. Shorten their lives a few years.'

"By the time I left, all three of 'em were trying to one-up each other. It was like the Marx Brothers."

"I'll bet he had nicknames for the other two guys, right?" Louie said.

"I didn't hear that. But he calls his grandsons Phil and Don."

John laughed. "As in, *Wake Up Little Susie*?" Louie nodded, the smirk now turning to a smile.

"That was my guess," I said.

"Their first, and *biggest* hit. A lotta groups influenced by The Everly Brothers," Louie said.

"A bigger hit than *Cathy's Clown*?" I asked.

"Yep. It was on the charts for more than six months. Number one four consecutive weeks."

John gave me a look similar to the one I often got from Becky each time Louie drifted into one of his Oldies routines.

"You ever see his Pop Music bible?" John asked.

"Yeah. He brought it to my house once," I said. "We were trying to settle a bet about some group."

"*Gimme Some Lovin'*," Louie said. He pointed at me and added, "*You* thought Traffic had it first. Just the other way around. The Spencer Davis Group had the hit in 1966. Steve Winwood then helped to form the group Traffic, and *they* had a cover hit five years later, 1971."

"Of course. I don't know why my kindergarten teacher didn't tell us that," I said.

"Didn't The Blues Brothers record it?" John asked.

"Yep. 1980. It's in the movie," Louie replied.

"I never get very far in these discussions. Could we talk about the Red Sox. Or the weather?" I said.

"It is because all that time you spent in radio," Louie was pointing at me again, "you *didn't pay attention* to the music."

"You're right, I know. You ... are... right."

One of the grandsons was standing at our table. "You gentlemen ready to order some breakfast?"

All three of us looked at the menus. John went first. I waited for Louie to ask the young man if he was Phil, or Don?

Twenty Five

While waiting for the food to arrive and talking about the Red Sox prospects for the season, Louie remembered Becky's request on the drive down and the promise to his wife that he would 'go easy' on Hanlon.

"I told you that my uncle brought me here when I was in high school," Louie said. Hanlon had just taken a swallow of coffee. He nodded in acknowledgement of the comment.

"This was, maybe 1980, I think. Yeah. Jimmy Carter was running for reelection."

"The year Ronald Reagan was elected," John said.

"Right." Louie laughed. He pointed at Willie, now seated at the counter, "You shoulda' heard him going after Reagan."

"I can only imagine," Hanlon said.

"He worked behind the counter then. Like that guy's doing now," Louie pointed at the grandson waiting on customers. "I just remember him pacing from one end of the counter to the other, pouring coffee, bringing food from the kitchen, clearing plates." Louie laughed out loud.

"He kept going back to this one older customer. A guy seated next to my uncle. Willie would pour the guy some coffee, then lean on the counter across from him. He'd wait a few seconds, then make some crack about Reagan. Things like, 'What's the Gipper gonna' do if he gets to Washington, call on Knute? Knute's *gone*, baby. Tough shit, Gipper'll have to figure it out on his own.'

"And what did this customer have to say?" Hanlon asked.

"I think the guy was a good sport. He was probably used to Willie's taunting and didn't go for the bait."

"Speaking of bait," Hanlon said. "You guys going to fish, or play golf?" Before either Louie or John could answer, Phil (or Don) was placing their breakfast in front of them.

Chief Peter Whalen and Officer Jeff Brutelli walked into Diner Shore at 9:02. A couple of men were just leaving their seats at the counter, so Whalen and Brutelli took their places.

Willie Ridell spotted the chief. He got up from his stool, went behind the counter, got two coffee mugs and a pot of coffee. He was moving more slowly than the grandson, but he was able to put the mugs on the counter in front of Whalen and the younger man.

"How's your dad coming along?" Willie asked as he

poured coffee into Whalen's mug.

"He's OK. And he's back home now. We'll see," Whalen answered.

"That's good. He's a tough guy. Tell him I said hello."

"Thanks. I will." Whalen didn't expand on his father's medical treatments.

Willie held the coffee pot in front of the other man.

Brutelli pushed the mug forward. "Please," he said. Willie filled the mug.

"You boys want some breakfast?" Will said.

"Yeah. Give us a minute," Whalen said. "Jeff better look at the menu. His first time here."

"Welcome," Willie said. He placed the pot back on the coffee warmer and went to the kitchen to get in the way.

"See what you think you like there," Whalen said, handing a menu to Brutelli. "Let's see if one of the booths clear out," he added, turning to look to the rear of the diner.

Hanlon saw Chief Whalen at the counter, but Whalen did not see him. He nudged Ragsdale's arm.

"Guy at the counter there," Hanlon said. "One with the tan and the short hair. He's the police chief in Sandwich."

"Peter Whalen," Ragsdale said, not looking up from his food. Hanlon looked at Louie.

"You know him?"

"In fact, I do." Ragsdale put his fork down and wiped

110

his mouth with a napkin.

"Jesus. You're just the all-around, go-to-guy fount of information, eh?"

"He's been out here a couple of years now. Used to be with the Mass State Police," Louie said, now looking in the direction of Whalen. "I did some work with him a few years back," he added.

"Task Force?" Hanlon said. Louie nodded.

"Might not recognize you all spiffed up," John Hill said.

"Probably think I'm George Clooney."

"Right," Hanlon said. "I think the guy on the stool to his left is one of his officers, Brutelli." Both cops were in civilian clothes. "He was the first to show up at the beach Friday afternoon."

Louie was back to his food, head forward, chewing a mouthful of pancakes. When he'd finished, he took a sip of coffee, wiped his mouth again and placed the crumpled napkin on the plate with his utensils. "We can say hello on the way out," Louie said. "You guys ready?"

"In a minute," John Hill said, swabbing up some egg with his toast.

"So, I didn't hear an answer to my question. Golfing or fishing?" Hanlon said.

"We're gonna go get the cottage set up at Corn Hill Beach. Put the groceries away, make up the beds," Ragsdale answered. "Becky and Angie should be here around one or so. Probably just hang out this afternoon. Go fishing tomorrow. I have to check the tide chart."

111

"Angie wants to go out to see Provincetown at some point," John added. This provoked a snicker from Louie.

"We go out there, I'll give you ten bucks to hold my hand while we walk through town," he said.

"Ah, here we go," Hanlon said, looking sideways at John. "Travelling with the Ambassador of Enlightenment."

Ragsdale patted Hanlon's cheek, puckered his lips and made a kissing sound.

Twenty Six

Donnie was on I-80 at the outskirts of Detroit by 10:15 Sunday morning, nine hours after he'd left the East coast. Following the Ohio Turnpike west and south of Cleveland, he avoided stopping off in Youngstown. He would visit home during the summer.

Before leaving Atlantic City, all live on smartphone camera, the packets of the $100 bills, along with the old newspapers, were placed back inside the suitcase. He spun the dials on the combination lock as requested. If the man at the other end of the call had any concerns about Donnie opening the case while travelling, he did not convey them. It was obvious that they had been shorted by a vastly substantial amount from what had been expected. So, the thought of one of these packets being lifted now, did not come up.

As far as Donnie was concerned, his job would be completed when he delivered the suitcase to Sal's office. After all of this fucking non-stop driving, he was looking forward to a few days off. Enough! He only hoped that the heat wave was not following behind him.

Sal sat perched on a rattan stool that had a rotating seat, one of three such stools arranged in front of a bar in his office. Every few seconds, he would give a little twist with his ass and make the seat turn ever so slightly, then turn back.

Seated on a worn leather sofa eight feet away, legs crossed, arms relaxed and folded across his lap, sat Nick, Sal's number one Safari Boy. Nick was 5' 9', stocky and in good condition. Looked like he probably did weights. He was wearing an expensive looking yellow zip-neck sweat shirt and matching sweat pants, brown loafers with tassels, no socks. Not likely an outfit that he wore in the gym, Sal surmised.

On the other hand, Sal was dressed pretty much the way he always dressed, Sunday morning or Tuesday night; very light tan linen slacks, tan linen vest over a lavender collar bar shirt with a box pattern lavender necktie. His shoes were highly polished black Italian loafers, not the handmade $5,000 a pair kind, but more in the range of $1,500 knock-offs.

Nick brought his arms up to his chest and folded them. He shook his head.

"This whole," he raised his right hand and gestured as though he was weighing a large cantaloupe, "good money chasing bad … *mess*. It has created, let us say, dissent among the boys." He shook his head again and offered a sardonic smile.

Sal didn't respond, but continued his little twisting maneuver on the stool. Nick went on.

"You see, Joe has this nephew back in Boston." Nick wiped a hand across his mouth like he was perspiring, but he wasn't. Sal knew it as one of his mannerisms.

"The nephew, *somehow*, convinces Big Joe – you know who Joe is?" Sal thought he knew which of Nick's associates he was talking about, but wasn't sure.

"The one with the tinted glasses? Could've played professional football," Sal replied.

"Or basketball, that's him. Joe is the pivot man for just about everything we do. Been around here for a long time. Or, another way of looking at it, *nothing* goes down without Big Joe being OK with it.

"Only this little number could cost a few important people more than $25 mil." Nick waited for Sal to respond. Sal stopped swiveling on the chair. He stared at Nick, placed his hands on his knees and leaned forward.

"More than *twenty-five million dollars*?" None of Sal's activities over all the years he'd been in Detroit had ever been in this league. He had managed to generate business fees that frequently boosted his annual income above $250,000. As a rule, his more-often-than-not proceeds from gambling jacked that amount up another hundred or hundred-fifty grand, most of which never found its way onto an IRS form. So, wherever this conversation was going with Nick, it was going to be new territory for Sal.

Nick was slowly nodding. Yes, more than twenty-five-million.

"The *dissent* I mention, it all has do with Joe's nephew, this hot damn computer kid out there in Boston. He and some of his pals, along with some other geeks from Brazil, they work up an internet scheme to bring in a lot of money from investors for a phony telecom business. Selling advertising online and some other get rich quick nonsense," Nick said, shaking his head.

"For more than a year, it's doing great. Joe gets a few other guys to pony up. Everybody's happy. Then, the shit hits the fan. Feds in Boston investigate what they call an 'international pyramid scheme'. One of the guys back there goes all friendly, pleads to a money-laundering charge, starts having numerous conversations with investigators.

"Before too long, we got the fucking Chief of Criminal Division for the Eastern District of Michigan out snooping around. You know about that, right?"

Sal nodded that yes, he did.

"Joe flips out, not a normal reaction from him, by the way. He tells the nephew and some of his pals to get the fucking money *out* and get it out *now*." Sal let that sink in.

"A plan comes together. Some of the cash is going to Atlantic City, find its way through the casinos." Nick was now rubbing his hands together as though they were cold, despite Sal's office being a comfortable 70 degrees.

116

"The cash there in Jersey, in the suitcase, is gonna be the first installment, according to Joe's nephew. 'More on the way,' the kid says. But, and a very unfortunate but, the nephew is not returning calls." Nick's eyes went a little wider and he dropped his arms back to the folded position across his lap.

"*And...* this part you already know, both the drop guy in Boston and the casino connection in Atlantic City, they have apparently gone off on a world cruise. These two are *not* returning any calls."

Sal listened to all of this while trying to stay ahead of Nick. Where was the part that involved anything further from Sal, or Donnie? He looked down at his watch as this thought held him: 10:30. He knew, and Nick knew, that Donnie was due in the next hour with the suitcase, the cash and the old newspapers.

Sal got up from the bar stool, folded his arms tight against the linen vest and lavender shirt, then twisted his neck a couple of times as though he was straightening out a crick.

"Are you telling me all of this," Sal said, "because you, uh," he unfolded his arms and stretched them out to his sides, "because when Donnie gets here, you expect that there is more work for us?"

Nick nodded. "That's it." They stared at each other, then Nick started in again.

"Joe doesn't want to make any contacts with anybody in Atlantic City or Boston. Providence, you name it. *Nobody* back East. And besides, your boy Donnie, he's already seen the drop guy at the Boston airport."

Sal reached up, pulled on his necktie and twisted his neck again. He made a show of holding his arm out to check his watch, again: 10:32.

Twenty Seven

"**Chief, Officer Brutelli. Good morning,**" I said. Both men swiveled around to face me. Louie and John were at the register paying one of the twins for our breakfast.

"Mr. Hanlon, small world. How're you doing?" Whalen replied.

"Mornin'," Brutelli said.

"I'm OK. I think you were right. Looks like the heat is gonna' break. Weather Underground says low 80s today. Maybe even a breeze," I said.

Whalen shook his head. "Really unusual for us to have temperatures like this and no winds. Especially so early. And for *three* consecutive days," he added, shaking his head.

"I think you may know a friend of mine here," I said, turning as Louie came up to stand next to me, smirk in place. He didn't look like George Clooney. But he didn't really look like an undercover guy, either.

"Chief," Louie said, extending his hand. "Lou Ragsdale. We worked together three years ago. Little group of shit

119

balls out in Pittsfield." Whalen sized him up, eyes squinting and a half-smile. He shook Louie's hand slowly while he nodded in recognition.

"You were one of the guys working out of Albany. With Marty Evans, DEA," Whalen said. Ragsdale nodded.

"Yeah, I was on loan from the Task Force. We knew two of the dealers from some of their previous handy work in Vermont," Louie said.

"Still on the job?" Whalen asked.

"Oh yeah. Mostly breaking in some of the new bucks." As he said this, Ragsdale's eyes automatically shifted to Brutelli, the one Hanlon had mentioned was the first cop on the scene two days earlier.

"Hey," Louie said, shaking hands with Brutelli. "What'd you do, bring some young guys down from Middleboro when you took the job here?" the question directed at Whalen.

"Nah, Jeff's a local. Grew up here. Worked on the force in Taunton. Joined us last year," Whalen said. Brutelli nodded without comment.

"So, you fellas planning to do some fishing?" Whalen asked.

"I might go for some stripers. Our wives are coming out this afternoon. We rented a cottage in Truro," Louie said.

"Try some of the smaller inlets," Whalen said. "Look for the birds, the fish are usually right behind' em."

"Yeah. I've been down here a few times. Usually have

some luck on Scorton Creek. And a few other spots."

"Guys with boats are taking some *big* stripers in the canal," Brutelli offered.

Ragsdale shook his head. "I'm a surf guy when I fish down here. Lots of places I can go out in a boat. I like wading."

Hanlon and John Hill had started moving to the door. Louie turned around to follow them, shaking hands again with Whalen.

"Go Minutemen," Ragsdale said.

Whalen pointed at him. "Right. You were at UMass Amherst. What year?"

"87."

"I was '86," Whalen said.

"I remember. You played on the baseball team while I played on the radio," Louie said.

Whalen looked out the door and pointed at Hanlon. "Is that how you two got together? He's old radio, right?" Louie shook his head.

"Long story. Yes, he was a fulltime radio news guy. But he doesn't know squat about music." Both men laughed.

As soon as Ragsdale, Hanlon and the other guy were gone, Whalen and Brutelli picked up their plates and coffee and moved to the booth the three men had just vacated.

"As I was starting to tell you a minute ago," Whalen said, "we're checking videos trying to see any vans that match up with the one Hanlon described."

"You said that he told you that he remembers it had Mass plates?"

"Yes. Says he's not a hundred per cent positive, but after thinking about it a little, he recalled turning around once to look back at his car while the van was still there. Pretty sure that what he saw was red numerals on a white background."

Brutelli ate his breakfast while listening to his boss.

"Everything we have is out on the HOTLINE frequency. You know from Taunton, all local departments, county law enforcement and state police monitor it. And the turnpike video control center in Boston knows about the van.

"Sergeant Murtaugh's guys will look at the video we get from town feeds." Whalen took a bite of his omelette and a drink of coffee before continuing.

"There are a number of private businesses in town that have security cameras. A few out along Main Street near the access road down to the beach."

Brutelli had finished eating. He sat back in the booth, gripped his coffee mug with both hands and continued to pay attention.

"I'll talk to Murtaugh. I'd like you, and probably one other officer, to spend the day tomorrow going to see the businesses and take a look at their video."

"OK with me," Brutelli replied. "I'm on 7 to 3 all this week."

"Let me talk to the Sergeant. Come see me when you get in tomorrow morning."

Twenty Eight

By noon I decided that I didn't need more beach time today. There was a small yard with three Adirondack style chairs and a hammock behind Jean McKearney's home. And there was some shade. A good spot to chill out and read.

We walked up the street to the Daniel Webster Inn where I bought both the *Sunday Boston Globe* and *The New York Times*. Nine bucks total, but it would give me reading all week long. Plus, I had some books in the back of the car.

Rocco was happy to lie down under the hammock. I watched him do the circling routine before getting settled. Every few seconds, his expressive eyebrows would jiggle one way or the other as a bird landed somewhere in the yard, but he didn't bolt. Eventually he fell asleep.

My stomach felt a little off. It had been like that a couple of times in the past week, but would then return to almost normal. Maybe I was drinking too much coffee. I didn't think that it was food related. I had been taking it easy, not eating too much, skipping the cookies and other sweets altogether.

Sunday newspaper reading, for me, always starts with the sports section, then working backward through news, the week in review, business, the arts and, if I have any patience left, I will look through the travel section. If the paper carries any comics, I will read *Shoe, Pearls Before Swine, Hagar The Horrible* and *Doonesbury*.

The Globe sports section had a rather lengthy article speculating on the potential for serious violence at the 2018 World Cup Games to be held in Russia a year from now. The story even included quotations from anonymous members of both English and Russian Football Hooligan groups who clashed at the 2016 Euro Cup. Great. Certainly made me want to go.

I recalled one of my winter indoor soccer games two years ago. Normally, everyone came for the exercise and the fun. We played reasonably hard, but we all wanted to be able to go to work the next day, so no one got out of hand. Friendly competition, in large part because we were all over 40.

On this particular evening a new guy showed up to play. Some people knew him, I didn't. We weren't into the match even ten minutes when the new guy was playing more hockey than soccer. Most of his aggressiveness was directed at one individual. Sure enough, at the beginning of the second half, they were going at in the corner, fists flying, knees coming up and the new guy bloodied and broke the nose of the regular. When it all finished up, the owner of the indoor facility banned both players for the rest of the year.

Bonnie had happened to be with me that night. On the ride home, she told me that she had overheard other spectators talking about 'bad blood' between the two that went all the way back to their teens.

"Give me a break," I'd said, when she told me this. "Don't we have to let certain things *go* at some point? Soccer's not supposed to be played that way. This is *not* fucking high school." I was surprised and more than a trifle exasperated by the occurrence. It had never happened before at a friendly soccer match with adults.

"You are naïve, I think, Michael," Bonnie had replied. "In small towns, sometimes even just a slight, or old family rivalries, can carry over to the next generation."

I put the newspaper down and thought about Bonnie. How many times had she heard me go popping off about something a little prematurely, only to then wait until I had finished and give me a reality check.

"Hey, Bonnie. Wanna go to Russia next summer?" I said out loud. Rocco sat up.

Sal, Donnie and Nick were in a private parking garage on Centre Street in Detroit. The van was pulled parallel to Sal's Jazz Blue Chrysler 300C. Donnie had moved the suitcase from the front to the rear of the van and they were about to open it.

Nick held up his right hand for Donnie to wait. The case was flipped on its side and both tailgate doors open.

"Let's do the phone thing," Nick said. He pulled his own phone from a pants pocket and handed it to Donnie. "I'll open the case, you get a close up of the cash." Donnie nodded, Sal looked on without comment.

"Ready?" Nick added. Donnie activated the video on the phone camera and nodded again.

Bending at the waist, Nick moved the four dials on the combination lock. Seconds later, he lifted up the top of the suitcase revealing all the packets of bills stacked on top of the newspapers. Motioning with his left hand, he tapped one of the packets.

"Show us each bundle as I bring it out," Nick said. Then he methodically removed one packet at a time and laid each on the interior deck of the van. When he'd finished, there were 187 packets in all. Nick stacked them next to each other as he counted off. He motioned for Donnie to get a close-up shot.

Donnie moved forward, held the phone inside the van and moved it slowly from right to left. The cash was $100 bills, a hundred to a pack making them $10,000 each. So, the total here was less than even two mil.

Backing out of the van, Donnie looked at Nick, who gave him a nod to stop shooting. He tapped the phone, looked at the screen for a second, then handed the phone back to Nick.

"Put it all back in the suitcase," Nick said. Donnie did as he was instructed.

Turning to face Sal, Nick placed the phone in his right pants pocket, wiped both hands across his head as though he were smoothing his hair, then adjusted the waist band on his designer sweat pants.

"I'm taking this to Big Joe," Nick said, gesturing with his left hand to the suitcase. "He's talking to some other people tonight. But like I said, I think we're gonna need some help from you two."

"Just tell me the plan, I'll tell you if we can do it," Sal said. Nick gave him a wordless stare.

"What I mean is," Sal quickly added, "we'll create the line-up card. But I gotta know *who* and *where*."

"No line-up card," Nick said. "If there's a plan, it will be you and him," he added, pointing at Donnie.

"OK. Just give me the word."

Donnie wheeled the suitcase to Nick's Lincoln MKZ and hefted it to the back.

"Thanks," Nick said, sliding in behind the wheel. He closed the door, started the engine, backed up, turned and slowly drove out of the garage.

Sal and Donnie watched the car descend to the street one level below. The brake lights flashed briefly as Nick made the turn, then he was gone.

Donnie turned to Sal. "What kind of *plan* are we considering here?"

"Let's see what they have in mind," Sal replied. He

opened the driver's door to the Chrysler and started to get in. He held the door open and looked back at Donnie.

"Good job. Sorry about the delay. Go home and get some sleep."

"I'm not real crazy about these guys knowing who I am," Donnie said.

Sal shook his head. "Not to worry. The Safari Boys are good. We're not gonna have any problems from them." Then just like Nick, Sal started his car, backed out and drove slowly down the ramp to the street.

Twenty Nine

After making the cottage comfortable and walking to look at the bay, the Ragsdales and the Hills plopped into four, lightweight folding camp chairs. Louie had unloaded the chairs and arranged them around a kettle charcoal grill in the tiny front yard of the cottage.

Angie had made a pitcher of red wine sangria. She brought four plastic tumblers with ice and served the drinks. Conveniently, each of the camp chairs had a cup holder, one of the best improvements in outdoor life since beach umbrellas.

"Is this the same concoction that got me into trouble couple summers ago?" Louie asked.

Angie laughed. "I don't put quite as much brandy in as I used to," she said.

"Still goes down way too easy," John said. "Be careful."

Louie took a small sip, waited, then took another. "Pretty fruity."

"Orange and apple slices, pomegranate juice," Angie replied.

"Did you say anything to Michael about coming out to eat with us?" Becky asked.

"Yeah. He's game," Louie said. He looked at his watch; 5:08. "Low tide is at 8:12."

"So, what does that mean?" Becky said.

"I was planning to fish down at the inlet."

"At exactly *8:12*?"

Louie rolled his eyes and looked at his brother-in-law. John was smart enough not to comment.

"Not exactly at 8:12. *But...* for the first couple of hours when the tide starts to come back in."

"So, if you didn't get down there until 8:30, would that work?"

"That would work fine," Louie answered, a trace of 'whatever you say' in his voice.

"Then why don't we plan to eat at 7. Earlier?" Becky said.

Angie shook her head. "Seven is good."

"You can call Michael," Becky said to her husband. "Tell him to come out around 6:30."

"I can do that." Louie placed his drink in the cup holder and went for his phone.

48 hours after the body was discovered at the Town Beach, no replies and no queries had come back. From *any* law enforcement agencies around the Northeast. Not one.

The Commonwealth, like many urban states in the US,

experiences too many cases of Missing and Unidentified Persons throughout a given year. Infants, young children, teenagers, college students, adults, people from other states, citizens from other countries. Just gone.

Not all the cases involve violence or death. There are parental kidnappings, for example. And runaways. There are cases when persons are found and returned to their homes. There are cases that go for years without a sign of any new evidence pertaining to the person's whereabouts. Some cases have remained 'cold' for decades. And some cases simply have *never* been solved.

According to statistics from the National Missing and Unidentified Persons Database – NamUs – there are more than 14,000 cases in the US. 80% of those cases, some 11,400+ are classified as being 'Open'. Another 2,700+ are listed as being 'Closed'. In Massachusetts, the numbers break down with a current total of 200 cases, with 56, or 28%, 'Closed' and 72%, 144 cases still 'Open'.

The rest of the New England states stack-up this way: Connecticut, 75 cases, 41% open and 59% closed; Maine, 16 cases, 88% are still open and only 12% closed; New Hampshire, 8 cases, with a similar 88% open and 12% closed; Rhode Island, 26 cases, with 96%, all but one, still open; and Vermont, also 26 cases, showing a 73% closed rate against 7 cases, or 27% still open.

Not surprisingly, the big population states have the big numbers. California, 2,400+ cases with 91% still open; Texas, 1,700+ cases, 82% open; and New York, 1,500+

cases and 86% still open. The case breakdown for each state reports gender, race, ethnicity, physical description, age and the last date the person was known to be alive.

Female, white, 5′ 9″, 150 pounds, brown hair, brown eyes – between 45 to 50 years-old. She has been found.

On a hot afternoon. In a town in Massachusetts.

Chief Peter Whalen sat in front of his computer on a Sunday evening. Phone calls, email. Read and reread the cases from each state listing people that had disappeared. Before the night was over, he would have looked at photos of more than 200 women from just the Northeast, and read whatever information was available about each of them.

Some had gone missing in recent days, some had been missing for weeks, months or years. Simply because this particular woman had been alive only a few days ago did not, at least for the moment, shed any light on when she had 'last been seen and known to be alive.' Or by whom. Or where.

So far, two days into the investigation, the chief held the belief that the woman was not from the immediate area, at least not recently. There were fourteen other police departments on the Cape and communication with each of them buttressed this belief. But nothing was for certain. Whalen knew that from all his years in working with the state police.

Before he would call it a night, Whalen would send an email to District Attorney O'Connell, suggesting wording to be included in the update for the media. O'Connell was likely to issue the statement on Monday afternoon. Whalen recognized that there were only so many ways one could write about 'investigation ongoing.'

DRAFT: Town Neck Beach, Sandwich - UPDATE

Additional information will be released and exhibits made available for reproduction by media outlets in connection with the investigation of the unidentified body discovered 5/26/17 near Town Neck Beach in Sandwich.

Sandwich Police Chief Peter Whalen, and Captain Christopher Dixon of the Massachusetts State Police Detective Unit assigned to the Cape & Islands District, are working with District Attorney Martin O'Connell's Office in an effort to engage the public's assistance in the investigation.

The victim is a female, approximately 5' 9" in height, weight of 150 pounds. Believed to have been between the ages of 45 and 50 years-old. The victim has brown hair, brown eyes and was wearing a white jumpsuit with long sleeves. Tattoos in different locations of the victim's body may aid officials in positive identification. Cause of death was asphyxiation; the victim had been smothered.

Sandwich Police Chief Peter Whalen adds that police are seeking information regarding a dark-colored panel van. The truck is believed to have a Massachusetts registration. A vehicle fitting this description was seen in the parking area near the beach shortly before discovery of the body.

(**Note to MO**: see PR excerpt from 5/27 copied below)

Chief Whalen said that the body could have come from anywhere in New England and that he did not believe the murder had occurred in Sandwich. Preliminary autopsy results indicate that the victim had been dead between two and three days prior to being left at the beach. The body had been wrapped in blue industrial tarps and bound with white nylon rope.

O'Connell stated that Massachusetts State Police were assisting with the investigation and that anyone with information should contact the Sandwich PD at 508.295.7171.

Whalen read over the email a second time. O'Connell had the final say on wording and was more experienced in responding to the media. Both men knew that a follow-up would be required in the next week, the timing subject to progress of the investigation and any new information that might come from the public.

Whalen clicked SEND, logged off, closed his computer and went home.

Thirty

As soon as we had finished eating – roasted pepper and Asiago chicken sausage on the charcoal grill, homemade red-skin potato salad, a green salad and pieces of focaccia – Louie had his fly rod rigged and was ready to hustle down the beach to the Pamet River inlet.

It was five after eight and the sun was setting. We would have another forty-minutes or so of twilight. Those out in boats and using *nautical* twilight as their guide, technically, would have an hour-and-a-half. The weather was back near the normal range, the thermometer on the side of the cottage showing 62.

John and Angie Hill had volunteered to clean up the food and dishes and were going to stay at the cottage to read. Becky and I agreed to chaperone her husband to see if he got into any stripers. We both knew that he would stay on the water for at least a couple of hours, possibly all night if left to his own wishes.

"You two go on. I want to get a jacket," Becky said.

Ragsdale was wearing a lightweight parka over his waders but under his fishing vest. I had pulled on a holey old LL Bean wool sweater from the back of my car.

Rocco bounded out in front of us, starting up the beach until I whistled. He saw that we were going the other way, turned and ran ahead of us. No one else was on the beach that we could see. Covering the first fifty yards without conversation, Louie stopped and looked back. I turned as well and saw that Becky had just come out onto the sand.

"I'll wait. Go see if they're moving in yet," I said. Louie looked at his watch and began walking at a faster pace. I called Rocco back and made him stay until Becky reached us.

It took ten minutes to reach the inlet. Louie had made his way down over some big rocks, was standing in water up to his hips and retrieving the line he'd put out that was now drifting below him. We watched him cast and retrieve three more times. If any stripers were coming in with the tide, they were avoiding a hook-up with Louie.

Rocco was behind us and had waded out to some other rocks along the jetty. I whistled. He looked back, but stayed in place, ears up, water splashing at his underside. I walked in that direction and Becky followed. We could see that he was nosing around some kelp on the rocks.

"Leave it," I yelled. He stared at me for a couple of seconds, bent his head forward for one more sniff, then came out of the water toward us. When he got close, I held a hand up. He stopped, stared and then did exactly what we knew he would do; shook his head and body to rid himself of excess water.

"Rocco, come," Becky said, kneeling on the sand to greet him. He bounded straight at her, big licks and wet ears against her face. She hugged him.

I nearly lost it. Jesus, that could've been Bonnie kneeling there in the dusk holding her dog. I took a big breath in through my nose and held it. Wait, repeat. Becky was fussing over Rocco. I doubted that she could hear my deep-cleansing-breath routine above the noise of the surf.

She stood, brushed off sand and water while Rocco made a circle around her, head up for more of the love pats. I reached into my pocket for a treat.

"Bonus," I said, extending my hand. He wheeled away from Becky, shook off more water on his way to be *my* pal. He stopped in front of me and sat. I gave him the treat.

"Good boy," I said, scratching his head.

"Do you want to stay down here with Louie? I'm going to go back," Becky said.

"Nah. I'll walk back with you. Your husband is even less social when he's on the water. Besides, I would just give him helpful pointers on his casting which would really piss him off."

She walked to a spot where Louie could hear her and said, "We're going back to the cottage." He raised his left arm and waved.

Coming across the bay was a boat heading for the inlet where Ragsdale was fishing. I watched the bow lights, saw the boat slow as it got closer and knew that it would take its time maneuvering past him on its way to the marina a little farther up river.

"You didn't talk much at dinner," Becky said as we started walking.

"Eh-h. Guess I'm tapped out for a bit. Sorry."

"You don't have to apologize. You were just kind of quiet." Two more steps and she added, "How are you doing?"

When she asked this, I struggled not to drop into another spell of '*I'm so lonesome I could cry*'. Except that it would more likely be, 'I'm so *sad* that I think that I *will* cry. Any minute now.' I stopped walking. I placed my left arm across my chest and held my right hand over my mouth. Becky stopped.

"You know, the strangest thing that I've been doing, for two weeks now, is that I will be thinking of something, or I will see something, and I just start this *conversation...* with Bonnie." I shook my head, offered a half-hearted laugh and held my hands up.

"If Rocket Boy here is around when I do it, he just stops and looks at me." On cue, Rocco stopped walking when he heard me say his name. He looked back at us. Becky laughed.

"I'm probably going to send the dog into therapy just from the different names I call him."

"Did you and Louie have a chance to talk?" Becky asked.

"Yeah. A little. Like you on the phone the other night, he says get rid of the guilt. Easier said than done."

"It takes time. And every day helps," Becky said.

"He did talk about some of the things that he saw during his army days in Kuwait. Young soldiers surviving when some of their close friends and fellow-soldiers did not."

"He never talks to me about any of that," she replied.

"Not surprised. Some guys just don't care to share it. But he wanted me to know that the whole 'survivor's guilt' thing is pretty common, in all kinds of situations.

"It's not as though I haven't had experience with grief before," I went on. "My mother died when I was in my early twenties. And I've had other relatives and friends die. Had a *really* hard time just a few years ago when my dad died. But this, with Bonnie. God, she was just *so young*."

Becky placed a hand on my right arm. I shook my head and did the deep inhalation again.

"You know, she was just really happy that she was going to get married. And I can't *tell* you how much she was looking forward to starting a family." Becky left her hand resting on my arm but didn't speak.

"I know that I have to get beyond this. If she were here now, she would talk to me about young children who get sick and die without *ever* having a chance at a life. Or how so many others are gone suddenly and leave families distraught. That it happens all the time, just a part of life."

I patted Becky's hand, turned and we started to walk again.

"Give it all the time you need, Michael. Don't be afraid to talk to me. Or to Louie. *Anyone*. When you feel like it.

"And keep having the conversations with Bonnie," she added.

On the drive back to Sandwich, the emotions continued to boil up to a point that I pulled the car to the side of the road and put my emergency flashers on. Turning in to the edge of somebody's driveway, I stopped.

Rocco sat up on the back seat. There was no traffic coming in either direction and no cops stopping to check on me.

Burying my face in both hands I was able to control the convulsions and the heaving in my chest, but felt as though I was about to get sick. Fortunately, that didn't happen. After another minute, I had myself under control and turned to look at Rocco. He was like one of those dog statues you see on a front lawn. Except that he was wet and smelled like Cape Cod Bay. I gave him a pat, checked my mirrors and eased back onto a still empty road.

Twenty minutes later we were in the back yard behind the guest bunk house. I opened a beer and sat in one of the Adirondack chairs, Rocco on the grass at my feet. He'd apparently had enough sniffing back at the beach and was content to chill out.

I thought of Becky's encouragement to keep having the talks with Bonnie. So, in my head and not aloud this time, I took another whack at explaining to Bonnie and to myself, how much she – and 69 other airline passengers and crew whom I had never known – would be missed for a long, long time. By so many people who loved them.

Thirty One

The Sunday night call from Nick made it official. Sal and Donnie were about to engage in the next step to, a) help the Safari Boys find some geeky guys in Boston who'd fucked them over; b) *also* locate Big Joe's nephew before someone else located him; and c) maybe track down a lot more of the Detroit 'investors pool' of money that probably shouldn't have gone east in the first place.

The call didn't come as a surprise. Nick had said that when he 'knew what the plan was' he would be in touch. Nonetheless, what *was* a surprise was the nature of the plan, at least as far as Nick was explaining it.

"Joe is confident that we can get the registration on the car, the guy who did the handover at Logan. He's OK with asking for a little help on that. But nobody back *there* needs to know that anyone from out *here* is coming to look for that car," Nick said. "We can pass it off as 'just lookin', future reference for other activity, you might say."

Sal thought about that.

"So. I would be correct in thinking that Joe is not placing a call to the Department of Motor Vehicles in Rhode Island to obtain this information," Sal said.

"We have, let's call it, 'professional courtesy' on some things. Like tracking a car, or a not well-known address," Nick replied. "It gets done all the time. Small favors back and forth. We'll do that for you, could you maybe help us with *this*?"

"The east coast guys that you don't want to be in bed with, they farm it out?"

"Exactly. Small potatoes. And we ain't about to form a partnership anytime soon. So nobody's 'expectations' get cranked up to unreasonable, if you follow."

Sal did follow. Even before this latest job and Donnie's assignment to play the 'courier with a suitcase', it was pretty obvious to anyone paying attention that factions of gangsters in one part of the country were in no big hurry to be cooperative with gangsters operating somewhere else. There were, of course, exceptions; larger cities where someone at the top enforced cooperation among rivals in a geographic region.

As a young man growing up in northeastern Ohio, one thing Sal had observed about crooks was how ethnicity came into play on the big jobs. Or at least the big jobs that became public knowledge. After he had been in Detroit for a short time and had started to offer his own services, it didn't take long to realize that there were some jobs that never made it into the public spotlight.

No sensational newspaper stories, no investigative TV reports, no Grand Jury hearings. Things just 'happened.'

Sal had concluded that much of the distrust that the Safari Boys held for their counterparts in the East, and probably on the west coast, too, was a deeply-rooted allegiance to their ethnic communities. Everybody knew, or believed, that all the control in the East was in the hands of Italians and Jews. That could be changing these days with Russians, Asians and some Latinos. And there was no small number of these groups in Michigan, but the mix within the Safari Boys, as far as Sal could glean, was primarily of Greek ancestry.

A shifting demographic in metro Detroit of Greeks, Poles, Albanians, Italians, Asian and some Middle Eastern groups, all had recently been overwhelmed by African Americans. The crime competition was at its highest level in his time in the city. And not for a second did Sal see any of *his* clients teaming-up with blacks. Just was not going to happen.

Since this suitcase deal had started coming apart when Donnie's Atlantic City contact failed to arrive, Sal had speculated about where things would go. That was before he realized the scope of what was in play; 'more than 25 mil.'

Now, listening and waiting for details of what would be asked of him and Donnie, and what the fees would be, Sal shoved all these ethnic calculations to the back of his mind. He worked for only one small group.

"Tell me as much as you can. And when. I'll tell you if we can do it and we can talk fees," Sal said.

Nick continued laying it out, Sal remained silent.

Thirty Two

Monday morning media commentary and analysis:

BOSTON (AP) – Ninety-three US attorneys serve the designated regional districts around the country. The Massachusetts District US Attorney's office, operating under the Department of Justice and the Attorney General, has three divisions and fourteen units, all based in Boston.

One of those units is ECU – the Economic Crimes Unit – which investigates and prosecutes a variety of crimes, including bank fraud, bankruptcy fraud, advance fee schemes, insurance fraud, 'con man' schemes, money laundering offenses, tax offenses, securities fraud and other economic shenanigans. The Unit also handles complex computer-related crimes. It has a Financial Auditor who is available to help other Assistant US Attorneys in the other divisions.

Unlike the so-called 'sexy' or 'high visibility' crimes that often create headlines, such as narcotics, money laundering, organized crime, racketeering and gangs, as well as the more recent national security and cybercrimes, the ECU is not likely to be the model used for any online or network TV series to run on Sunday nights.

On the other hand, this unit is *dogged* in chasing ill-gotten revenue. In cooperation with the FBI and the IRS, it is pretty good at locating those who perpetrate fraud and bringing them to court.

The ECU does find misappropriated assets and has facilitated the return of those assets to people who were scammed.

One current case involves numerous individuals operating within Massachusetts and at least one other country, Brazil, in defrauding investors and customers who were promised future payments and huge profits. The scam revolved around the sale of 'Voice over Internet Protocol' services, VOIP, as it is commonly known, as well as the selling of advertising that never appeared.

To date, numerous federal prosecutors have compiled extensive evidence showing that thousands of customers of a company using the name *PhoneDat Global* (PDG), were promised large payouts from online advertising. Prosecutors say that no advertising was ever placed and no services have been provided. The early investors in the company were paid with money that came from more recent investors, typical of many pyramid schemes.

One source close to the current investigation has said that as much as $2 billion has been swindled from more than a million people in countries around the world. Prosecutors reportedly have interviewed former employees of *PhoneDat Global* and, according to the anonymous source, some of the former employees are now assisting with the investigation.

Charges are expected to be filed in federal court in Boston in June.

São Paulo (AFP) – Business scams are not new here.

With a population of more than 200 million in a country covering 5.3 million square miles, the fifth largest land mass in the world, Brazil's major city is the most populous city in the Southern Hemisphere and has a long history of 'white collar' crime.

More than 12 million live in this southeastern metropolis. It is also the 12th largest city in the world. Not surprisingly, one major crime is that of Identity Theft. What is *new* in the vast array of South American fraudulent activities, is the sky rocketing number of ordinary citizens drawn into internet scams on a daily basis.

At of the end of 2016, stories about cybercrime were peaking in Brazil with multiple reports of hackers obtaining sensitive information, credit card numbers and personal security codes, bank account numbers and passwords. According to one report, the country ranks near the top of the list in the world for online banking fraud.

As recently as March, a major Brazilian financial company with hundreds of branches, including in the US, learned that *all* online customers had their transactions rerouted to perfectly constructed fake sites of that bank's properties. Just on one weekend afternoon, the online customers willingly handed over their account information. According to a report, the unnamed bank with 5 million-plus customers and more than $25 billion in assets, has yet to disclose the full extent of damage caused by this one incident.

These stories could be – and are being – reported around the globe. Here in Brazil, however, a shift is occurring; citizens providing personal information and making payments for non-bank related services and for products that they will never receive.

Government investigations, judicial actions and fines related to corporate corruption and scandals are often widely reported in the press. It is believed by many, however, that the clearly illegal and extremely profitable activities of international hackers have yet to receive similar coverage.

Thirty Three

Louie Ragsdale stayed on the water until 11 o'clock. He only came in then because his wife had trudged back down the beach with a flashlight. She asked him if he knew what time it was?

"Time to call it a night," he responded, reeling in his line and attaching the artificial fly to the keeper at the base of the rod. He wore a headlamp, which he clicked on, and began moving slowly back to shore from waist deep water. Becky waited. He carefully came up over the rocks and joined her on the beach.

"You must've been having a grand time," she said.

Switching off the headlamp, he carefully turned his fly rod around so the tip was behind him, moved the rod to his left hand and gave Becky a hug with his right arm.

"If I'd stayed another half-an-hour, I might have had twenty fish."

"Wow. That good?"

"Yep. They started coming in," he looked at his watch,

153

"about an hour ago. Mostly small school fish, but I had one that was close to legal."

"What's legal?"

"The minimum length to keep a fish is twenty-eight inches. This one was... maybe just over two feet, not quite there," he added.

They continued in silence, Becky taking Louie's right hand as they walked. There was just a sliver of a waxing crescent moon. Ambient light from street lights along the road near the cottages up ahead of them helped. The surf was rolling to the beach only ten feet away.

"Hanlon go back to Sandwich?" Louie asked.

"Yes. We talked a little, but he wanted to take Rocco back. He said that he would call you in the morning."

"How do you think he's coming along?"

Becky sighed. She thought for a few seconds.

"I *think* that he's slightly better than he was two nights ago. Hard to say for sure."

Another dozen steps up the beach, another fifteen seconds of silence.

"Why do you think that he didn't want to fish with you?" Becky said.

"He didn't bring any gear with him."

"But *you* have extra gear. I heard you tell him that before dinner."

Five more steps. They were still maybe thirty or forty yards from the cottage.

"Truth is," Louie said, "it's just one more issue that

154

he's beating himself up about."

"What, *fishing*?"

"Nah, not just fishing. He likes to get on the water. You know that he was fine with that bone fishing in the Bahamas last winter."

"I thought that he had a great time," Becky said.

"He did. And bone fish are strong. You're lucky if you can land one. It's only the *trout and salmon* fishing that can make Hanlon go weak in the knees."

Becky stopped and looked up at Louie. "What does that mean?"

"Ah-h, back when he and Bonnie were together, he tried to get her into fishing. She was a good sport, tried it a couple of times. But, the way Hanlon tells it, they were coming back from Maine where he'd taken her to try for landlock salmon."

"Yes. So what happened?"

"Apparently, he was giving her the whole catechism on the practice of catch and release. Water temperatures and how long you should play a fish when you hook-up. Being careful handling them when you go to release the fish back to the water, not just tossing them in."

"I know. I've heard you talk about it. And I've seen a couple of those programs you watch," she said.

"Well," Louie laughed, "Hanlon was really giving her the 'sell' on this drive home. Told her that he would buy her some gear." He laughed again.

"And?"

"Bonnie listened without saying much for a while. Then about ten minutes later, they're at a stop sign, and she said to him, 'So you guys really have a great time with catch and release. Probably not a lot of fun for the fish."

Becky laughed. "Bonnie makes him feel guilty about tormenting fish. Great."

"She didn't *make him* feel guilty. He *chooses* to debate with himself the pleasure of many outdoor pursuits versus being one thoughtful and caring guy." Now Louie laughed again.

"You need to remember, Michael Hanlon would *choose* to feel conflicted about a lot of things that the rest of us don't have any problems with."

"I guess," she said.

"That's one of the reasons that he's such a knee-jerk liberal. He would fret over *killing a wasp*. I think the 'being kind to fish' is just part of the whole package."

Thirty Four

At 8:30 Monday morning, two Sandwich police officers, Jeff Brutelli and Kathleen Michado, started with drop-ins to businesses all along Route 6A, Main Street. They would ask permission to look at any security videos recorded the previous Friday.

Back at headquarters, the Sergeant in charge of the Detective Unit had begun making courtesy phone calls to the businesses to give them a heads-up that they would shortly be receiving a visit.

Not all of the local businesses were equipped with video surveillance. As the police department already knew, some establishments might have cameras mounted as a preventive measure, to thwart shoplifting or vandalism, even though the cameras weren't actually connected to a recording device. From those businesses that did have video, the police were only interested in exterior mounted cameras or possible interior cameras with an angle facing the street.

Brutelli and Michado had clear instructions from Chief Whalen and the supervising Detective Sergeant; *any* dark-colored vans that show up on *any* video, we need to know where and what time. In short, a lot of what the two officers would be doing could be considered preliminary 'grunt work'. Should a suspect vehicle appear in videos recorded by a private business, the Sandwich PD Detective Unit would take over. And they would follow the lead of the State Police Crime Prevention and Control Unit.

Starting at the west end of 6A – the corner of Main Street and Dewey Avenue – the two officers split up. They would work an area near one exit of the network of streets leading to Boardwalk Road and Town Neck Beach. Michado began with businesses on the opposite side of the street, while Brutelli hit those abutting the beach neighborhood.

Making their way toward the center of town, and determined by what might be discovered and how long it took, they would move farther out to the businesses at the west end of town where Main Street intersected with Route 130.

It might be tedious work, but it sure beat sitting in a cramped office looking at the videos.

"**Final report from the ME** probably not ready before the end of the week," Whalen said. "My guys say there were no obvious wounds from what they could see."

"No phone calls from any of the local residents about a woman reported as missing?" said State Police Detective

Lieutenant Brian Metcalf. Assigned to the Troop D Unit in Bourne, Metcalf frequently worked closely with the town police departments and with the District Attorney's office.

"Nothing," Whalen replied.

"You know the drill, Peter. For the record, CPAC takes it from here. But, we'll take all the help you can give us."

"And then some," Whalen said. "More than once during my time with the states, we were able to leap-frog a lot of small stuff thanks to local cops doing the work for us."

"Your witness, this man who says he saw the van. He's credible?"

"Yeah. Mere coincidence, but the guy actually does PI work in Vermont. He's down here on a vacation trip with a fishing pal, who just happens to be an undercover drug cop. You know the Task Force DEA runs out of New York for all of the Northeast?"

"Yeah. We've done a little with 'em," Metcalf replied.

"As we all have. I was part of big bust out in Pittsfield a few years back. This guy was there."

"Six degrees of separation. And all that 'small world' theory, right?"

"Something like that," Whalen said.

"OK, Thanks for the call. Let's stay in touch here. I'm sure that I'll see you at O'Connell's office real soon."

The phone call ended, Whalen got up to go check in with his own Detective Sergeant just down the hall.

Sal Hurley had considered and then reconsidered the proposal. If it really worked for them, even if only partially successful, maybe it would give him a 'lock' on a whole variety of tasks coming from the Safari Boys.

Maybe develop another associate of Donnie's caliber. Maybe get some help with the 'heavy lifting' or 'muscle' jobs when it was called for. And certainly, it would provide an opportunity for a lot more in fees. No maybe there.

A plan had come together, just as Nick had surmised the night before. Go to Boston, connect with the nephew, whereabouts unknown. Then try to find the handoff guy from Logan Airport who drove the Tesla. While Big Joe was playing kickass uncle and persuading the nephew to help out or else, Sal and Donnie would coax, negotiate, bribe if necessary, to find others involved and getting their hands on the rest of the money.

The timeline was urgent, Nick said. Leave like this afternoon, no later than tonight.

There were flights from Detroit Metropolitan Airport nearly every hour and the trip was under two hours. Plan on staying several days. A little side excursion down to Atlantic City was a possibility, depending on information from the nephew. If armed assistance was needed, not a problem. However, as Nick had made it clear, guys with guns would have to come by car. And they would only be dispatched if Sal concluded that it was the only option.

Walking around in his office, imagining how such a trip could play out, Sal didn't see any real downside. From everything Nick had told him, the nephew was smart and perhaps too slick for his own good, but not a tough guy. At least according to Big Joe, the kid was extremely unlikely to engage in violence. It wasn't in him, Joe had said.

How smart could the fucking kid be if he was stealing from his uncle? Somebody forgot to tell him that Big Joe didn't get his money from savings bonds? Or that he was not the type of guy who just shrugged off this kind of loss as another 'risk of doing business'?

Sal tapped his phone to call Donnie. Two rings and he answered.

"We can do this," Sal said.

"No doubt in my mind, Sal. You are the real 'Sunshine Superman.' But," Donnie added, "what is *this* that we can do?"

"They want us to go to Boston, find the nephew."

"Wonderful. You're driving, yes?" Donnie preferred not to spend another long haul in the van. And he knew that Sal wanted to spend no time at all riding in the van, across town or across the country.

"We're flying. How soon can you be ready?" Sal said.

"I'm, uh, not at my place at the moment. Spent the night with a friend." Donnie cupped his friend's right breast as she slowly turned over in bed to watch him talking on the phone. He removed his hand, stretched his arm to look at his watch; 9:02 AM.

"How about sometime later, after lunch. Maybe two o'clock?" Donnie said. His friend gave him a little bite on his right shoulder.

"Let me see what's going on with flights," Sal said. "I'll call you back."

Thirty Five

I wasn't surprised when Ragsdale told me he'd agreed to go shopping with Becky. Not his preference for a way to spend the morning, but he was an accommodating guy. Plus, his wife had more than earned just a little bit of his vacation time.

They were heading to a mall in Hyannis while his brother-in-law and wife were going to play golf. I knew that was the trade-off; Louie would find plenty of ways to avoid being coerced into golfing. So the shopping was not a big deal, even if he would have to endure numerous stores and offer his opinion on minor purchases.

We agreed to meet for dinner, this time at Captain Scott's in Sandwich. That gave me the rest of the day. The forecast was for sun and more reasonable temperatures, mid-70s. Rocco's morning walk completed, I went back to the *The Barnstable Patriot* guide book on places to see. More beach time at the moment held no interest. And I wasn't going to drive out to Provincetown as that was likely to be a group trip later in the week.

One possibility was a visit to the Heritage Museums and Gardens. I brought their website up on my phone to see what the hours were. Twenty minutes later I parked in one of their lots, partially lowered the windows in the car, opened the moon roof half way for Rocco's benefit, and went to the ticket booth.

What grabs your attention first at the Heritage are the gardens and grounds. A lot of color with perennials and annuals along the paths, rhododendrons, manicured lawns, healthy looking trees and bushes. A hundred acres with a windmill, a round barn, multiple paths through the woods and a fountain.

But what really drew me here from the website was the antique auto collection. I spent two hours in the round stone barn up close looking over a 1932 Auburn Boattail Speedster; a 1910 Cadillac Roadster; a 1930 Cadillac Convertible Coupe with a *V16* engine; a 1937 Cord 812 Phaeton; and my favorite of the group, a 1930 Duesenberg Model J Derham Tourster, primrose yellow with a light green trim. Originally owned by Gary Cooper it had been carefully restored and it was just spectacular.

After slowly circling the car twice and stretching over to inspect the interior, I chuckled and in a voice that no one else could hear, whispered a tribute to Irving Berlin, Gene Wilder and Peter Boyle; 'Super. Duper'.

Back at my aging Honda CR-V, I took Rocco out for a short walk, gave him a big drink of water, told him that I would bring him a treat and then let him leap back into the car. Ten minutes later, my lunch was a grilled chicken sandwich and a glass of iced tea at The Magnolia Café on the museum grounds. I saved a little piece of the sandwich for Rocco.

Relaxing at the outdoor table finishing the iced tea, I logged on to the Sandwich Police Department website and read a Press Release about the body at the beach. It described the victim as a female, approximately 5' 9" in height, weight of 150 pounds.

The information went on to say that the woman was between the ages of 45 and 50, she had brown hair, brown eyes and that she was wearing a white jumpsuit. There were some tattoos on the victim's body which the police hoped would help them with a positive ID. The cause of death was asphyxiation; in this case, the victim appeared to have been smothered.

When I had stopped by two days ago to tell Whalen about my recollection of the license plate with red numerals, he had confirmed that the body was a woman but had not shared the details now included for public knowledge. I assumed that they had just received the confirmation from the ME on the cause of death.

The statement referred to the District Attorney, one Martin O'Connell, and asked that anyone with information regarding a dark colored panel van contact the Sandwich

PD. A phone number was listed. In my years as a reporter I had read plenty of 'Press Releases'. This was short and to the point, with enough information to fulfill the public's 'right to know' and a plea for additional information should someone have same.

I knew that any reporter with two ounces of hustle would stay after the DA and Chief Whalen. The TV crews and the newspapers would offer supporting video and photos. How the story was treated would depend a lot on who was writing it, who their audience was and what other stories were in play at the time. While I was curious, I didn't feel a need to see any reports on TV. I probably would buy a copy of the local paper.

Walking back to the car I wondered about the victim. Where was she from? What kind of person was she? What did she do for work, what about her family?

Thinking back two weeks to when I heard the radio report that alerted me to the plane crash in which Bonnie and 69 others had died, here was an instance where there was a possibility that *someone* was going to hear about this crime and then have to identify the body.

A close friend, an acquaintance, maybe a co-worker or a relative? Not an easy task for anybody.

Thirty Six

I arrived at the restaurant at 5:20. Louie and Becky were nowhere in sight, so I asked the hostess for an outside table for three and told her that my friends would be there shortly.

No sooner had she seated me at a round table with an umbrella when I spotted the Ragsdale's pulling into the lot. A young man appeared at the table with a carafe of ice water and some menus tucked under his left arm. He filled the glass in front of me and started to place the carafe on the table.

"You might as well fill two more glasses," I said. "My friends are in coming in right now." I pointed behind him as Becky and Louie came up the steps to the restaurant. The server filled two other glasses, placed the menus on the table, then looked at the nearly empty carafe.

"I'll get more water and come back for your order," he said.

"Great. Just give us a few minutes. Thanks."

The hostess was bringing the Ragsdale's to the table. I gave a wave. Becky waved back, Louie had his head down as though he were deep in thought. Or perhaps watching the hostess walking in front of him. I stood when they got to the table.

"I've been here for almost an hour," I lied.

"You haven't," Becky said.

"Of course he hasn't," Louie said. "Probably just woke up from a nap."

"You wish. I haven't had a nap since the Sox lost that yawner down in Baltimore a few weeks ago." The truth was that I was not having *any* naps. And mostly irregular sleep.

Becky sat on my left, Louie took the deck chair on the right. He picked up one of the menus.

"Bit early for dinner, don't you think?" I said. Becky pointed at her husband. I nodded.

"When I saw your text, I thought, poor old guy, must have had a hard day. Then the bell went off, as in the *tide* bell, eh?" Without looking up from the menu, Louie gave a one-thumbs up.

"Why do you think that you will have a repeat of last night?" Becky asked.

"Might not," he said. "But if I'm not down there when they come in, the fish'll think I'm sick or somethin'."

"Yeah. Those stripers, never get enough attention," I offered.

"Louie said that you didn't bring any fishing gear,"

Becky said. I shrugged. "You don't like fishing for striped bass?"

"No, that's not it. I've had a lot of fun on the coast of Maine fishing with a friend. The stripers show up there a little later than they do here," I said. Becky waited for more. "Maybe it's like an old friend of mine who quit drinking. When he told me that, he could see that I was surprised. He said, 'I've had my share'." Louie looked at me when I said this. I stared back at him, then laughed. "Come on. I was pretty hard core for a *long* time. Fished early mornings before going to work. Fished most evenings and weekends. Ask my former wife."

"Was that an issue?" Becky asked.

"No, not really. She was OK with it. I was just being a smartass. But for the most part, I'm just not as eager as I used to be."

"*Who* is getting old?" Louie cracked.

"I don't mind all the fishing he does," Becky said, pointing at her husband. "I've gone out a few times with Louie. And he's tried to show me the casting, but I can't get the hang of it."

The young man had returned to our table ready to take drink and food orders. Becky turned back to study the menu.

"Beer. Tell us what you have on tap," I said.

He ticked off a half-dozen choices. I ordered a local favorite, according to the waiter, Cape Cod Beer IPA. Louie ordered a bottle of Sam Adams Summer Ale. Becky asked for a glass of Pinot Grigio. The kid left to get our drinks, giving us more time to think about what we wanted to eat.

Seafood all around: Becky ordered scallops, Louie went for the salmon scampi and I stayed on the light side with broiled haddock and a small green salad. Since a big lunch on Friday down in Woods Hole, my appetite was behaving like it was on finicky cruise control and off just a bit.

"You took Bonnie fly fishing a few times," Becky said. "How was that? Did she like it?"

The question caught me off guard. I looked at Becky.

"I'm sorry. We don't have to talk about..."

I held my hand up. "No, that's fine," I said. "In fact, she was really quick to pick up the casting. I was really surprised."

"So, when you were together, did she fish with you a lot?"

"At first. I mean, she did *want to learn* all the little details, how to hold the rod, how to present the fly in a way that didn't splash the hell out of the water. How to keep her back cast up. Which fly patterns and which size to use. I was all set to buy her some gear."

"What happened?" Becky said. I shook my head, shrugged and held my hand up while I had a drink of beer.

"We had this long car ride back from Maine. It'll be two years in October. We were talking about a lot of different things. I think she was a little moody at the time." I took a deep breath, exhaled, then laughed. "We eventually got

170

into talking about fishing, the different techniques people use. I think now, looking back, that I was starting to go all purist on her, yapping about catch and release."

Becky said nothing, watching as I placed my glass of beer back on the table.

"After a while, we switched subjects, maybe she didn't like the music I was playing, I don't know. She looked at me, not *angry*, more matter-of-fact. And she said, "The catch and release method. It's probably not a lot of fun for the fish." Louie now joined Becky in the 'let's watch Hanlon' mode.

"Ah-h, I don't know. You knew her." Becky nodded. "She wasn't the type to just say something to provoke you," I added. "I think she really felt that about the fish and never showed any interest after that. Then, we were only together another couple of months after that trip."

Becky reached over and covered my left hand with both of her hands. "I'm sorry. I shouldn't have asked you that."

"No, no. It's fine. You two got along. She was a lovely person."

"She really was," Becky said. "I'm glad that I got to know her."

I almost lost it.

"Excuse me a minute. I'm gonna wash my face. Be right back." I got up and headed for the men's room.

Thirty Seven

7:28 PM – Monday, May 29th – Memorial Day, DELTA Airbus flight 154 touched down at Logan International Airport, five minutes ahead of its scheduled arrival. Total flying time from Detroit, one-hour-and-fifty-one minutes.

A holiday flight and more than one-third of the 180 seats were empty. Sal and Donnie were in the last group to come off the plane. Moving up the jetway, Donnie had a duffel slung over his shoulder and Sal wheeled a black carry-on. They had agreed before departure that if they were in Boston longer than a couple of days, they could buy additional clothing.

Inside, they stopped just beyond the gate boarding area. Sal saw the signs pointing to Ground Transportation and Rental Cars. He motioned with his right arm in that direction. Anyone watching, as in airport security cameras, would have noted two regular guys, possibly brothers, making their way through the crowd of other passengers.

On the flight, Sal had outlined what they would do as soon as they picked up a car.

"Nick got an address where the nephew is supposed to be living," he said, looking at the screen on his phone. "One of the suburbs; Hopkinton." Donnie listened.

"We find the place and watch. If he's *there*, we wait until later, maybe 11:30 or so, then ring the doorbell." Sal paused. Donnie had shifted in his seat but said nothing. "That is, we go to the door *only* if we think he's alone. Any sign that he has company, we wait until morning."

Donnie had spread his hands apart and tilted his head toward Sal, a half-smile on his face as though he were pretending to be astonished. "It's not like we're coming in for Saturday night in Waco," Donnie said. "No guns, no problems, right?"

"Correct. In theory. That ain't saying that *he* doesn't have a gun. Or, someone there with him could have a weapon." Donnie switched back to listen only mode as Sal continued.

"He may or may not be surprised when we show up. Nick says the kid may actually believe that losing that kind of money is part of some game, it's just money, right? A game that he thinks Uncle Joe knows all about. And that he's more than likely lost similar amounts before. What's the big deal?"

"Twenty-five million," Donnie whispered, raising his eyebrows and tilting the back of his head against the seat. "Who loses that kind of money and doesn't get a *little* pissed off?"

"Correct again. Pissed off as in, 'excuse me, nephew,

we have a minor problem here'."

Neither man spoke for a minute. Donnie had shifted forward, looked out the window of the plane for a few seconds, then turned back to Sal.

"So, we have an address. What's the nephew's name?"

"Dyson. Dyson Manetas," Sal replied.

"Dyson," Donnie repeated in his whispering tone, nodding slightly. "Guess it's better than Little Joe, huh?"

Two hours after leaving the airport in a National Rental Car new white Buick Verano with only 3,400 miles on the odometer, Sal and Donnie pulled to the curb across from 5406 West End Circle in Hopkinton. If anyone was at home, there were no signs of activity. The garage door was closed.

The house was completely dark, where other homes in the neighborhood had lights on. A couple of houses had outside lights on at the front door. There were a few fake gas lamps on posts scattered up and down the street. One house, two doors down, had its garage door open with an empty space next to a pick-up truck. But all was quiet.

In addition to the rental, there were other cars parked on both sides of the street, not like in the city, but as though someone might be visiting and chose not to park in a driveway. So the Buick didn't look out of place.

Sal and Donnie settled in to wait.

Thirty Eight

The two dispatchers were not surprised to see Chief Peter Whalen back at the station on a Monday evening. They were accustomed to his off-hours visits to the office. He poked his head around the door of the communications room to let them know that he was in the building.

The Sandwich PD has a fulltime staff of 35, with nine additional people sharing the responsibilities of staffing a crowded joint police and fire dispatch center 24/7. The communications office is housed in the police station, with the town fire department located next door.

Normal shifts have a Sergeant and two officers on duty for each eight hour rotation. The Patrol Operations is the backbone of the force, responding to calls for service and the 9-1-1 emergencies. While officers are generally out somewhere driving around through neighborhoods, the Sergeant spends most of his shift at the station, unless an event or activity requires his presence with the patrol officers.

That was the case on this Monday holiday evening

when Whalen had come back to the station: the shift Sergeant had been called to join an officer investigating a report of loud music and rowdiness at a private home. Whalen was there to look over the report by Brutelli and Michado on their visits to businesses looking at videos in the search for the dark colored van. A copy of the report was on his desk.

A total of 23 businesses had been contacted, 11 of which had video surveillance. As he scanned the list and the notes written by the two officers, nothing jumped out at him. Unfortunately, only three of the businesses with cameras had an angle that picked up shots from the street. Most cameras that had exterior views were focused on the parking lots or the entrance and exit doors of the business.

Of the three with video showing traffic on Main Street, just one was mounted at a height that could pick up an entire vehicle as it passed by.

Whalen flipped to the second page of the report. At the top of the sheet the day and date were in bold type: **FRI – 26 MAY 2017.** Beneath the heading were four black and white photos of vans. The third page also had four photos and the three subsequent pages had additional shots, for a total of 17 photos. There was a date and time stamp on each photo, ranging from 6:05 AM to 11:26 PM.

He recognized some of the vans as belonging to local businesses, lettering on the side panels. Not all were dark colored; three appeared to be tan, light brown, or a neutral color, and two vans were clearly white. But the main problem with the photos was that none had a view of a license plate.

One photo did show a dark van that appeared to be traveling west. He would have to confirm that. There was no lettering or other markings on the vehicle. The driver's window was closed and it would be next to impossible to get a close-up of the driver's face. CPAC and the DA's guys would have to work on that. It was a long-shot *maybe*, at best. The time stamp on the photo was 3:37 PM.

Whalen circled that photo. He suspected that Brutelli and Michado had flagged it as well on the original report. He placed the copy back on his desk and started to switch off the light in his office, but stopped. He went back to the report. He hadn't paid close enough attention to where this camera was located that had all the street angle shots.

It was at a home business, one that he knew about, attached to a guy's garage at the east end of Main Street; Dave's Tackle & Fly Shop. It was located across from one of the side streets that led to Town Neck Beach.

Thirty Nine

The retching had come in spasms and went on for more than an hour. Just when I thought it was over, a new wave of nausea welled up and I was bending over the toilet, gripping my knees and waiting for my breathing to return to normal.

Rocco wasn't sure what to make of all the noise and my trips in and out of the tiny bathroom. He wasn't getting any sleep either. After the first run, which I had attributed to the culmination of my stomach being off and the dinner consumed a few hours earlier, I had very briefly amused myself with a memory of a conversation I'd had once with a Bahamian fishing guide.

What many in the US call 'driving the porcelain bus,' the guide had told me is often referred to in his country as 'dialing New York City.' Guess somebody from the island must've brought that experience back with them.

Didn't matter what you called it, it was not fun. And I had not experienced anything like this, ever. Nothing could be left inside me, yet my stomach felt as though it had some of those cartoon characters you see in commercials. They were down there jumping on a trampoline, taking turns punching me, trying to get out.

Finally, feeling that it might really have subsided, I sat on the floor with my head leaning back and resting on the edge of the bed. Rocco had moved up to lean against me and was giving me the expressive eyes. I put an arm around him.

I felt weak, clammy and right on the verge of whatever a total emotional breakdown must feel like. If reaction at dinner to Becky Ragsdale's questions about Bonnie had put me at a personal discomfort level of say a 5, then what I was feeling right now was pushing an 8.9.

You want to cry, but it won't come out. You take deep breaths, but need more air.

Maybe ten minutes passed before I felt that I could stand. I eased myself up, waited to see if it was going to make another run at me and was relieved when it didn't. My intestines seemed to be calming. The punching cartoon guys had been replaced by a feeling that my stomach was trying to find a pause on a conveyor belt that was vibrating ever so slightly, attempting to regain its alignment.

Patting Rocco, I said, "Hang on kid, I think we're OK." He gave me the look.

I imagined him replying, 'What is this *we*?'

Slowly, carefully, I slipped back into bed and pulled the sheet over me. As hot as it had been a few days earlier and as pleasant as it had been earlier this evening, I felt cold. I reached down and pulled up the cotton blanket on top of the sheet.

Not wanting to look at my watch, I would will myself back to sleep. Eventually.

Reverend Hugh Clarkson Mackin sat alone on the front screened porch of the parsonage. It was late, his wife was in bed, probably not asleep. Neither of them had had much sleep since their daughter's death.

But tonight was different. Three weeks since the plane crash. Twenty-three days of heartbreak, tears, prayers, hugs, bittersweet laughs at so many memories, phone conversations, and a near endless stream of condolences from friends and parishioners. All these things had the effect of making him feel as though he would awake from a dream any second.

Hughie had done something earlier in the evening, however, that now commanded his full concentration. After having initially – and deliberately – avoided reading the entire list of the names of the passengers and crew killed with his daughter, he had gone into his study after dinner and read the list.

Then he had pulled from his old desk a copy of *The Cincinnati Enquirer* that had been published the weekend after the crash. The newspaper had been sent to him by a classmate from The Wesley Theological Seminary who now lived in Covington, Kentucky, near where the plane had gone down.

When the paper had arrived, neither he nor his wife had read the stories about the crash. He'd simply put the paper away thinking that someday he would read it. Now, after slowly reading through the names on the list, he turned to the newspaper. That's when he connected the news stories with victims of the crash.

What he had done earlier with the list of names was something that he had always done, going back to his days in Viet Nam. It was a practice that he'd kept for nearly half a century. When he learned of someone's death, he would say that person's name aloud, think about them, then say their name again. In the past, he could always call up an image.

But he was having a difficult time trying to create an image to go with all the names on a list, perhaps because his mind could not get beyond thousands of stored images of his daughter.

From the list of those killed in the crash were many couples travelling together, according to the newspaper stories. And one father and son returning from a college visit in California. Of all the deceased, the story that now gripped him was that of a young couple. Husband 28, wife 23 and their three-year-old son. They had been flying to the wife's family reunion planned to be held in small coal mining community in western Pennsylvania.

Over the bank from the parsonage, spring peepers in a swamp were in full chorus. He listened for a while longer, closed his eyes and kept them closed, again thinking of Bonnie. Then he tried to imagine what the young family looked like, where they lived, what were their interests? What horrible news for their families to experience on the eve of a reunion.

Hughie picked up the passenger list again. There was barely enough light coming from the living room for him to read it. He put his glasses on, ran a finger down the page and stopped at the three names listed together. He stared at the names. He took off his glasses, placed them in his shirt pocket and closed his eyes again.

He said the names out loud, pausing a few seconds between each name, imagining.

Gilbert. He tried to envision what Gilbert looked like. Perhaps dark hair and handsome. Quiet smile.

Linda. Smart, lively personality, pretty face. A good mother.

Randy. Big blue eyes, curly red hair, full of energy. So incredibly young and so full of promise.

Forty

The front door was locked. A back door and a side door to the garage were both locked. The double-wide garage door at the right front of the house was locked. Sal and Donnie were back in the car. It was 11:38 PM.

"Guess we aren't gonna meet *Dyson* tonight," Donnie said, exaggerating the pronunciation of the name. Sal was slowly checking out the other houses to see if anyone had spotted them walking around 5406. Nothing.

"No, I would say that we are not going to meet him tonight."

"So, what now?" Donnie said, stifling a yawn. Sal put his right foot on the brake and pushed the ignition button to start the Buick.

"Let's go find us a room. We'll come back here in the morning."

They followed West End Circle until it came back to West Main, which took them to 495 and the neighboring community of Westborough. They saw a Residence Inn and got a room.

What they didn't see was the car that left West End Circle five seconds after they pulled out. *That* car took another turn and was waiting off West Main when the Buick turned right toward 495. The unnoticed car stayed back and followed them to the Residence Inn parking lot.

After watching Sal and Donnie go into the hotel, the driver of the unnoticed car – a stripped-down older Toyota Sienna, not dissimilar to Donnie's van – waited for five minutes before he returned to the highway and back to West End Circle.

Once he had parked again, in the same spot four houses back and on the opposite side of the street from 5406, he took out his phone and sent a text.

'2 men cased 5406. Rntl white Buick now @ Res Inn Westborough. Bk here for t/night.'

The driver put his ear buds in, slouched behind the wheel and with Joshua Redman's *Walking Shadows* on his iPod, resumed watching an empty house on a quiet street late at night.

Dyson Manetas had not been home in two days. His anxiety level was beginning to pump non-stop. He needed to get back out to the house ASAP. If he didn't, he was convinced that things would turn ugly fast and he was not prepared for ugly. Dyson simply wanted to be somewhere else.

The previous Thursday night and again the next morning, Dyson had spotted what he believed to be a strange car parked on the street near his home. The car, Dyson thought, looked like every stake-out car he'd ever seen in movies or on TV; an older model, non-descript medium blue Ford without hubcaps. He recalled reading an article about the US Government spending nearly $300 million on new, fuel-efficient cars. The larger group of the cars were Fords.

Thursday night was *before* the suitcase had been delivered to the van pick-up guy in the parking garage at Logan Airport. So, he was certain that if someone *was* watching his house, it wouldn't be anyone from Uncle Joe and his associates in Detroit. Way too soon for any of them to know that most of the cash they were expecting had been 're-allocated'.

Hiding out in a friend's cramped apartment in Boston sure as hell beat going to a hotel. A side benefit was that he was close to the Huntington Ave Y where he could go work out. He'd returned home to get clothes and some personal items on Friday evening. Another odd car was on the street then. He was in and out of the house in minutes and had stayed away since then.

His friend was coming back at the end of the week. She would not have any interest in allowing Dyson to hang around. The place was too small. And she wouldn't share her bedroom; extra benefits or privileges of that nature were not part of the friendship. He still had limited access to leased office space at one of the Boston sites for PDG. But that could end any minute, so he wasn't going to sleep there.

Everyone knew that at least one former employee was now cooperating with the feds. 'Volatile' was the operative word. So he was not inclined to work at the office, either. He had his computer, his phone, his passport and enough cash to sweat it out for a while, if necessary.

Imagining a dozen scenarios that would take him back to the house was easy. And he'd almost tried one of them Sunday night. After persuading himself that he was being paranoid and that those cars on the street were nothing, even though he had most definitely seen a man behind the wheel Friday morning and again that evening, he got cold feet. *Somebody* was watching.

Dyson convinced himself that only two parties had an interest in his whereabouts; the US Attorney's office, and some disgruntled investors. Now his uncle had joined the latter group, which created a third front to watch.

Options were thinning out fast. Maybe the best play was to face the music and explain the problem to Uncle Joe. Before finally returning one of his uncle's calls, Dyson flipped open the cover on his iPad and began searching for flights to Detroit.

"Nobody here," Sal said into the phone. "We watched 'til midnight. Walked around the house twice, all of the doors are locked. No lights on."

It was now 8:30 on Tuesday morning. Sal and Donnie were back on the street. They had watched vehicles leave from different houses, one man out jogging, and a woman walking with her dog. But nothing at 5406 West End Circle.

"Stay there for the time being," Nick said. "Let me talk to Joe. He may want you to go find the kid's office."

"We can do that. Just don't wanna spook anybody, get 'em calling the police. This looks very much like a family neighborhood." Both Sal and Donnie watched other houses to see who came out and went in.

"Understood," Nick said. "Stay with it a while longer. I'll get back to you soon." He clicked off.

The woman was coming back up the street with her dog, an older German Shepherd. She appeared to be in her sixties, Sal thought. Stopping to pull a newspaper from a tube next to the mailbox, she looked at the paper for a minute, turned, then continued walking to her door while reading the paper and not looking at cars parked on the street.

"That Shepard looks like he has a few miles on him," Donnie said. No reply from Sal.

Nick had become the de-facto 'do it' guy for Big Joe. It had started at the very beginning of their alliance. When both men were younger and starting to make their way in Detroit, Nick was the one who remained calm no matter what, offering quiet, sound advice to Joe in all matters.

187

Excitable and compulsive, Joe could ratchet up in seconds, maybe heading for a big confrontation over what often turned out to be trivial issues.

Time and experience had brought Joe in bounds, for the most part. But the fuse was always there. Nick could usually crimp it before things got too hot. His fear at this moment was the whole 'family' thing. It had been a long time since he'd seen Joe become borderline apoplectic over a deal going bad. And it was the fucking nephew.

The arrangement with Sal Hurley had always been for handling errands, using his network of gophers. It kept what nowadays is called a 'firewall' between potentially messy situations and the police. So far, anyway, nothing major had been traced back to Joe's diverse, profitable enterprises. Then again, with all of the spreading crime activity in the greater Detroit area, it wasn't as though the cops and the prosecutors were likely to spend too much time chasing small stuff.

That was Nick's challenge now; keep this small. Don't go enlisting help from people who would be too happy to see Big Joe *not* in the race. Counseling Joe on 'who do we get' to go east to assist Sal? What was the best way to exert influence on the nephew and his friends? These were the immediate concerns.

Maybe the best suggestion would be that Nick should go himself.

It was the Ford Taurus now parked on West End Circle, part of the rotation with the Toyota minivan. The driver had expected to see the Buick rental car return and there it was, four houses down. Two men in the Buick when it went by. Now they parked at an angle across from 5406.

But where was Mister 'I Am Smarter Than You' who *lived* at 5406?

Five days and counting. This could go on for a while. Not sure what this guy was up to, but *someone* back at the 10 Causeway complex was anxious to find him.

The driver in the Taurus reclined his seat and took a sip of coffee. He looked at his watch; 8:37 AM.

Forty One

If we were doing ratings again this morning 0-10, I would be lucky to hit a 3. Achy neck, stiff shoulders, legs that felt as though I was wearing two cinder blocks, mild headache and a nervous stomach.

One could almost believe the theory that dogs are attuned to how their human companions are feeling, even young dogs with too much energy. Rocco wasn't subdued, but seemed willing to cut me a little slack. Maybe all the retching got his attention. Whatever the reason, I was glad that he wasn't leaning into the harness as we came back to the cottage after the morning walk.

Ragsdale's truck was parked next to car. He was sitting in one of the Adirondack chairs and drinking from a travel mug when he saw us coming across the lawn.

"I'll bet you could make a little pocket money walking dogs there in Quechee," he said.

I didn't go for it. Rocco did, tail wagging and giving Louie the full on sniff; pants first, then shoes, back to the pants, then moving in closer to check out the travel mug. I held the leash so he wouldn't try to climb up.

Easing myself into one of the other chairs, I released the snap on Rocco's collar and rolled up the leash into my right hand, not saying anything to Louie. He was giving me the smirk.

"You really don't look so good. Are you OK?" Despite his facial expression, his tone sounded sincere. I shrugged in response.

"Seriously," he added. "You're as pale as the proverbial ghost."

"Eh-h," I wobbled my left hand. "Bad night. I think I'm better now." He just stared at me. Rocco was back sniffing Louie's shoes.

We didn't talk for about a minute. I leaned my head back to let the sun hit me. Louie was scratching Rocco's ears. "He really is a good-looking dog," he said, stroking Rocco's back. "What, he's three now?"

"Two-and-a-half. Born in November. Thanksgiving Day 2014."

"Gobble, gobble," Louie said, giving the dog a pat on the rump. "Normally takes most breeds about four years or so before they stop all the silly stuff. Depends a lot on training."

I tilted my head forward and looked at Rocco. He gave me a glance, but remained focused on Louie.

"Bonnie was good at taking him to obedience training. When he was a pup, then again last summer," I said. "He's pretty good at the basic commands, for the most part. Just has a *lot* of energy."

"So, what's going on, Michael?" Louie never calls me by my first name. Absolutely *never*. I looked at him.

"You've been talking to your wife," I said. "She sent you here to hold my hand." He waved me off.

"Nah. I'm trying a new tact. Civil and polite from now on. With everybody."

I laughed. "It will make the world a better place."

He took another drink from the travel mug, tilting it nearly upside down.

"Let's go get some breakfast," he said, getting up from the chair. I held my hand up.

"I don't know about that. Might try some black coffee."

"Whatever. Let's go out to Willie's. See who he's givin' it to this morning."

I got up from my chair and made the kiss noise with my mouth. Rocco looked up. I showed him the leash and his ears went up.

"Where's Becky. And the Hills?" I asked.

"You did such a bang-up on the Heritage last night at dinner, she and Angie are heading there this morning. Probably spend the whole day. And I'll let you guess where Johnny boy is off to," he added.

"Has he always been this obsessed with golf?" I asked, starting toward my car.

"Nope. Started two years ago. You know how some guys get, all rinky-dink about some new hobby for a while.

Then they get bored and try something else. Probably sell his golf clubs next year and take up mountain biking."

"Let's go in my car," I said, opening the back door for Rocco. He jumped up and turned around. Louie got in the passenger's side.

I got behind the wheel, put the key in the switch, pulled the strap around for my seat belt and clicked it. Louie fastened his belt, took off his faded old baseball cap and scratched his forehead. We sat for a couple of seconds before I started the engine.

"Tell me something," I said.

"You name it. I am *here* to help."

"Right. All civil and polite." He nodded, putting his cap back on.

"Do you have a glossary somewhere of all your little expressions?" He squinted, eyes barely open, and spread his hands apart, but offered no verbal reply.

"Rinky-dink?" I said.

He pointed at the key in the switch.

Forty Two

The early crowd was gone from Diner Shore. We took seats at the counter. Willie was at his usual spot to our left, newspaper folded on the counter in front of him. He had his back to us and was joking with three men seated in a booth.

As one of the grandsons brought us coffee, Willie was giving it to the guys in the booth.

"Do federal authorities know about the three of you? Immigration and Customs Enforcement maybe? We *know* you're price fixing rug imports."

As soon as he said this, I turned to look at the guys in the booth. All three of them were about his age, most likely born sometime between the late 1920s and 1940. I recognized two of the men as having been here the first morning I had stopped by. Then, Willie had ragged them about calibrating a barometer and made a crack about their ethnicity.

"Never mind old hostilities and genocide, do you know

why Armenians and Turks *still* don't get along?" one of the men said. He wore a golfer's hat with the US Open logo above the brim.

"No, but I'm sure that you can tell me, Arem," Willie retorted.

"Because *we* get better prices for our rugs than the Turks do," the man said.

Willie laughed, the Arem guy laughed, the two other men laughed. I suspected they had heard the line before.

"And it just so happens, Maestro Ridell," the Arem guy added, pointing at Willie, "we are *not* talking about rugs."

"Let me take a guess. Picking a winner for the Belmont Stakes? Plotting a march on Washington?"

"We are discussing … *violins*."

"Oh, Sweet Jesus," Willie said, turning back to face the counter. "Fritz Kreisler lives. You're out of my league now."

The other men laughed some more, while the Arem guy admonished Willie, "And don't you *forget it*, pal."

Louie ordered corned-beef hash and toast, I asked for a dry English muffin and coffee. Before he could begin his therapist routine, I made a preventive plea.

"Listen, Becky is really trying to help me with all this stuff about Bonnie. And I know that she's telling you to go easy on me. I honestly appreciate the support. From both of you." He sipped his coffee and stared straight ahead.

"I was up for most of the night, got very little sleep. Vomiting, sweating a lot. Then shivering and cold. Pretty

195

unpleasant." Now he turned to face me, but said nothing.

"It's not really surprising. I haven't felt right since the memorial service. And the butterflies in the stomach, it's been relentless. From the day of the plane crash." His look of concern was as serious as I had ever seen from him.

"Have you considered seeing your doctor? Maybe get some counseling?" he said. I nodded.

"Yes. But I thought this trip would help. I'll probably call for an appointment when I go back."

"Good idea," he said.

"I don't like taking meds, you know that. Pretty good chance he'll want to give me a prescription."

"Could help. Or," he hesitated, then added, "get some professional help. Grief counseling *does* work."

"Maybe."

We sat in silence for a minute, then Louie switched the subject.

"Of course, you didn't need to be the one finding the woman's body, either. Holy high tide," he said, shaking his head. "I mean, I know that I'm on vacation," he continued. "That kind of shit happens *way too often* in my work. I've seen enough of it to not get too stressed out." He looked at me before going on. "You just did *not* need that at this moment now. Not on top of the crash."

I inhaled through my nose, held the breath, then blew out.

"Yeah, you're right. I didn't need it. But..." He waited for me to finish. "To quote that old radio philosopher who gave me my first real job, 'Suck it up. There's a helluva lot more work to be done here."

One of the twins, Alan, I think, arrived with the food. I avoided looking at the hash, but it smelled good. I took a small bite of the English muffin.

The old guys in the booth were now up and paying for their breakfast. Willie was at the register and, as far as I could make out, must have been telling a *really* off-color joke because he was whispering. The Arem guy had to lean in to hear. Then they both erupted in laughter and Willie slapped Arem on the shoulder.

Our breakfast finished, we were back in the car. Louie wanted to show me some of his favorite fishing spots, so I drove as he gave directions.

"You know, we didn't talk about this last night, but I went to the Sandwich PD web site yesterday afternoon and read the Press Release about the body."

"Yes?" Louie said.

"They did a good job. Just the facts, hoping somebody will call if they saw the van. Or anything else."

"They would keep a couple of details out of the press release. See what any potential witnesses had to offer. Corroboration," he said.

"Sure. But one thing they did include was what the woman was wearing: a white jump suit."

"We talking fashion runway jump suit, or Jiffy Lube technician jump suit?"

I shrugged. "Didn't say. I took it to mean more fashion than a mechanic."

"How old did they say she was?" Louie said.

"Forty-five to fifty."

"Really hard to say. You have a better idea about the woman, where she was from, what she did for work, it'd tell you something about her clothes."

"Is that detective work? Think you might be able to teach me some of that?"

"Guess you're feeling better," he replied.

"Sorry, you gave me an easy shot."

"It's OK. I like to help."

"But, let me tell you this," I said. "You know about that big hot air balloon festival they have every summer in Quechee?"

"Kinda' right there in your back yard, isn't it? Yes, I know about it. You remember that Becky and I visited two years ago, right after they'd held it and the balloons never got to go up? Shitty weather."

"Yes, I do remember. But *last* summer, it went off without a hitch. Lot of people, traffic jams on Route 4, the balloons went up five or six times that weekend"

"Great. Sorry I missed it."

"I went over one evening," I continued. "They had a local bluegrass group I wanted to hear, before the balloon launch. So, I had a beer and some ribs, just hanging out at one of the tables, watching all the crews get the balloons ready. They roll out the balloon, hook up the basket and ignite the burners to heat the air. There's a person driving a chase vehicle with a trailer for when the balloon comes down."

"I've seen it on TV. Never in person," Louie said.

"I was watching one crew. A tall, attractive blonde woman was running the show. Not the pilot, but directing the ground crew. And she was wearing an all-white, one piece *jump suit*. Could've been Amazon Women running the show here, thank you."

We were at a STOP sign. No other traffic. Louie looked at me, I looked at him.

"Huh," he said.

"Yeah. Huh."

Forty Three

Whalen, and his Detective Sergeant Terence Murtaugh, made the short drive to Barnstable, where they had a meeting scheduled with Cape and Islands District Attorney, Martin O'Connell.

As is the case with all homicides in this jurisdiction, O'Connell's office was the hub for the investigation. With assistance from Massachusetts State Police detectives, the staff also works with municipal police departments. While the victim found at Town Neck Beach in Sandwich might have been murdered elsewhere, at least for the present the case would remain with the DA's office.

After a late Saturday morning briefing with a few local reporters, less than 24 hours after the body had been discovered, today's meeting was planned as the first in-person update for all law enforcement agencies involved. It followed on the heels of O'Connell's second Press Release to the media on Monday.

The photo of the van had immediately been distributed

to state police and other agencies earlier in the morning. Subject to any new information that O'Connell might have received and not yet shared, Whalen's department was prepared to expand the local search for other video images of the vehicle.

The Sandwich cops were first to arrive at O'Connell's office. Whalen expected the meeting to run no longer than ninety minutes. Before it was over, he knew that another half-dozen people would participate.

One Mass Department of Transportation Information Technology employee had the sense to begin reviewing video from booths and electronic toll gantries on the Mass Pike, *starting* with Exit 26 at Logan Airport. It was the last numbered exit coming east, but the *first* entrance for vehicles heading west.

At 6:17 PM, FRI 5-26-17, a Chevrolet van looking very much like the one in the Sandwich PD photo, entered the west bound lane. The driver took the turnpike card from the automated dispenser. No camera angle to catch the driver's face, but the arm reaching for the ticket appeared to be that of a man wearing a short-sleeved shirt.

No license plate on the front. The rear plate was a blue, white and gold Pennsylvania – **YT 15315**.

Checking video from another twenty-five toll booths and electronic gantries covering more than 220 miles all the way to the New York border would take some time. But if it turned out to be the same van as the one recorded in Sandwich, this was a start.

Of course, if the van was entering the Mass Pike at this location, there was a high probability that one of the video feeds from Logan Airport might also have recorded it. Departures/Arrivals, the Central Parking Garage? There are hundreds of cameras functioning as part of the airport's consolidated camera surveillance system. The security covers four terminals, all exterior parking and the Mass State Police building adjacent to the terminals. Many other cameras record at the rental car lots and at hotels within the airport perimeter.

Step one, notify the Sandwich PD and the state police. Step two, send over a date and time-frame notice to the Massport Control Center in South Boston.

Chevy van, PA registration **YT 15315,** is on video somewhere else. Only a matter of time to establish where and when.

Forty Four

Sal's phone vibrated. He looked at the screen; 313 area code. He recognized it as one of the numbers used by Nick, a land line.

"Mahoning Enterprises," he answered, just in case.

"It's Nick. Are you still at the house?"

"Yeah. Still here. No sign of your boy Dyson."

"Stay there a while longer. How quick for you to get to the airport?" Nick said.

"Maybe an hour. Depends on traffic."

"I'm flying out. You can meet me."

"Sure. When're you coming?" Sal asked.

"Just as soon as I can get a flight. I'll try to be there this afternoon."

"Let me know as soon as you know. We'll be there," Sal said.

"You'll hear from me." Nick ended the call.

Sal placed his phone back on the console between them, took a sip of his coffee and looked at the cup. The coffee was going from warm to cold.

"What's that?" Donnie asked.

"Nick's coming to join us," Sal answered.

"And the plan *is* ...? We're going to do *what* with little nephew Dyson?"

"He'll tell us the plan when he gets here." Sal put the coffee back in the cup holder. "Nick's not big on sharing information in advance. One of those 'need to know' guys. As far as Dyson goes, I think the first thing we need to do is *find him*," Sal added.

Donnie nodded.

Placing the call to his uncle was proving to be harder than Dyson had imagined. Big Joe had been a reluctant 'sell' on the investment scheme. Dyson had visited Detroit and his uncle during the Christmas holidays three years earlier, accompanied by one of his techie pals from Boston. It had worked.

Joe had finally agreed to throw in five hundred grand at the outset. If they could deliver the returns they boasted about, he would come in with more on a second round. They did, sending four quarterly payments of $100,000 each over the first year.

Then Joe had come in with the much larger chunk of $2.5 million the previous summer. Dyson and friends promised that Joe's total investment would be doubled within in two years. They told him that he was their first big investor and was first in line as the profits began to flow, projecting them to do so at an accelerated pace as thousands of smaller investors came on board.

Things changed at the beginning of 2017. That's when the feds began to act. Within weeks, it became clear that it was not just the US Attorney's office in Boston, but police and federal prosecutors in Brazil were involved with the investigation.

By the end of March, charges were brought against six US citizens in three cities – Atlanta, Boston and Dallas – as well as in São Paulo. In both countries, more than a dozen people had been ordered to surrender their passports while the investigation moved forward. Speculation had been that the scam, when all was known, could reach more than $2 billion.

At the center of the US probe was *PhoneDat Global*. Dyson knew that numerous people higher up the food chain than himself were in the crosshairs of the investigators. He knew that the little side show that he and three associates had schemed up was relatively minor in scope. And, as of two weeks ago, he also knew that this venture was ending. It was time to take the money and run.

So, what had been a plan to leave with a shitload of cash to be deposited outside the US, all of a sudden was morphing into a last resort plan to call Uncle Joe. Explain the situation, get help, get protection. And move the cash to Detroit.

The concept was easy. Dyson *thought* that he was prepared to watch his uncle and his associates take the bulk of the money. Then the wavering set in. Foolishly, he'd sent only a small installment in the suitcase a few days earlier. Now, three of his own cohorts in Boston, in addition to Uncle Joe, were very eager to have a word.

Dyson stopped pacing. Instead of calling Joe right now, he would go over to the Y and work out. Nobody there would know him. He would clear his head, revise his plan, then act.

He slipped the phone into his duffel with the exercise clothes and running shoes. It was 11:23 AM.

Listening to WBZ News Radio 1030, the driver of the Ford Taurus parked on West End Circle had just relieved himself by pissing into an empty, half-gallon plastic orange juice jug. He put the cap back on the jug and carefully placed it on the passenger side floor.

Just up the street the two men in the Buick hadn't moved. He'd been able to get a glance of the driver through his compact binoculars. And he had taken a photo of the rental car. But neither man had gotten out of the vehicle. They had been watching the house for over three hours.

The woman announcer on the radio was giving the weather, something this station did every ten minutes, along with news and sports headlines and traffic updates. The driver of the Taurus thought that he could lip sync with the forecast, ending with 'traffic and weather together on the threes.'

He switched the station to WRKO AM 680 to listen to a business/financial show. The guy hosting the program was talking about a study showing how much soda the average American consumed: nearly fifty gallons a year, which translated to nearly forty pounds of sugar from popular soft drinks. The same announcer went on to report the annual sales of the top soft drink companies in the US.

Up ahead, the car was pulling away from the curb. The driver in the Taurus picked up his phone and sent a text message; Buick leaving, 11:28 AM.

Forty Five

Driving around, with occasional stops, Louie and I had run through what seemed like the gamut of cases involving homicides that he personally knew about, both through experience as a municipal cop, and now as a member of a multi-state task force focused on drug trafficking in the Northeast.

"I haven't looked at the statistics recently, but more cases than you might think remain open for a long time," he said. "Nationally, something like maybe a third."

He was looking at houses while he talked; we were coming into Sandwich. Rocco was asleep on the back seat. Middle of the day, more traffic on Main Street and we were two minutes away from my rental unit at the east end of the village.

"Some cops blame prosecutors. You hear a lot about a increased demand for the 'open and shut cases' and plea bargains."

"That kidnaping and murder case in Maine three years

ago," I said. "A conversation I had with the FBI agent in charge..."

Louie cut me off with a laugh. "Special Agent Gary Guidi," he said.

"One and the same."

"Some of the Maine State Police guys are still pissed about his arrogance."

"Nah, he was OK. It was some of his colleagues down *here* who had the attitude. Anyway, what I remember him talking about was the clearance rate of murder cases being just that, slightly under sixty-five percent."

I pulled into the driveway and stopped. Rocco sat up.

"Think I'll take a run down to see Chief Whalen. Need to shower first," I said. "You want to stick around for a few minutes?" He shook his head and opened the door to get out.

"Wanna try out a cool new fly pattern I read about. I'm going to tie some up later this afternoon and then go get lobsters for dinner. You wanna to come out?"

"Eh, maybe not." I clipped Rocco's leash and let him out of the backseat. "I was going to drive over to Bourne and watch some high school baseball."

"You change your mind, just let me know" he said, getting behind the wheel of his pickup.

At precisely two o'clock, I showed up at the Sandwich PD unannounced. If Whalen wasn't around, I would ask to see the Detective Sergeant, Murtaugh.

A minute after talking to the unseen voice over the intercom, a Lieutenant Kane came out to the lobby and told me that the chief was on a phone call and would be available in a few minutes.

"I can wait, thanks," I said. Kane went back behind the security door.

On the glass display case in the reception area were several different brochures. I took one for something called Massachusetts 2-1-1, a new statewide phone link allowing residents to have immediate access to local contacts for a variety of services. I was sitting in the same chair I'd sat in three days earlier and was reading through the brochure when Whalen came out and invited me back to his office.

"Any luck yet on the van?" I said, taking a seat across from him.

"Nothing definitive." Still standing, he opened a folder on his desk, looked at sheet of paper, flipped to the next page, studied it for a couple seconds, removed a paper clip and handed some of the pages to me. "Take a look at the one marked with an arrow," he added.

There were several black and white photos of different vans, four to a page. I turned to the third group and saw the red arrow that he was talking about.

"Think it looks like the van you saw at the beach?"

I pulled the photo closer, maybe eight inches from my face. My eyes shifted over the other photos on the page, then back to the one he'd marked. I looked up at Whalen.

"Maybe. Better idea if it was in color," I said.

He nodded. "Yeah."

"Where was this taken?" I asked.

"It's from a security camera at a home business right across from one of the streets that connect with Town Neck Beach. About a hundred yards from where you're staying."

I looked more closely at the photo and saw the date and time stamp in the lower right corner; 05/26/2017-3:37 PM.

"Can't see the license plate there," he said, pointing at the photos I was holding. "We have another van leaving Logan Airport only a few hours later. Pennsylvania plate."

"White background, blue numerals," I said, my native state. He nodded in agreement.

"It may be nothing. We're likely to see hundreds of different images, maybe thousands, before this is over."

I handed the photos back to him. He clipped them together with the papers on his desk and placed them back inside the folder.

"Boy, I *still* think the plate I saw had red numerals," I said.

"If this is our van, may not be the same one they got up in Boston," he said.

"The reason I stopped in," I began, shifting in the chair to get comfortable, "is that I had another thought."

Whalen looked at me, clasped his hands, sat back and gave an expression that suggested 'Let's hear it.'

I told him about reading the DA's most recent Press Release on his department's web page. Then I told him a somewhat abbreviated story about the Quechee, Vermont Balloon Festival from a year ago, when I'd seen the woman in the white jump suit. As I was describing this, he cocked his head a bit and his expression changed slightly. When I'd finished, he didn't say anything, but then he stood up.

"Excuse me for a second. I'd like Sergeant Murtaugh to hear this." Whalen left the office and came back in less than thirty seconds with Murtaugh in tow.

"Mister Hanlon just told me a story about a woman in a white jump suit," Whalen said. Murtaugh looked at the chief, then at me.

"Would you mind taking a run through that again?" Whalen asked me, gesturing with his left hand toward Murtaugh.

I proceeded to repeat the story, then added the observation about the woman that I'd seen that evening last summer as having been taller than average, near six feet. "Solid figure and big boned," I said.

Murtaugh shook his head. "Our vic is five-eight," he said. "Maybe 160 pounds, tops." Now Whalen was shaking his head.

"If that is some *standard uniform* for those... balloon people," Whalen offered, spreading his hands apart. He looked at Murtaugh, then at me.

Murtaugh's eyes acknowledged that he got the point before the chief could say more. He folded his arms and nodded in agreement.

"Lot of balloon events," the sergeant said. "And we're right at the beginning of the season."

Forty Six

DELTA flight 1398 non-stop from Detroit landed at 3:54 PM. Nick was a First Class passenger seated in the front of the plane. He was inside the terminal thirty seconds after the attendant opened the door.

Five minutes later, standing at the passenger pick up area outside the lower level of Terminal A, he saw the white Buick approaching. Sal was driving. When the car stopped, Nick opened the rear passenger door, put his valise in first and climbed in behind it.

Both Sal and Donnie turned to look at Nick. Nobody said anything for a few seconds, then Nick pulled his seat belt strap across his lap and inserted the fastener.

"Was the grass cut?" Nick asked. Sal stared at him.

"At the house. Had the lawn been mowed recently?" Nick added. Donnie and Sal looked at each other, then Sal nodded.

"Yeah. *All* the lawns had been mowed. It's that kind of neighborhood. Maybe on the same day, by the same guy,"

Sal replied.

"Pool?"

"No pool. Small patio at the back of the house. That's it."

"Any buildings, like a garden shed?" Nick said. Sal shook his head.

"Not at 5406. Nothing I could see. Think there might be some small building on the lot next door, one of the neighbor's," Sal said.

A Massachusetts State Policeman tapped on the driver side window. Sal turned and hit the button to lower the window. The cop motioned for him to move the car. He slipped it into gear, checked to his left and pulled away from the curb.

Merging with shuttle buses and other traffic, Sal circled around until he saw the sign for the Airport Exit. He put his blinker on and moved to the right.

"Where now?" he said, looking in the mirror at Nick.

"Downtown. I've got the address for his office," Nick said, taking his phone from a side pocket of his sport coat. "You're looking for," he tapped the screen, then tapped it again. "Huntington Avenue. 109."

Sal followed a cab to the Sumner Tunnel under Boston Harbor and watched for signs to downtown.

The easy workout at the Y had helped. Thirty minutes alternating the pace on a spinning bike, followed by twenty minutes of easy laps in the pool, a long, hot shower and Dyson was more relaxed. Maybe not as good as racquet ball, but he was avoiding his regular court partners and hadn't played in nearly a month.

Back at the apartment, he was psyching himself for next move. Just no way around talking with Uncle Joe. Depending on how that played would determine where Dyson would go; Detroit, Atlanta or out of the country.

The cash that he'd managed to send in the suitcase, just under two million, as far as Dyson was concerned, had been a sign of good intention that he would get most of his uncle's money back. He did regret filling the suitcase with newspapers and the note. That had been Ramon's idea and Dyson, foolishly, thought that it would be funny. Now, fucking Ramon was back in Providence or somewhere else. He was on Dyson's 'paranoid list' and not likely to come around again anytime soon. Dyson had not told Ramon or *anyone* about this apartment.

Pouring pomegranate seltzer from a plastic bottle into a glass full of ice cubes, Dyson cut a wedge of lemon and dropped it in. After drinking half of it in one long swallow, he put the glass down and picked up his phone.

On the fifth floor at 109 Huntington Avenue, the company's name was embossed on a door at the end of a long corridor. The door was locked, no lights visible behind the glass.

Nick took the elevator back to the lobby, stopped and looked at the building directory again. Businesses were listed by floor. PhoneDat Global – Suite 520. None of the other businesses on the directory appeared to have any connection to the one that held his interest. Other than one lawyer's office on the second floor, none of the offices listed a person's name.

The Buick, engine idling, was double-parked across the street next to a locked Fiat 500. Nick went to the crosswalk on the corner, waited for the pedestrian signal, walked back to the car and got in.

"That was quick," Sal said.

"Closed for the holidays," Nick said. Sal gave him a quizzical expression via the rearview mirror. Donnie watched people going by on the sidewalk and kept his mouth shut.

"Memorial Day?" Sal said.

"Memorial Day, Father's Day, Fourth of fucking July. All of 'em. Closed for *any* holiday when we give your money back." Nick also took a look at the people on the sidewalk. "How long to get to the house?" he asked.

"Half-an-hour, maybe forty minutes," Sal replied.

Right hand resting on his thigh, Nick tapped his fingers rapidly as though he were sending Morse code.

"Let's find a bar. I need to talk to Big Joe before we go out there."

Forty Seven

The high school baseball game was a Sectional Playoff in Bourne against Martha's Vineyard. Great effort by the home team with three runs in the seventh for a come from behind 4-2 win. I was impressed by the umpires, as well.

A pleasant evening, a good crowd and fun to watch some spirited teenagers with talent, skills and plenty of determination. And Rocco got a lot of attention from others at the game but was reasonably well behaved.

Driving back to Sandwich I thought about getting something to eat. Just the English muffin this morning and a couple of crackers and a bottle of water before we left for the game. I hoped that my stomach was back to normal, but didn't want to push my luck. No fried clams or some other 'not so wise' selection. I compromised; ham and cheese on a whole-wheat bulkie from a deli/convenience store, along with a can of diet ginger ale.

My stay on Cape Cod had now been almost a week. Other than a quick hello to the other guests and some small talk with the owner of the guest cottages, Jean McKearney, I had deliberately maintained a low profile. All of the activity after the body at the beach had thrown me off the first couple of days.

Vermont plates on my car almost always draw some comment when I'm visiting elsewhere. One of the couples staying next door had been eager to talk about Bernie Sanders. I was polite, but had feigned little interest. Not anything I care to talk about right now, thank you. I didn't actually say that. Ragsdale might have, given the chance.

Could've been my imagination, but in addition to sensing that my stomach and my nerves might be settling, thoughts about Bonnie seemed to be shifting to the more humorous and happier memories. The 'you could lose it here at any minute' feeling had dissipated. There were still instances of me saying something out loud and using her name when nobody else was around, but it was now accompanied by at least a smile, maybe a laugh.

The nice thing about staying at a simple housekeeping place like this was that you were not distracted by TV. I knew that didn't work for some people, but right now, for me, it was a treat. A half-a-dozen library books were in the back of my car and I pulled out *2016 - The Best American Science and Nature Writing*, a collection of essays from 25 different writers, including a story about a three-week mission on the US Navy *RV Atlantis* in the Gulf of Mexico and a mini-submarine dive to 5,300 feet.

By 9:30, I was ready for bed. Early, but I hoped that

tonight might get me back on even keel. If I was lucky, tomorrow I might be able to resume some half-hearted exercise regimen.

The email attachments that Sergeant Murtaugh had sent to his boss listed 22 hot air balloon festivals, rallies and events around the Mid-Atlantic states and New England, with dates ranging from mid-March in Georgia through early October in both New York and Vermont. Another list included 68 different clubs and associations affiliated with ballooning.

A more important list, however, for the Sandwich PD and the Cape and Islands District Attorney's Office, was a roster of 231 balloon owners, operators and pilots. It was from this list, Murtaugh believed, that they would have the better chance of obtaining information about female crew members.

Of course, there was also the very real possibility that the jumpsuit worn by the homicide victim had nothing to do with hot air balloons. The suit was also similar to that worn by pro golf caddies at the big tournaments. Murtaugh and Whalen had discussed that after Hanlon had left the police station. Nonetheless, they agreed that this was an interesting hunch and worth investigating.

Media reports citing unidentified persons – dead or alive – routinely refer to said person as John Doe, or Jane Doe. Law enforcement agencies frequently do the same. And while the Medical Examiners are responsible for the administrative work and official forms that go along with a body, ME's can provide an interim ID variation by filling in something like 'New Orleans Jane Doe', or 'Chicago John Doe'.

Reporters are quick to pick up on the 'location specific' usage. It helps their story. As recently as the summer of 2014, only the torso of an African American man was discovered in Sandwich, not very far from the same Town Neck Beach location as this most recent female homicide.

While news reports referenced the 2014 discovery, a case still unsolved and identity unknown, few speculative stories had surfaced citing 'Sandwich John Doe'. How it was playing with residents, and those free to gossip and speculate any way they choose, was unknown. Unless, of course, you were privy to the local gossip.

As far as Chief Peter Whalen and the Sandwich Police Department were concerned, and everyone at the station knew this, the policy was to 'keep your mouth shut, your ears and eyes open.' Interaction and conversations with members of the community are certainly important to any municipal department. Town employees cannot predict or anticipate the nature of all comments from a neighbor, or someone after church, or at a Rotary Club function. But if you work for the town, *not* a good idea to be the one to initiate such discussions. Even if you're related.

Although jurisdictions in some states liked to hang onto their discovery work, Chief Whalen was perfectly OK with 'official' information for this particular case to flow through the DA's office just up the road in Barnstable.

Martin O'Connell, first elected as District Attorney fifteen years ago, had an impressive resume. Having prosecuted cases for twenty years as an Assistant DA before winning this job, O'Connell had earned his JD degree by attending law school classes at night. He had done this while he was working as a small-town police officer, a job where he was awarded a Medal of Merit for Bravery.

Members of the legal community knew that O'Connell has brought to conclusion more than 250 court cases, including the successful prosecution of 20 homicide trials. He was the recipient of numerous awards and citations from state and national associations, and was a Fellow in the American College of Trial Lawyers, a position attained by invitation only.

Ask some of the people who know O'Connell well and they would likely tell you about his professionalism, his dedication to public service, and both his commitment *to* and involvement *with* the community at large. They would also tell you that he knows a little bit about politics.

Fortunately, cases like this one involved an absolute minimum of politics. Public Relations, of course. Find any position with a high profile and there was no small amount of PR required. But having a competent, experienced staff and the support of cooperating law enforcement agencies made a DA happy to show up for work regardless of how unpleasant the details of the current caseload.

Forty Eight

Nick had spent more time on the phone in the last
three hours than he might spend during an entire week
back in Michigan. But he sensed that progress was shifting
in his direction.

The first call to Big Joe, after finding the *PhoneDat
Global* offices closed and locked, triggered a sequence of
events that began with Nick, Sal and Donnie going into a
holding pattern. The afternoon flight from Detroit fresh in
his mind caused Nick to think of what was happening right
now as being analogous to a plane circling an airport,
waiting for permission to land.

By coincidence – Nick was skeptical here – Joe had
just spoken with his ingrate nephew. The kid had finally
called. According to Joe, young Dyson had realized that
allegiance to his east coast frat buddies and some fast
talking crook from Brazil, was really not the way to go. He
regretted the ill-conceived jerk-around that they had tried
with the suitcase and the cash a few days earlier. Dyson –

and *not one* of his Boston associates – knew the location of the rest of the cash, reportedly several million.

Five more calls, including one brief conversation with Dyson, and Nick was also skeptical about 'several million.' But Nick did work for Joe. And here he was, already in Boston, hanging out in a suburban hotel room with Sal and Donnie, two men not usually seated in the same section of the plane as Big Joe, Nick and their 'select crowd' back in Detroit.

"How's it look?" Sal asked. Nick stared at him.

It was one thing to be waiting for permission to land, but Nick's patience in sharing information that he didn't have was not making things better. He slowly brushed the creases of his slacks, stood and walked to the hotel room door. He stared at the door, then turned and came back to where Sal, shoes off, was stretched out on a bed. Donnie had gone down to get more ice.

"How it looks," Nick began, "is that Big Joe is still working it out with *Dyson*," his tone reverting to sarcasm, "on just *when* we're going to stop this fucking little hide and seek. And *when* we will have the money and be on our way back home."

"Everybody confident that the kid actually *has* the money?" Sal asked.

The door clicked open. Donnie came into the room with a small plastic bucket of crushed ice. He placed it on a tray near the microwave oven, then sat in the wing chair next to the window. Nick looked at him, then back to Sal.

"No, that would be going a little too far to say that *everybody* is confident. But Uncle Big-fucking Joe seems to be buying it," Nick said.

Hearing Nick's tone, observing his body language, Donnie had the sense not to ask what Big Joe was buying. Clearly, he'd missed an important part of the conversation. He scooped ice into a glass and poured in some Dr. Pepper.

Nick looked at his watch; 10:57 PM.

"Would you switch that to CNN. And turn the volume up?" Nick said, pointing at the TV. "Let's see what else is going on in the world. Maybe my cousins in Greece and the fucking Germans have come up with a new plan to goose the world economy."

Checking his paranoia yet again, Dyson Manetas promised his uncle that he would meet with the Detroit guys who were now in Boston. His first reaction, upon learning that the men had been dispatched to find him, was a momentary lapse into the state of accepting that his life was about to end.

His uncle jerked him back from the edge. It was Joe's clever and effective habit of lecturing Dyson on 'family.' He was one of the best at trotting out *familia supra omnia*.' But this time, Dyson was a believer. No matter all the various aspects one could imagine of 'everything,' he was now ready more than he had ever been to fully embrace

226

'family.' Starting with Uncle Joe. And the money.

What they worked out was that Dyson would spend the next day misdirecting two of his cohorts by proposing a plan when they could meet. The meeting would be on Friday night, 72 hours from now. Dyson would plan a rendezvous to retrieve the money, to be evenly divided among the three of them before anybody else got nabbed by the feds.

The real rendezvous would come sooner. Probably tomorrow night. For all anyone knew, investigators could be just minutes away from putting the cuffs on a few more of *PhoneDat Global's* employees or former employees, disgruntled or not. It didn't take a Brazilian whiz brain to know that 'cooperation' was likely to begin shortly after the cuffs went click.

Everyone knew that the mastermind of the entire scam, going back five years, was the Brazilian now hiding somewhere in São Paulo. Not everyone knew, however, that much of the ill-gotten cash was still in the US. Dyson knew. And now his uncle knew.

Big Joe again had Dyson's promise: by five o'clock tomorrow, he would be ready to meet with Nick and the two others and take them to where the money was hidden. If all went according to this *new* plan, Nick, his two side men, and Dyson would remove several million dollars in cash and drive it back to Michigan immediately.

Now, a few minutes before midnight and adrenaline-juiced like some swimmer who had just qualified for the

Olympics, Dyson was happy to be hunkered-down in the tiny borrowed apartment. He did not expect to get any sleep during the next twenty-four hours.

Forty Nine

Wednesday morning I had gotten up early, had taken Rocco for a walk and was back at the bunk house by 6:45. After fifteen minutes of stretching, push-ups and sit-ups, I was actually hungry. I called Louie.

"Wanna get some breakfast, or have you guys already eaten?" I said.

"No, I'm the only one awake. Just putting water on for coffee."

"I was out for a walk with Wonder Dog and he asked if we could go see the diner guy."

"Why not?" Louie said. "Let me see what the plan is here. What, maybe forty-five minutes or an hour?"

I looked at my watch. "That can work. Call me back."

Rocco had lapped up a full bowl of water so I filled it again. Then I poured water in the little two-cup, automatic coffee maker and waited for it to drip through. Looking out at the two other rental units, it seemed that no one else was stirring yet. Everybody must be catching up on sleep with the cool night.

After a shower, it took me fifteen minutes to read most of the *Cape Cod Times* that I'd purchased on the way back from the walk. There was an article on Cape Cod Breeds by The Bite, reporting different incidents of dogs biting *other* dogs, and biting humans. The story recounted some nasty attacks, coupled with varying opinions of local dog owners and animal control officers. Included was a chart covering a recent one year period of the reported bites by breed for each community. Based on this report, Pit bulls were the leading bad actors.

My phone vibrated; it was Ragsdale calling back.

"I'll meet you in twenty minutes," he said.

"Anybody else going to join us?"

"Nah, late night here. They're moving a little slowly. I'm gonna' come back after breakfast."

"OK. See you there." I put the phone in my pocket, snapped on Rocco's leash and headed for Barnstable.

Peter Whalen read over the lists of the hot air balloon events and clubs. He forwarded the email to the DA's office and offered to have his department begin making contact with some of the names.

He picked up the phone to call the Medical Examiner and ask about the jumpsuit. Might help if there was a manufacturer's label, size tag, or any other information attached.

The call went to voicemail and Whalen left a message.

Daily briefings with the top officers of the Sandwich PD were held in the conference room and usually lasted thirty to forty-five minutes. Subject to what might be going on with any active investigations, others might be included or Whalen would meet separately with a sergeant and his officers. That was his plan this morning. Once the briefing was over, he would spend time with Detective Sergeant Murtaugh and two other officers who could be assigned to help with still more grunt work, i.e. working the phones.

Before going to the conference room, he spotted an email reply from Martin O'Connell: 'I'm in court til noon. Let's talk then.'

Louie was at the counter talking with Willie Ridell when I arrived. The booths were full, but nobody else was seated on the stools near Louie. I sat on his right. He turned and acknowledged my arrival but was listening to Willie.

"He was going to play in the World Cup," Willie was saying, turning his head toward one of the booths behind him. "Now he's here in the states. Living with a coupla' sweethearts there."

I looked at the people Willie seemed to be discussing. It was a young guy with longish brown hair, a three-day beard and two very attractive young women seated in the booth across from him. All three of them looked as though they might be in college, or recently out, in their twenties.

"How do you *know* all this, Willie?" Ragsdale asked.

Willie held up two fingers and pointed at his eyes, then at his right ear. "I was in Navy intelligence. Before they turned me into a cook," he laughed.

"Really?" Ragsdale said.

"Absolutely. I was *intelligent* enough not to mess with the SPs."

Ragsdale shook his head, then turned to me. Willie got up slowly and started back toward the booths to visit with customers.

"What was that all about?" I asked.

Louie laughed and gestured with his left thumb. "See the young guy with the babes back there?" I nodded.

"Willie says he is a big-time soccer star from France. Has been visiting the Cape for the past few summers. Says his grandsons know him."

"Did he tell you his name?" I looked at the guy in the booth again.

"Brewitt, maybe." I leaned away from Louie to get a better look at the guy, trying not to be too obvious.

"Bruit. Like Dewey. Marcel 'Beaucoup' Bruit," I said. I got the Ragsdale eye roll and tilt of the head.

"You actually *know* who he is?"

"Yeah," I said. "Certainly looks like him. He plays for FC Barcelona. I think he's had some minor health issues." I took another look at the man in the booth. "But how does *Willie* know the first thing about French soccer players?" I added.

"Probably from the twins," Louie said, pointing toward the kitchen. "I think they both play in an amateur league around here somewhere."

One of the twins came out and was ready to take our breakfast order. Louie went for bacon, scrambled eggs and homemade white toast. I ordered the mushroom omelette and homemade wheat toast. The grandson filled our coffee mugs and went back to the kitchen.

Our conversation went from the Scrabble showdown that had apparently gone on until midnight, through talk about a planned day trip out to Provincetown, and back eventually to how I was doing. Even though I was pretty sure that Becky had worked on him, I was still touched by what seemed to be Ragsdale's genuine concern for my emotional well-being.

"Considerably better, I think. Just before I went to the baseball game last night, my sister finally called back. She and her husband have been gone for two weeks." Louie nodded. I went on. "She's always ready to buck me up and offer a ten-point plan on how to move forward, no matter what the crisis. She's been that way ever since we were teenagers."

"Good that you're friends," Louie offered.

"Yeah. And she has good antennae, quick to pick up on how somebody's feeling. Talking and laughing with her helped, but I think watching the kids and the crowd at the baseball game reminded me that life does go on. Man, if you're fortunate enough to have your health ..." Louie cut me off.

"Count your blessings," he said.

"You're not making fun of me?"

He shook his head. "Hey, I've known that most of my life." He took a sip of coffee. "It's just hanging around with you and *hearing* it all of the time, I'm in."

I studied him for a second, then patted his shoulder. "You might be what Bonnie's father Hughie would think of as an unsuspecting convert. You can be saved," I offered.

"Don't tell him."

Fifty

Nick, Sal and Donnie had done a drive by 5406 West
End Circle, but with no reason to stick around they had
returned to the hotel. Big Joe told Nick that Dyson was in
Boston and that was where they would meet him that
evening. The only remaining glitch was for Dyson to deal
with his techie sidekicks and throw them off his trail.

Maybe. Nick was not convinced that Dyson was as
clever, nor as reliable, as his uncle believed, now that he
had brought him to heel. But Nick hadn't become a close,
trusted associate of Joe by always second-guessing him.
Listening, analyzing and then tactfully persuading. Nick
thought this was the better approach, especially when Joe
believed that it was really *his* idea. It had worked more
often than not.

"Let's check out the aquarium," Nick said, putting his
phone away. He'd been scrolling through a list of sites and
attractions in Boston.

Sal looked at him, then looked at Donnie.

"It's good for me," Donnie said.

"OK, I like fish," Sal said. He stood up and looked at the window. "We checking out, or think we'll be back here tonight?"

"Better keep the room," Nick said. "If we do head back tonight, you can call the front desk when we're on our way."

Dyson met with two of his PDG associates: Kurt, an American who had been a fellow participant in a coding boot camp Dyson had attended; and João Pedro, a grad student from Brazil brought on the previous summer when the company was flying high.

Both these men were very smart, had worked and *would work* extremely long hours; and both were just gullible enough to accept most of the spin that came down from the brain trust behind the scam. As a person with both IT skills and something of a 'Midas touch,' Dyson had been drawn into that brain trust. Now, with PDG people beginning to scramble for any safe spot other than Boston, Dyson had become the last man who knew more than most and was still in town.

Kurt and João Pedro had been hired by Dyson and remained loyal to him. In talking to them on the phone, Dyson had determined that neither man expected to have his job back. With assurances from Dyson, neither one of them really feared going to jail, because they hadn't done anything illegal. Of course, if what Dyson was now laying out before them came to fruition, they would be doing something very illegal; stealing money from people who had already stolen it from others.

It was all a smokescreen, probably unnecessary, but something that Dyson felt he needed to do. If he could convince the two subordinates that they were about to have a 'shitload of money' and that they would be able to 'go anywhere away from here' then he was confident they would come on board.

"High key' was his signature expression. He used it now, followed with the suggestion that they meet on Friday, 5 o'clock, the Lookout at The Envoy Hotel. They agreed.

All of this acting and sucking-up simply bought Dyson more time. He hoped that it would throw confusion at anyone closely affiliated with PDG: a former superior, or any other person who might be looking for the chance to ask Dyson a few relevant questions.

The feds were another matter, but for the moment he was still a free man. As far as stakeout cars back in his Hopkinton neighborhood, Dyson was uncertain. Probably feds, but maybe somebody delegated by Whiz Brain. He might get the answer to that when he got home.

And home it would be, sometime later tonight.

Dyson took his phone out. Time to tell Uncle Joe what to tell his guys in Boston.

"Says they are a 'Global leader in ocean exploration and marine conservation," Nick read from a visitor's brochure at the New England Aquarium.

After forking over eighty-five-bucks for three tickets, the men joined a large crowd of young parents, kids, senior citizens and students on school trips, all trying to enter the 75,000 square-foot facility located right on the wharf of Boston Harbor.

"Twice as big as Sea Life," Nick said, referring to the largest aquarium in Michigan.

"Never been there," Sal said.

"Auburn Hills. You go to all those fucking games at The Palace and you never been to Sea Life?" Nick asked. Sal shook his head.

"Donnie. How about you? *You* have been to Sea Life."

"Nope," Donnie said. Nick made a show of throwing his hands up to the sky. The brochure fell to the sidewalk. Donnie picked it up and they moved inside the building.

"Guess you fellows made it out of Ohio not a day too soon," Nick added, taking the brochure back. He looked at an illustrated floor plan, studied it for a few seconds, then turned to his left and pointed. "Giant Pacific octopus. Let's go this way."

Sal and Donnie fell in behind their tour guide.

For nearly three hours they saw more fish species, seals, turtles and penguins than Nick could ever have imagined. He would have kept them going but his phone buzzed. It was Big Joe.

"Let me call you right back," Nick said, motioning to Sal and Donnie that he was going back outside.

Walking in slow, wide circles, Nick listened as Joe did most of the talking. He sounded excited. And a hell of lot more convinced about Dyson's 'playing it straight now' than Nick thought wise.

With only a few short questions about 'what if', Nick told Big Joe that they would proceed and that he would call at the first sign of things going south.

Slipping the phone into his pocket, he turned back to the entrance of the aquarium. He could see Sal and Donnie standing right where he'd left them.

Fifty One

We'd finished our breakfast, including listening to an exchange between Willie and Marcel Bruit, the French soccer hotshot. Willie was telling him that he would give him an authentic Diner Shore tee shirt if Marcel could arrange a professional try out for his grandsons.

"I think their mother has some French blood," Willie said. "Isn't that right, Brandon?" One of the twins was standing at the counter looking slightly embarrassed by his grandfather's antics.

"Oui?" Marcel replied. The twin, quickly shaking his head, tapped two fingers to his temple and rolled his eyes at Willie.

"Hey, Alan," Willie shouted to the other twin back in the kitchen. "Your brother is confused. Come out here and set the record straight."

Marcel, laughing, shook hands with Willie, then with the twin at the counter. He gave a thumbs-up to the other twin and walked out with the two young women.

As I paid for breakfast, Ragsdale went back over to the counter. He put his arm around Willie's shoulder. Willie was still grinning from the brief exchange with Marcel, or perhaps because of the young women.

"You know something, Admiral," Ragsdale said. "I don't think you know jackshit about soccer."

Willie pretended to be offended. He closed his eyes in a mock expression of concentration, looked to the ceiling and then held up his right hand. "Wait. Does Pele count?" Grinning now, he looked at Ragsdale. "How about Walter Bahr?"

"Keep him honest, boys" Louie said to the twins, then slapped Willie on the back.

Leaving Barnstable, we headed to the rental cottage at Corn Hill Beach. Becky, Angie and John had finished their breakfast and were waiting on the front lawn.

After a brief discussion about cars, the five of us were on our way to Provincetown. Becky and Louie were riding with me, Louie in the backseat with Rocco, and John and Angie were ahead in their car. The first stop was going to be the Marconi Wireless Site in South Wellfleet. Two old radio guys like Ragsdale and me wanted to see the spot of the first transatlantic communication between the US and Europe.

The rest of the itinerary included a stop at North Truro Beach, a drive to the Race Point Lighthouse, some shops and galleries, and dinner in Provincetown. One thing I had learned from the first time Rocco came to stay with me was to always travel with bowls, food and water, so he was good for the duration.

All afternoon, Becky stayed close to me. Several times, she took Rocco's leash. For all I knew, he would leave with any woman who smiled and scratched his ears. But it worked, except when Louie and I would forget that she was trailing behind us. Becky was a good sport. Her brother and his wife were not as distracted as we were and they adjusted their pace to Becky's.

Going on six o'clock we'd had enough. Sightseeing done for the day, we decided we had better find a restaurant. I first fed Rocco, then threw the ball for five minutes, cleaned up after him and took him back to the car. Becky and Angie had picked a place called Fanizzi's. It looked pretty casual and had a dining room that offered a view out to the bay.

As soon as everyone had given the waitress their food and drink orders, Louie was eyeballing me while scooting his chair closer to his brother-in-law. I anticipated some wisecrack about golf, but that wasn't what he had in mind.

"John, tell Hanlon the story you were telling us last night," Ragsdale said. John raised his eyebrows and looked at Louie. "We were playing Scrabble. You were losing, by the way. The *body*! The one they found out here back in the 70s," Louie said.

"Oh. Lady of the Dunes," John replied. "Yeah. 1974. It

was my sophomore summer. A friend of mine had a job as a waiter over in Harwichport. A buddy and I came down a couple of times to see him."

"You told us they were filming *Jaws*," Louie said.

"Yeah, over on Martha's Vineyard. But we didn't know anything about it at the time. It was *later* that that came into the speculation."

I had a sneaky feeling that I was being set up and that Louie had conned his brother-in-law to play along. "OK," I said. "Where we going with this, guys?"

"No, this is legit," Louie said. John was nodding.

"Yeah. The story was that a young girl, maybe thirteen or fourteen, was out walking her dog," John said, looking out the window. "Somewhere in the dunes not far from here. And she comes across a body, a woman."

I glanced at Becky and Angie to get some clue. Both were straight-faced. John went on.

"The body had been there maybe two weeks or more. It was all over the papers and on the news. They never identified her, I don't think to this day. Later, some convict claimed that he'd done it, but the cops didn't believe him. I think he claimed a couple of other murders they thought he was lying about."

John sounded convincing, so I decided that maybe this wasn't a spoof.

"After *Jaws* became a big hit, there was speculation that the dead woman might've been an extra in the film. I guess there was a crowd scene with a young woman who looks like what they reconstructed of her face."

"What about the Whitey Bulger angle?" Louie said. Again, I watched for a hint that this was fiction.

"Then, a couple of years ago, the cops were looking into a new report that Whitey had been in Provincetown earlier that summer and had been with a woman that matched the description of the victim."

"1974?" I said. John nodded. It was the year that I was in third grade, Louie would've been in the fourth.

Nobody said anything for a minute. The women looked pretty grim, but they'd heard the story twice now. Louie was giving me a look and I knew that he was about to say something serious.

"What he's leaving out is," Louie looked at John, then continued, "they think that she had been strangled."

"Yeah," John said. "That's what I remember. The Globe had an update after all the stuff came out about Bulger's serial murders."

"What, they finally arrested him somewhere out in California?" I asked.

"Fucking scumbag," Louie said. Becky hit him on the shoulder for the F bomb. Louie pointed two fingers at me and ignored his wife. "Let's talk to Whalen about this when we see him," he said. This surprised me, as I didn't know that 'we' were planning to see Whalen again. Louie and I stared at each other.

"I can only *imagine* how many women are killed each year – just in the US – by strangulation." I said. "Maybe the latest being the body in Sandwich. But I think they're saying she suffocated. Forty-some years is a long time..." I was interrupted when two servers brought food to our table.

After everyone had a chance to start eating, Louie resumed the conversation.

"I'm not suggesting there's any connection. Cape Cod's a popular place. Probably some other nasty deeds here we've never heard about." He was spreading butter on a roll and looking only at me. The women were checking the salad dressing, John was listening to Louie.

"But I'd like to hear about some of the psychological profiling they're doing these days," Louie said. "Whalen was with the state police before he came out here." He took a bite of his roll, then picked up a fork and held it above his plate. When he finished chewing, he continued.

"I read a lot of material and have some idea - my work, for ten years now - that it's all drug related. We see our share of murders. But they're straight out violent and connected to knocking off shitbags who maybe shouldn't be here anyway."

I'd taken a couple of bites of my tortellini with scallops while Louie was talking. He stopped and started eating his meal, a Cajun Seafood dish. It all went quiet, everyone was eating now.

Putting my fork down and taking a sip of wine, I wiped my mouth.

"I can never quite predict just *who* is going to be nice

to you and who's gonna tell you to take a hike," I said to Louie. He shrugged. "Why would Whalen want to talk to you about profiling?"

"Professional courtesy," he managed to get out, not quite finished chewing. "I'm just curious. He seems like a good guy," he added. "And I'm on vacation. Just want to stop in, say hello, how's it going?"

"Yes," Becky chimed in. "You *are* on vacation."

I watched them looking at each other and wondered which had the ultimate stare.

Fifty Two

What Nick had explained to Sal and Donnie was that a plan was coming together. A meeting with Dyson Manetas, venue still to be determined. What he had *not* told them was that his patience was approaching empty.

Fucking family. How did Joe let the twerp nephew jerk him around like this?

But, they had come to Boston to: a) find the nephew and, b) bring back the rest of the money. Maybe it was actually going to happen. One thing for certain, if this kid was really dumb enough to screw with his uncle a *second* time, a meeting with Nick, Sal and Donnie would be only the beginning of his headaches.

"Do we have a time?" Sal asked. "Are we going back to his house, maybe?"

Nick didn't answer. He'd turned his back to them and was looking out at Boston Harbor. The last surge from the crowd in the aquarium was slowly departing. People were drinking sodas and having snacks on the pavilion outside.

Still others were having drinks and eating at Legal Sea Food's outdoor café.

Nick turned back to face Sal and Donnie. He looked beyond them to the café across the street. Their appeared to be two or three empty tables. Nick started walking in that direction.

"Let's get some food," he said, stepping past Sal.

There were tables available. A hostess showed them to one, gave them menus and said that someone would take their orders shortly.

When the hostess had gone, Nick wiped his mouth a couple of times, more as a nervous gesture than checking his lips for dryness. Now he was holding his right hand over his mouth and rocking his upper body ever so slightly. He continued that for several seconds, stopped abruptly, folded his arms and sat back in the chair, his eyes first on Donnie, then shifting his gaze to Sal.

"You wouldn't know this," Nick began, "but this entire fiasco has been going in the shitter ever since that suitcase showed up with more weight in old newspapers than the cash." Now he looked at Donnie again.

"Hey, you *saw* me open it, right? What was there, was *there*," Donnie said, holding both hands up as though he were deflecting an accusation. Nick was shaking his head. He held up his right arm.

"Easy. I'm not suggesting that you took any money. *Yes*, we watched you open it. OK?"

Donnie backed off. Sal was waiting to hear where this

might go.

"What I'm trying to say is, Joe fucking near had a stroke when he saw the smartass note with the money. And the fucking newspapers. Then we had no other contact with the nephew, or the guy in Atlantic City, or *anybody*.

"If it was only Joe's money, maybe not such a big deal. Eventually the nephew's gonna show up, right? But..." he paused for effect, "*But*, Joe got a friend to come in for a mil. And even maybe *that* is not such a big deal." Nick took drink of water, put the glass down, leaned forward and folded his arms to rest on the table. Alternating his gaze between Sal and Donnie, Nick resumed.

"For a year now," Nick was speaking softly now, "Joe is not the same guy that I've known for thirty-five years. Even little things get him all jammed up. Worries about something for days. Weeks! Things that are *nothing*. And he's not about to be down a million bucks to a friend. It's crazy. Five, ten years ago, everyone would be ripped, but would laugh off something like this. Chalk it up to a lesson learned. Maybe find some macho way to wager it all back, so everybody's even."

A waiter came to their table. Before he could speak, Nick held up an arm.

"We need a few minutes," he said to the waiter. The guy nodded, turned and went to another table. "Couple of us have been worried for a while now. I'm the one closest to Joe, so everybody is watching me. Only I'm here in *Boston*." Nick's eyes went wide to emphasize his point. "If

Joe doesn't pull all of this mess together with the fucking nephew, guys back in Detroit – *our guys* – are going to eat sawdust and shit two by fours."

Sal took the opening to ask another question. And to show commitment to Nick, possibly the new leader of the Safari Boys.

"What else can we do here," Sal gestured to Donnie and himself, "that we are not doing, that can help you out? Do you want us to go bust in the house?"

Nick was shaking his head at this suggestion. "No. We're not going to do that. Yet. You just need to know that ever since this started coming apart last week, I'm getting, let me say, contradictory moves from Big Joe."

The hostess walked past them leading two women to a remaining empty table. Their waiter came back over. Nick nodded to the waiter, then gestured to Sal and Donnie.

"Let's hear about the specials," Nick said.

It was a great temptation to send Uncle Joe's guys to the house. Dyson knew that if that *was* an undercover fed car parked out on West End Circle and Joe's men got nailed, he would be leaving the country immediately. And that thought caused an alarm to go off. Maybe, in fact likely, Dyson's name was on some watch list with the TSA.

The last time he'd gone through Logan was a round trip to Atlanta in March, before the shit really hit the fan at PDG. And he knew all about several Brazilians having their passports lifted by their government. Sure, *they* might be able to get hold of fakes somewhere. Dyson didn't have the first *clue* about trying to find a counterfeit passport.

After playing around with the idea of sending decoys to the house, Dyson was right back where he'd been earlier with his uncle: call this Nick and just set up the meeting. They all would go to the house together. Maybe this Nick character could figure out a way to distract the stakeout car.

"Dyson. Just call him," he said to himself.

Fifty Three

Driving back to Corn Hill Beach, we talked about which towns were part of the Upper Cape, Mid Cape and Lower Cape. Louie had a good handle on it and I had read about it when I'd arrived in Sandwich. Becky, on the other hand, wasn't so sure.

"I think it helps if you're actually looking at a map. It did for me, anyway," I said.

"And don't forget there's Outer Cape," Louie added.

"That's where we were?" Becky said, "Provincetown." For the ride home, she was now sitting in the back seat with Rocco. I glanced at her in the mirror.

"And Truro. Wellfleet. Eastham, I think," Louie added.

"That's part of the confusion. That hook of the land looks *upper*, doesn't it?" Becky said.

"Maybe think of it the way you think about the part of Maine they call Downeast," I said.

"Not the same," Louie said.

"But that part of the coastline, it's the *lower* region of Maine. It comes down around toward the *east*, maybe not as much as here."

"I'm pretty sure that Downeast actually comes from early sailing days," Louie replied.

"So how many towns altogether on Cape Cod?" Becky asked.

"Fifteen. All in one county. Conterminus," I declared.

"Oh, mother," Louie said.

"Hey. I read about it. It means common boundary."

"Thank you for that."

When we decided to drop it, I turned the radio on. I already knew that the oldies station with the best signal was Cool 102, so I tapped the seek button until we got it, just in time to hear a set with The Doobie Brothers *Long Train Runnin*, ending with *Listen to the Music*.

"I've had an idea for a while. Tell me what you think," Ragsdale said, like he was back hosting his Oldies Show. "Sometimes you're in restaurant, maybe some store and they're playing this kind of music." He pointed at the radio.

"Yeah. Happens a lot," I said. The station segued to Crosby, Stills & Nash with *Suite: Judy Blue Eyes*.

"Well, some of these songs are *so good*, people oughta just shut up and listen."

"I agree. You hear something that you really like and people are talking." Louie reached over and turned the volume up and looked at me. I got the hint.

As the song ended, the woman DJ immediately went to

253

commercials.

"So, your big idea. Is it that people should just put a lid on it and show more respect for *your* favorites?" He was shaking his head.

"Even better than that. I think that we should start a movement, petition the FCC, that because you get this music for *free*, that there are certain songs, maybe pick ten for every decade, specific songs that when you are driving and they come on the radio, you are *required* to open all your windows and crank up the volume." He was watching me for a response. Becky beat me to it.

"Marvelous idea, Louie. But what if I'm driving through a small town late at night?" He threw his hands up before she could continue.

"Hey. You hear a *really* outstanding song, give 'em a little excitement! They're probably watching the news and getting depressed anyway."

"Wait a second. Are you suggesting that the FCC gets to compile the *list* of songs? What if I *hate* that song and am ready to switch stations?" I said.

"Could be like the All-Star Game. Maybe like that People's Choice Awards routine. Let the listeners vote. The FCC updates the list every ten years, like the census."

"And all this time you've had me believing that you were a Libertarian. Now you're gonna make me *vote for songs* with the 'we're not political' Federal Communications Commission? I think not."

"OK. No voting," he replied. I could tell that he wasn't

ready to give it up. We were now into our third back-to-back commercial on Cool 102. Louie was thinking.

"Maybe it could be by genre," Becky said. "Pick the all-time best Top 40 of say, Country, R & B, Easy Hits, Classic Rock, Oldies..."

"*No!* No Easy Hits!" Louie said. "That stuff really does belong on elevators. In *Supermarkets!* And your dentist's office."

The woman DJ came back on and did too long of an intro to *Proud Mary*. I turned the volume up and, for a millisecond, thought about opening the windows. I decided against it.

When Creedence Clearwater Revival had finished and there was a segue to the next song, I lowered the volume.

"What about cover versions?" I said. "Or, we only follow this new law for *original* performances?"

Louie pointed at the radio. "Originals only. Like the one we just heard," he said.

"But other artists have their take on a particular song. How about Tina Turner?"

"Look it up, hotshot. Nobody ever has – and nobody ever will – do a *better* version of that song," he said. "Not Tina, not Elvis. C-C-R. Period."

Ragsdale was never shy about his opinions when it came to pop music. Never mind the inconvenient fact that his tastes in music, kind of like mine, were slogging around in another era.

"I once heard this local band at a club in Morgantown,

255

West Virginia. They were pretty good," I said.

"Oh, I'll just bet they were. Made the cover of *Rolling Stone*, right?"

Fortunately, we had arrived at their cottage. The Hills had beaten us back and were either inside or out at the beach.

As Becky got out of the car, she nuzzled with Rocco and gave him the double ear-scratch, getting a lick in return.

"Are you going out to fish?" I asked Louie. He looked at his watch.

"Nah. Tide's not right."

"Maybe you can start drafting your petition. You need some paper?" I reached under my seat and pulled out a reporter's spiral bound note pad.

"I got a new word for Scrabble. I'm going to show Johnny boy," he was pointing at the cottage with his left thumb, "he better stick to golf."

"Thanks for dinner. And the tour," I said. I started to back up. Louie whacked the side of the passenger door. I stopped and he came around to my side.

"They're going to a quilting museum tomorrow." Again, he was making the thumb gesture toward the cottage. "Let's go see Whalen."

"What, offer our services?" Louie stared at me. Then I added, "Woodchuk Investigators, Limited, but not very. We're here to help."

He was shaking his head.

"I wanna talk to him. Like I said, he's a good guy. If there's anything that we don't need to know, he sure as hell is not going to tell us."

"What time?" I said.

"Mid-morning. That'll be best for him. Staff meetings over and before he heads out somewhere."

"Think maybe we should *call* him first?" This thought caused Louie to give me the two-finger point and thumb-up fake pistol shot as he moved backward away from the car.

"I'll call him. Then I'll call you." He looked back at the cottage, adding, "John can drop me at your place when he goes to play golf."

"Just text me. We'll be around," I said.

Fifty Four

Dyson Manetas told Nick that he would meet them in the parking lot at JJ's Sports Bar & Grill in Northborough, about a ten minute drive west from the hotel where Nick said they had a room. They settled on nine o'clock. Dyson said that he would be driving a BMW M4 convertible, silver with a black top.

Before coming to Boston, Nick had given Sal a contact and had arranged for Sal to buy a couple of guns. On the drive to the airport to get Nick, Sal and Donnie simply had to connect with a guy at a triple-decker in Dorchester. They did, gave the guy a thousand bucks for two Compact Glock 19s and a box of 9MM ammo, which they placed in the trunk of the rental car.

Nick expected absolutely no fireworks here. Joe had made it clear; if things do get nasty, we'll go at it from a different angle. They did not anticipate any dumb, firearm silliness from the nephew. At the same time, Joe was still hoping to avoid asking for any local help. Nick agreed. But he would not be caught off guard should Dyson have friends who were less amenable to a positive solution.

Stopping back at the Residence Inn before meeting with Dyson, Nick had Sal get the guns from the trunk and keep them in the front of the car. You never knew.

At 8:56 PM, they watched the Beemer convertible pull into the lot. It moved slowly through the lane and past the cars parked at an adjacent motel, coming to a stop when the driver spotted their white Buick. The driver got out.

Nick recognized Dyson from the only other time he'd seen him. The kid had been in Detroit a couple of years back to visit with Big Joe. Dyson appeared to be alone. Nick climbed out of the Buick, brushed the wrinkles from his slacks, then walked toward Dyson.

"Sorry about the secret rendezvous nonsense," Dyson said, extending his hand to Nick.

"It's OK. We're here now." They shook hands.

"There really are some people looking for me." Dyson took a quick glance around looking at the other cars and a few motorcycles in the lot.

"So, we hear," Nick replied. He was going to let the kid talk. His single objective was to get the money. He was pretty sure that Dyson understood this.

"Don't think we wanna go inside," Dyson said, pointing at the sports bar. "It gets pretty loud." Nick nodded.

Neither man said anything for a few seconds. Dyson continued checking out all directions around the lot, then he looked at the two men in the car with Nick. He pointed at them.

"They work for Joe? He said he had some guys here."

"They work for me. *I* work for your uncle," Nick said.

"Got it."

"We can talk in the car," Nick said, pointing to the Buick. "That work for you?" Dyson looked at him for a few seconds, then nodded.

"Let me pull out of the way." He got back in the BMW, pulled it around to a space in front of the motel, then walked back to the Buick.

Nick had a back door open. He went around the other side where Donnie was getting out to move up front with Sal.

It was the Ford Taurus in the rotation and back on West End Circle in Hopkinton. The driver had the seat reclined. Even should someone living in the neighborhood report the presence of his car, or the Toyota minivan, the Hopkinton Police Department would have their way of explaining the situation. They had been alerted on day one. Patrol cars had come through a few times but did not draw attention to the parked vehicles.

While the drivers of the Ford and the Toyota were not privy to all details, they believed that their superiors, more than likely, had already interviewed some of the neighbors of 5406. There didn't appear to be any young children around, so it wasn't like a couple of 'sex offenders' casing the neighborhood. It was a little after nine o'clock. Walkers and joggers were all back in their houses. Listen to the ball game on the radio. Play words with friends on his phone. Text his girlfriend. Read some magazines.

Wait. The driver was accustomed to this aspect of the job.

Tough work, but somebody's gotta...

Hours before the face to face meeting, Nick had the beginning of *his* plan. If Joe was correct about his nephew being ready to help 'get things right,' then it was simple. Where is the money? How do we retrieve it?

There *was* the thought that one of Dyson's geeky pals, or someone else for that matter, might already *have* the money. Could be headed for Mongolia, or New Zealand. But Nick had to go with what he knew. What he knew was that Big Joe, and now Nick himself, had to believe that Dyson was on the level and that the money was still here. Somewhere.

Seated in the backseat of the Buick, Dyson right next to him, Nick stayed with that premise. He decided not to fuck around, to go direct.

"The money. It's at the house, yes?" he said.

Dyson didn't respond, but tilted his head, avoiding eye contact. Then he scratched his nose with his left hand, the fingers of his right hand nervously flexing back and forth on his thigh.

Sal and Donnie remained silent. Nick waited.

"Some of it is there," Dyson finally replied. He looked at Nick.

"Some of it? You can tell me how much 'some of it' is?"

"About half," Dyson said.

"And half would be how much?"

"Ten million."

Nick nodded. He looked out the window at the parking lot. People were coming out of JJ's Sport Bar. There was noise from the traffic on the road behind them. He turned back to Dyson.

"And the other half?"

"It's in a friend's apartment," Dyson said.

"Where you've been hiding, back in Boston?"

Dyson shook his head. "Just a few minutes from here. A woman I knew in school. We were together for a while, then we broke up. But I still see her off and on. She lets me store cartons in her basement."

"These 'cartons' have the other half of all this money, what you've been discussing with your uncle? Don't jerk me around here, Dyson. I lost my patience as soon as I got off that plane. And Joe could go down the shoot really fast. Your problems could get much worse than you can even imagine." Nick's tone had changed enough to cause Sal to shift in the seat upfront.

"I told you on the phone," Dyson pleaded. "We can get *all* of the money and take it to Uncle Joe."

"That would be a good thing. So, where to first?" Nick asked.

Fifteen minutes later, Nick riding in the BMW with Dyson driving, Sal and Donnie following in the Buick, they arrived outside a modest looking raised ranch house on a quiet cul-de-sac in Westborough. It was 9:30 PM.

Dyson parked at the curb. Sal drove past and parked in front of him. Nobody got out. Inside the house, there were lights on in the room facing the street. A Volkswagen Passat was parked in front of the house, no garage.

On the drive over, Dyson had explained that his old girlfriend, Kayla, was living in her grandmother's house. After the grandmother died, Kayla had moved there the previous autumn. Dyson had helped her with the move. She lived alone.

Dyson had called Kayla before they made the trip and told her that one of his associates urgently needed to find a file contained in one of the boxes in her basement. She had said OK, but not too late.

At the front door, Dyson introduced Nick and Kayla. After a minute of small talk, he led Nick to the basement. Sure enough, at the far end of an unfinished room with a concrete floor, there were eight white banker's boxes in stacks of two. The boxes appeared to be new. Each box had been labeled with writing on the end, in black Sharpie – PhoneDat Global, 2016, then marked A-C, D-F, G-I and so on.

Nick untied the string and button closure on the A-C box and opened it. Stacks of bills in mustard colored straps indicating $10,000 each. The stacks were also wrapped in

263

clear plastic. Nick closed that carton, then opened three more at random, shuffling and lifting packets of money from the bottom. They appeared to be the same.

After replacing the packets of cash, closing each box and aligning them as they had appeared a few minutes earlier, Nick turned to Dyson. He decided the kid might be telling the truth, at least about the money stored here.

"Tell her that you want to come back in the morning and get *all* the boxes. Couldn't find what I was looking for and that we'll need to go through them," Nick said.

They had earlier discussed how the money would be transported to Detroit. Nick had told Dyson not to worry about that, Sal and Donnie would take care of it.

Again upstairs, Dyson gave Kayla the story. She said that she needed to leave for work at 6:30 in the morning, but could leave the side door unlocked and that Dyson could lock everything once they had removed the boxes. Nick thanked her and said that there would be a payment for the short-term use of her basement.

Back at the car, Nick told Sal that they would follow him to the hotel. They would discuss the plan to get a van and retrun in the morning, as well as the timing and what might be the best approach to get inside Dyson's house in Hopkinton.

At 10:20, all four men were back in the room at the Residence Inn.

Fifty Five

Walk, throw the ball, read the newspaper. It was 9:30 Thursday morning when Louie's text came. I was on the front porch at Beth's Bakery & Cafe eating a stuffed French toast panini and drinking some really good coffee. Rocco was lying at my feet, *not* asleep.

'P Whalen will see us @ 10:30.' So, I guess the old UMass connection really worked. Or, maybe it was in fact, 'professional courtesy'. Never know when the Sandwich PD might need a favor from one of the senior guys at the Joint Northeast Counter-Drug Task Force.

I texted back. 'Downtown. Will head back. John will drop you?' Five seconds went by.

'Yes.'

Folding the paper, I took another drink of the coffee. I was glad that my appetite was back and that I felt OK. I gave Rocco a last bite of the panini, placed a tip on the table and we left.

At twenty-five after ten, Ragsdale and I were in the

reception area at the police station. I was trying to read the small engraving on the different sports trophies in the case when Chief Whalen came out and invited us to the conference room. Louie took a seat, I sat across from him and Whalen sat to my left.

"So you want to hear about psych profiling?" Whalen said, looking at Louie. "I can give you general information, an overview. You want the seminar, 'fraid you will need to hook-up with Metcalf at the state police." Ragsdale was getting settled in the swivel chair.

"Truth is, we were talking last night about that cold case out in Provincetown from back in the 70s," Louie said.

"Lady of the Dunes," Whalen said, shaking his head. "They still don't know."

"My brother-in-law's down here with us. He's the one that seemed to know something about it. Said there was a story speculating about a Whitey Bulger connection."

"I've heard that," Whalen replied.

"The woman was strangled?"

"Yes. ME said that was the ultimate cause of death."

"And you get this woman's body last week? How'd she die?" At this, Whalen was shaking his head.

"Official report still not in. But, from what I understand about the Dunes woman, *really* nasty death. I think that she was nearly decapitated."

"And that was a long time ago, I know. My training goes back to the stone age. Just curious what aspects and characteristics you look at these days when you have a murder by strangulation? Or, asphyxiation?" Louie said.

"I can set you up to talk with a state police detective." Whalen was replying to Ragsdale, but he looked at me when he said this. "We're not making a lot of progress on the van," he said, as though he was reading my mind. "But," he looked at Ragsdale and then back to me, "your tip on the hot air balloon angle?" I nodded. "Two of our guys are working with the DA's office chasing balloon clubs and owners all over the east. See if we can get anything on a woman who fits the description of our victim."

"Gotta be a huge number of vans registered around the Northeast," Louie said.

"A few thousand just in Massachusetts alone," Whalen said.

Louie got up from his chair. I got up and Whalen stood as well.

"I know you're busy," Louie said. "Thanks for taking the time." He shook Whalen's hand.

"My pleasure," Whalen said. I did not detect sarcasm. If the guy had wished that we had not come by, he wasn't showing it.

I shook hands with Whalen, and Ragsdale and I were back in the car a minute later.

"You want to get a sandwich?" Louie asked as soon as he closed his door.

"I had a pretty big breakfast. But, if you're hungry... "

267

"Let's take a run out to Willie's." He chuckled when he said this.

"Why not?"

"Maybe your French soccer playboy is in the parking lot tutoring the grandsons," Ragsdale cracked.

"Phil and Don," I said.

"He's a *bird dog*, Rocco," Louie said, reaching back and giving him a pat.

Fifty Six

Sal and Donnie were inside a Penske Truck Rental office in Framingham. Once they finished with the paperwork and deposit, Donnie would drive the rental back to the hotel. Sal would ride with Donnie, Nick and Dyson in the BMW, all heading to Kayla's house for the eight banker's boxes in the basement.

The twelve-foot Penske cargo van had a capacity for 450 cubic feet and could handle a load of up to 3,100 pounds, far more than what they needed. The cartons weighed approximately 25 pounds each, while the boxes at Dyson's house, he said, weighed more because they were larger moving cartons.

At the same time while Sal and Donnie were off getting the cargo van, Nick convinced Dyson to take him to his neighborhood in Hopkinton. Nick wanted to see if there really was a stakeout car as Dyson had claimed. For that reason, Sal and Donnie had taken the BMW and Dyson was now driving the Buick rental.

The thought was that once they had cruised down West End Circle by Dyson's home, they would then head straight to Westborough to retrieve the banker's boxes. A decision for a return trip to West End Circle to get the rest of the money would hinge on what they saw on the street, the only reason for the reconnaissance drive by.

And what they saw was zip. No suspicious looking unmarked cars, like the Ford Taurus that Dyson claimed had been there on two previous occasions.

"We'll come back," Nick said. Dyson turned the corner. "But tonight. Probably not a great idea to have neighbors see you hauling boxes out of the house in the middle of the day."

"And if the there's a car here when we come back?" Dyson said. "Then what?"

Nick looked at him before responding. "Let's swim in that lane when we see what's here, OK?"

Dyson didn't say 'OK'. He didn't nod. He just stared back at Nick. He flipped the turn signal, made another turn heading for Westborough and to go get those cartons at Kayla's house.

After a few minutes of driving, while Nick was texting Sal, Dyson acknowledged that maybe he had overreacted. Perhaps the Ford Taurus was just some guy waiting there to see somebody else, maybe sneaking in for a quickie with somebody's wife. Or husband.

"Doesn't matter," Nick said. "If the car is there when we come back, we'll deal with it."

Whalen checked on his detectives making the phone calls. Slow going and they were not a quarter of the way through the list.

"I'll talk with O'Connell," the chief said. "Could be that we will have to go wider, make calls outside the Northeast. That body could have come from anywhere."

The DA had the same thought; expand the queries. The estimate from the Medical Examiner had placed the time of death as being 24 to 36 hours before the body was discovered. The state parkways, turnpikes, the interstate highway system, all made it possible to drive to Cape Cod from Akron, Ohio, or Roanoke, Virginia, or Durham, North Carolina and many points in between, in less than twelve hours.

Whalen and O'Connell talked about the lists of balloon events, owners, clubs and associations.

"Have Murtaugh and his helper stay with what they're doing," O'Connell said. "If they can finish up with New York and Pennsylvania, great. We can split up the Mid-Atlantic states, maybe down to Florida. And out to the Mid-West. I have two people here that can start on those calls."

"You know that we now have *two* bulletins out on the HOTLINE?" Whalen said.

"Yes. If we're lucky, might get a response."

"I'll call you back," Whalen said.

"Peter, you may have to tap your overtime budget," O'Connell replied. "Let's stay on this."

The driver in the Toyota minivan had the dayshift. He'd been parked on West End Circle since 7:30 AM. His routine for staying alert was to read magazine articles aloud in between hour-long segments of listening to music, either on his iPod or on the radio. He couldn't deal with all of the non-stop, 'urgent' news/talk noise.

A little after ten, the White Buick rental moved slowly down the street, driver and one passenger. The car didn't stop. Thinking that the Buick might come around again and park, the driver in the minivan had his camera ready should the two men get out of the car.

They did not come back.

Fifty Seven

Diner Shore was light on lunch, as in the total number of patrons late on this Thursday morning. Each time that I'd been there at breakfast, it had been either packed or had had maybe one or two seats at the counter. When Louie and I arrived at 11:15, there were only six people visible; one of them was Willie.

"You boys back to steal our secrets, open a chain of diners in Vermont?" he asked as soon as we walked in. "You'll have do better than that fancy cheese and maple syrup," he added.

Ragsdale put an arm around Willie's shoulder.

"Lord help me," Willie said. "He's gonna try to give me a kiss."

"Wllie, you've insulted enough people down here, don't ya think? Why don't you retire, move to Vermont? Let your grandsons take over. Maybe class this place up a little." Willie, with the two day whiskers and a half-grin, looked at Ragsdale.

"I'll come on two conditions," he said.

"Anything you want," Louie said.

"One, we have to use my name. And I get fifty-one percent of net profits." Louie was nodding in agreement.

"And two, if Bernie Sanders comes in, he gets VIP treatment. All the time."

"That could be a deal breaker," Louie said.

"Think about it. Let me know by fall. May have to go out to Vegas, or Hollywood." He looked back at the kitchen and jerked his head in that direction. "The boys might be ready by then."

Louie pulled away his arm and patted Willie on the shoulder.

"You gentlemen have a seat there in the Blue Room," Willie added. "Alan will bring you a menu."

Louie and I went to one of the empty booths. Another booth was presently occupied by a young man and a woman, both perhaps early-thirties. As soon as we were seated, one of the twins was at the table with menus and glasses of water. I asked for a grilled-cheese on rye with tomato and onion and a side of coleslaw. Louie went for 'Willie's Wonder', a cheeseburger and French fries with gravy.

Over lunch, and I should have seen this coming, Louie expounded on his thoughts and experiences on how some law enforcement agencies work well together, while some others don't. When we left Whalen back at the Sandwich PD, I knew that Louie was still processing what he had observed during the brief visit.

"Whalen's got bit of a leg up. He's worked as a state policeman, probably knows every other cop in this corner of the state. And he's clearly not a showboat," Louie said.

"That would be my impression," I replied.

"This body back at the beach. Yes, it's in the town of Sandwich and it's his department, but the system down here actually places the District Attorney in charge of the investigation."

"That's not so different from Vermont. We have the State's Attorney. Same thing, yes?"

Louie was shaking his head. "Yes and no. In Vermont, and probably most other states, too, you scratch a little on the surface, you're going to find that any State's Attorney has roots in one of the major political parties."

"For God's sake, this is Massachusetts," I said. "You are not suggesting that the DA is *removed* from politics?"

"Not at all. But how they get along, how they perceive their colleagues, level of respect they hold for the other guys, all of that makes a *tremendous* difference in the chemistry, how they work a case."

"OK, but..." I started. Louie didn't let me go on with the thought.

"They're all professionals. The basic training they get, compared to what existed *twenty-five years ago*, is much better. Despite what you see on TV, *far and away*, cops in smaller communities, they're already doing 'community policing'."

"Most of what's in the news, at least the worst stories, are inner cities. The big population centers," I said. "We've talked about this before."

"Yeah, that we have. But what I'm suggesting here is, an unidentified body on a beach, scam artists on the phone working on senior citizens, a bunch of sleazebags running drugs. *All* of those demand different skills, resources and experience to clean up." He watched me, then added, "I don't know a lot about inner cities. You couldn't pay me enough."

We finished our lunch, but Louie had a post script.

"This O'Connell, the DA," he said.

"Yes?"

"I Googled him. You can bet your ass the fact that he started out as a local cop," Louie was taking on the smirk expression, "that'll keep a few defense attorneys on their toes."

Fifty Eight

The eight banker's boxes were loaded into the Penske cargo van. Dyson locked the front and side doors of his former girlfriend's house and joined the three other men. Sal and Donnie stood at the rear of the truck, Nick at the edge of the grass along the driveway.

"Let's go back to the hotel," Nick said. "We need to walk this through before we go to Hopkinton," he added, pointing at Dyson.

Donnie got behind the wheel of the van, Sal in the passenger seat. Nick and Dyson went to the Buick parked on the street. It would take them ten minutes to get to the Northborough Residence Inn.

With Dyson driving, Nick placed a call to Big Joe to let him know that they had the first cartons of cash in their possession.

"We'll go to the house late tonight," Nick said into the phone. "Split it up. Let Dyson and Sal go over first." This caused Dyson to glance at Nick. Nick held his left hand up to cut off any comment should Dyson feel the need to speak up. He continued his conversation with Joe.

"Dyson thought that he saw a car hanging around a few days ago. Said that he saw it twice. We went by this morning, nothing. Looks pretty normal."

Nick listened to Joe's response for a few seconds, then said, "Yes. It'll be late. But I will call as soon as we're on the road."

Nearly 5,000 miles away from Boston, in São Paulo, 'slush fund' cash floats around all the time. It is unknown if any of the money is stashed in bankers boxes.

But earlier in the spring, more than seventy company executives of a giant Latin American construction firm, were negotiating plea bargain agreements with Brazilian authorities. Might've been some cash involved.

According to several media reports, in what was being described as the world's largest leniency deal with US and Swiss authorities, *one group* of executives had confessed to corruption charges and faced more than *$2 billion* in fines and jail time. It was a big story outside the US.

One of the executives, a few rungs down the ladder, perhaps, was well-known among former associates back in Massachusetts, as 'Whiz Brain.' His involvement with and consultation for *PhoneDat Global*, had yet to surface publicly. An undetermined amount of cash, likely hidden in different locations in the US, was not at the top his worry chart. At least not today.

Twenty million US - stowed away in Massachusetts - out of a billion, is comparable to a twenty-dollar bill out of thousand dollars. Two tickets to a movie, maybe a low-end bottle of wine during the 2016 Olympics in Rio.

If and when all of this story is pieced together, an enterprising reporter might make the comparison between the amounts that multi-national firms pay in what *appear to be* huge fines, to say that of some astronomical salaries and bonuses being paid to a few Super Star athletes. US dollars (USD) converted at an exchange rate of 3.25 to Brazilian reals (BRL), it all starts to add up.

Since the top company execs are prepared to pay these large amounts in fines, might we have a look at *their* tax returns?

Having listened to Nick on the phone earlier, and again now explaining how they would execute the retrieval of the balance of the $20 million, Dyson Manetas had nearly forgotten the anxiety he'd felt only two weeks ago when his life, at least at *PDG*, had appeared to be spiraling out of control.

Watching Nick speak, with long pauses and using a minimum of carefully selected words, it surprised Dyson that he could place so much trust in a man that he'd known for less than 24 hours. But his uncle had told him as much during the phone calls, saying 'Nick will take care of it. Tell him everything and do *not* lie to him.'

At least part of the proof was outside in the back of the rental truck. This time tomorrow, *all* the money would be out of Massachusetts and not on its way to Brazil. *PDG* would be history. Let the fuck-ups here and in Atlanta deal with prosecutors. Dyson would be on his way to Detroit.

He was beginning to find a trace of optimism that he could work with his Uncle Joe. And, certainly, with this guy Nick.

Fifty Nine

It was 5:19 PM when the Sandwich PD got the call. It came from a man in Great Barrington, out at the western end of the state. The man was a hot air balloon pilot.

The man's name was Jack Ryan. His former wife, also a balloonist and now living in the Great Lakes region of Michigan, told him that a friend had gone missing. The friend, Geri Stuart, had not returned phone calls, email or text messages in over a week.

"I was on the phone with a pilot in Connecticut. We're trying to put together a crew for an event in August. He told me about your call on a woman's body. Said it was found near a beach someplace," Ryan had said.

Detective Sergeant Murtaugh was now on the phone with the man, telling him the same thing that he'd been telling other balloonists all day long, describing the murder victim and then the mention of the white jumpsuit.

"Oh, God," Ryan said. "That could be Geri."

"Geri? This is someone that you know personally?" Murtaugh asked. He heard the man take a breath.

"Yes. We were friends a few years back. My wife and I, we've been divorced since 2009. All of us spent a lot of time together. Geri worked with my crew at some of the festivals."

Ryan explained the phone call from his ex-wife, to which he had not given much thought, *until* the phone conversation with the other pilot in Connecticut.

"Do you know where this woman has been living?" Murtaugh asked.

"No, but Carol does."

"That's your ex?"

"Yeah. She lives in Michigan, the U P."

"I'm sorry, U P?"

"Upper Peninsula, the northern section of the state."

"Maybe we could speak with her. Could I get a phone number?" Murtaugh asked.

"Hang on a minute."

Murtaugh placed his next phone call to a Carol Fletcher in Manistique, Michigan. When the woman answered, he introduced himself, told her about his conversation with Jack Ryan and the circumstances of that call.

"Has something happened to Geri? I didn't know that she was back in New England?"

"We can't say that for certain," Murtaugh replied. "A woman's body was discovered here last week. She had no identification."

"I don't understand," Fletcher said. "Why would Jack think that it could be Geri?"

Murtaugh hesitated, but only for a second, then said, "The woman was wearing a white jumpsuit that is similar, from what we understand, to those worn by some balloon crew members."

"But Geri lives out here, down near Detroit. She hasn't been in Massachusetts for years."

"I think we can clear this up," Murtaugh offered, "a couple of ways. I would like to send you an email with the contact information for our department. Or, we can handle it through your local police department there, if you would rather do that. They can contact us directly."

"But like I said, Geri lives *downstate*, not here." The woman sounded agitated. Aware of all manner of phone scams, Murtaugh was reluctant to press further questions. Follow protocol.

"I'm suggesting that you might be more comfortable speaking with people you know, at your police department there in Michigan." He'd already pulled up the info for the Manistique Public Safety Department on his computer and was looking at it as they spoke.

"You can ask them to call me. Do you have a pen?"

Ten minutes after giving his phone number to Carol Fletcher, Murtaugh got the call from a Chief Ken Garlow, the Public Safety Director for the Town of Manistique. He went through the story about the body, the tip about the jumpsuit and his conversation with Carol Fletcher.

"She said that her friend lives near Detroit. If we could get an address, that'd be a start," Murtaugh said.

"OK," Garlow replied.

"See what she says about this woman's disappearance. When did she last see her, or speak with her? And if she has any recent photos of the friend. Maybe you could send us one?"

"Give me a few minutes. I'll call back."

"Thank you," Murtaugh said.

At 5:52, they were back on the phone. Murtaugh was writing down an address in Southgate, Michigan for Geri and Richard Stuart.

"Mrs. Fletcher is going to send a photo. I'll forward it as soon as we have it," Garlow added.

Before making the call to the Southgate PD, Murtaugh went for a cup of coffee and to see if Chief Whalen was still in his office. He was. Murtaugh stuck his head in the door.

"Might have something."

"Yes?" Whalen said.

"Got a call from a balloonist in Great Barrington. His ex-wife now lives out in Michigan. She has a friend who apparently dropped out of sight a few days ago. The friend

284

has worked as a team member with balloonists," Murtaugh said.

"*Michigan*?" Whalen said. Murtaugh nodded.

"Chief in a town called Manistique, up near the lakes. He's getting us a photo."

"OK. Let me know how it goes."

Murtaugh went to the men's room, got a cup of coffee and went back to his desk. He found the phone number for police in Southgate, Michigan and placed still another call.

Sixty

A patrol car from the Southgate PD stopped in front of the stone façade, two-level home at 16 Riverview Road, the home of Richard and Geri Stuart. There was extensive landscaping, a stone wall around one corner of the lot, a large RV parked behind the house. And nobody home.

It was 6:45 PM. After repeatedly trying the door bell and waiting, the officer got in his cruiser and called back to the station. He had a brief exchange with the dispatcher before his duty Sergeant instructed him to leave a card in the front door and make another pass in thirty minutes. An earlier call placed by the sergeant to the Stuart home had gone to an answering machine.

A subsequent visit by the same patrol officer produced the same result; no response to knocking at the front door, at a rear entrance off the stone patio, and at a third door that appeared to be from a bedroom. Draperies were drawn closed. The garage door was locked as well.

Speaking with a man next door, the cop was told by that neighbor that he thought the Stuarts were out of town, that he hadn't seen either of them in over a week. The man speculated that they might have gone off on one of their balloon trips. He said they left in the husband's SUV with matching cargo carriers mounted on the roof, something that he had seen them do on previous trips.

Back at the station, this information was relayed to the police detective in Sandwich, Massachusetts.

Murtaugh received the email from the Police Chief in Manistique at 7:20. A photo was attached. He clicked on it.

There on the screen was a photo of two women, sitting on a bench, a small white dog resting between them. Based on how they were dressed, it appeared to be a summer photo. One woman had dark hair and was smiling. She had a hand resting on the dog. The other woman appeared to be taller, with light brown hair, not blonde, and she had a more restrained smile.

Murtaugh leaned closer to study the snapshot. His gut told him that he was looking at a photo of the same woman who had been rolled inside a tarp and left at Town Neck Beach.

He placed another call to the chief in Manistique. When Garlow was on with him, the chief told him about the cops in Southgate and no one presently at the Stuarts home.

"Too soon to know for certain, but this looks like our victim. Can you go see Mrs. Fletcher, see if she has other photos? Doesn't have to be recent, but maybe something with a close-up of the Stuart woman?"

At 7:30 PM, after the update from Murtaugh, Chief Whalen called District Attorney Martin O'Connell at home to tell him what was happening. They talked for five minutes, O'Connell asking short questions and Whalen giving short answers. Then O'Connell cut to the chase.

"Send what you have to the ME. If Murtaugh gets a better photo, send that to her. Anything else that comes from the cops in her hometown, if they speak with the husband – or any other members of the family – we need to know just as soon as they know."

"Will do," Whalen said.

"Chief, tell me again where you came up with this slant on hot air balloons?"

"Guy from Vermont, the one who was walking his dog and discovered the body."

"Seriously?"

"Yes. And, you ready for this? He used to be one your favorite kind of people."

"Yeah. What's that?" O'Connell asked.

"A reporter."

"Oh, joy!"

"Now he's some kind of PI/Security guy."

"Sounds like a dangerous combination."

Whalen laughed. "I think he's all right. He's down here with a fishing buddy, an undercover cop with the Northeast Counter-Drug Task Force. Can't be too flaky, I don't think this guy would hang out with him."

"O-kay," O'Connell said. "If you say so. Anyway, this goes the way I *hope* that it will, I'd like to meet this guy at some point."

Sixty One

Nick and Sal were walking the perimeter of the parking lot. Anyone watching from one of the hotel rooms or the lobby might believe that they were in town for a funeral, or here to visit a dying relative. Back at the room, Donnie was keeping an eye of Dyson, both men content to watch the NBA Championship on TV.

Keeping a slow pace, stopping occasionally to look at Sal, only to offer some terse reply, Nick had his plan down and appeared to be almost in a state of Zen. The same could not be said for Sal, but even he was beginning to settle into an accommodating role of 'just do what you're asked to do and we'll all be out of here in a few hours.'

"And the Buick?" Sal asked.

"We'll leave it here. When we have the rest of the money *and* we're on the road home, you can call the rental people and tell 'em where it is. So maybe you pay an extra fee for a pick-up." They were back at the hotel entrance.

"Leave the keys in the room. Tell 'em an emergency came up, you forgot," Nick added.

Returning to the room, Sal gave a quiet knock on the door. Donnie opened it, Sal and Nick came inside.

"Gentlemen," Nick said, "I suggest that we go have a nice, relaxing dinner. Might be a long night."

A dark red Chevy Malibu hybrid was parked on West End Circle this quiet Thursday evening. The driver was new to this rotation, but certainly not new to watching others. He thought of himself as one might think of a substitute teacher; call me, tell me where I need to be and when, I can handle it from there.

Tonight, it was in Hopkinton. Tomorrow, maybe up to Gloucester. Or Fitchburg. Just stay awake, report anything unusual, your replacement will be there at 7:00 in the morning.

Unlike some of the younger types who pulled stake-out duty, this man, technically retired but available per diem, was not inclined to listen to what he considered as either the 'white boy, bone rattling, progressive schlock' or the 'Straight outa Worcester, let's pretend we're black' kind of music that he'd heard called Rap. And he had precious little patience for radio shows that pandered to those who began their call-in with, 'I'm a long-time listener, first time caller.'

Good for you. But I am not listening, thank you.

Low volume, good speakers, 99.5 FM Classical Radio Boston, WCRB. At this very moment he was listening to The PhilHarmonia Octet: Music for Wind Instruments. Sure, many people knew some of the music of Beethoven and Mozart. How many knew about the Czech composer Gideon Klein?

He could multi-task and did not need the reminder, 'while you're listening, be on the lookout for a silver BMW M4 convertible, Mass plate 10787. And a white Buick Verano four-door rental, also with Mass plates.'

The restaurant they selected was Carbone's on Cedar Street in Hopkinton, an Italian establishment operated by the same family for more than eighty years. Dyson had done the research.

"I've never had a meal there, but I hear it has great seafood." He lived only five minutes from the place. "Good pasta too," he added.

"No Greek restaurants around?" Nick asked.

"Sure, if you don't mind going to Framingham," Dyson replied.

"How far?"

"Half an hour, maybe less," Dyson said.

"It's out where we got the truck," Donnie added. Nick was shaking his head.

"I'm good for Italian."

The four of them went in the Buick, Sal driving. After dinner, they would return to the hotel and switch to the BMW and the rental cargo van. As soon as they were parked in front of the restaurant, Nick turned to look at Dyson and Donnie in the back seat. He held up his hand as though he were throwing a slow-motion, left-handed pass.

"A nice meal, a little wine. No hurry," Nick said.

"Great," Dyson said.

"Works for me," Donnie offered. Sal nodded, the men got out of the car and went inside.

"Welcome to Carbone's," a young man said, greeting them at the door.

Sixty Two

I sat with Rocco watching the twilight and listening to the traffic passing on the street. Our evening routine was becoming second nature, no matter where we were. Once he'd had some exercise, a good long walk or running after the ball for fifteen minutes, I could count on him to stretch out and relax. That's what he was doing right now, while I was getting a little ansty.

After nearly a week of having gone to my laptop only a couple of times, I now felt an urge to plop into a chair, log on and do a little research. Among the numerous things that Bonnie used to chide me about was the fact that I still preferred using a laptop.

She'd said that 'everyone' had moved on to smaller tablets, or larger phones. My response had been 'bully for them.' She would shake her head and leave me to it.

What I wanted to do at this moment was to look into something that Louie and I had discussed; cold cases and missing persons. When we'd talked about it at lunch, it had been apparent that he was more up to speed than I was. Then again, he'd been at this for most of his adult life. My transition to 'investigative research' was still somewhat of a work in progress. Didn't matter how eager I might be, nothing would substitute the for actual experience.

Coaxing Rocco to come inside, I sat down and opened my laptop.

Almost like searching for weather services or travel online. Type in some key words, say 'Missing Persons' and *bang*, you're looking at dozens of links. States with the most OPEN Missing Persons cases; Missing in the US with maps; Kidnappings and Missing Persons; 48 Interesting FACTS about Missing People; you could wade through not dozens, but more like *thousands* of stories, statistics, photos and charts.

I started by first checking the source for each link, then narrowing my reading to a few, eventually coming to *NamUs*, where I created a profile and logged in to the *National Missing and Unidentified Persons System*. I spent over an hour going through just the cases listed for the Northeast. What an eye opener. Then I filtered down to Massachusetts, knowing that the body in Sandwich from a few days earlier was not yet included. They didn't know who she was. Or where she was missing from.

By the time I got around to reading the Department of Public Safety and Vermont State Police MISSING PERSONS page, I was beginning to feel a bit overwhelmed. Click on the map, see *silhouette figures* placed in different areas of the state. Click on the *figure* and get details: Name, Age, Gender, Date missing, missing from WHERE. Click *here* for More information. Click *here* to Submit a tip.

I logged off and shut down the computer. God.

"Bonnie. How bout helping me out here?"

Rocco looked up at me. Great eyes.

The second photo that Carol Fletcher gave to the police provided a much better look at Geri Stuart, a head and shoulders shot from two summers ago. Geri had come to visit and they had taken a drive to the Fayette State Park. In the photo, she was seated at an outdoor table, smiling at the camera. A close up photo.

Fletcher's hand was trembling and she was sobbing as she handed the photo to the policeman.

"I can't believe that this is happening," she said. "*Why* would someone want to kill Geri?" The policeman shook his head, but didn't reply as he accepted the photo.

"Please let me know what they say," she convulsed, put a hand to her mouth and turned away. When regained some composure, she turned to face the policeman again. "Pardon me, I'm sorry. You will tell me what they find out in Massachusetts?"

"Yes mam. The Chief will call you as soon as we know anything."

Ten minutes later, the new photo had been scanned, enlarged and emailed to the Sandwich PD.

Murtaugh immediately sent the photo on to both the DA and the ME, with a copy to his boss. Then he picked up the phone to call the Michigan police to thank them and ask another favor.

"I think this is it. It's a better photo, thanks for getting it. As soon as we get word, our DA's office is going want to talk with Mrs. Fletcher. See if she has insight about things that may have been going on with the victim, family issues or any problems with others. Can you help us set that up when he's ready?"

"Certainly," Ken Garlow replied. "Let me give you my mobile and home numbers."

It took all of two seconds for Dr. Katherine Lofgren to determine that the woman in the photo and the body at the morgue were the same person.

The confirmation would come when she went to her office in the morning and actually compared the photo with the corpse. The next step would be to obtain some form of DNA from the woman's home, dental records or finger prints. If a relative or friend could make a positive ID on the body, that would help closeout this phase. After that, Dr. Lofgren's involvement would be all paper work and likely testifying if and when a trial took place.

It was late, but she typed a very short email reply to Murtaugh; 'In the office 7:30 am. Will call.'

Carol Fletcher sat on the edge of her bed. The crying had stopped and she was beginning to feel numb. She would be alone until her husband got home from his job with the Michigan Department of Natural Resources, 45 miles away at the Sault Saint Marie State Forest. She'd spoken with him earlier on the phone, but hadn't shared any news in the past two hours.

Her friendship with Geri Stuart dated back to when both women were in their early twenties, single and living in Western Massachusetts. Carol was married for a few years, then divorced, moved to Michigan and remarried. She no longer participated in ballooning.

Geri, entangled in a 'on again/off again' relationship with an older man from Connecticut, had finally married the man. By coincidence, they'd moved to another part of Michigan and both were apparently still quite active in ballooning. They lived outside Detroit, nearly 400 miles away and a six-hour drive from the Fletchers on the Upper Peninsula.

Trance like, Carol sat thinking of a phone conversation she'd had with Geri, who had called her on the morning of her birthday, May 5th. As it fell on cinco de mayo, they'd laughed about some of the celebrating they had done when they were younger. Part of the conversation had skirted around some problems Geri and her husband had been having. She told Carol that she thought that they would 'get through it.'

Now, she remembered one of the last things that Geri had said to her at the end of the phone call.

"I know you think you're *old*, girl. But have at least *one* drink for me." Both of them loved a cocktail called Crouching Tiger. They had first had the drink back on Carol's 30th birthday.

Rising from the bed, she went to the window and stared out into the darkness. She could see the lake, red and green running lights from small boats, and the lights from some of other houses. She did not see car headlights.

Her husband wasn't due home for at least an hour. How long would it be before she heard anything from the police?

Sixty Three

Standing in the parking lot at the Residence Inn, Sal 's earlier concerns were starting to flare up again. He decided to keep them to himself.

Over dinner, Nick had detailed *how and what* the four men would do to get the remaining boxes of cash from Dyson's home. Now they were back at the hotel preparing to depart in two vehicles. Sal would ride with Dyson in the BMW; they would go first. Nick would ride with Donnie in the rental truck, the cargo van that already contained approximately $10 million in eight boxes.

Nothing about the plan was very complicated. Thirty minutes after Dyson and Sal were inside the home, Sal would call Donnie, who would then come to the house and back the truck into the driveway. With four men, the boxes could be out of the house and loaded into the van in less than five minutes, then straight to Detroit.

"At this point, there is no rush," Nick said, a variation on a comment he'd made twice already. "We go slowly, nobody in a hurry. Right?" He looked at each man. Donnie was nodding; Dyson gave two thumbs up; Sal's nod was borderline hesitant. Nick put a hand on Sal's shoulder.

"Now is not a good time to be nervous. Trust me," Nick said. Sal offered up a thin smile with a quick nod. "OK," Nick went on, looking at his watch. "It's 12:59. You two go ahead. We're staying right here. I'll wait for your call, then we'll head over."

Dyson got behind the wheel of the BMW, reached over to open the door for Sal and started the engine. Ten seconds later the car eased out of the hotel lot and turned onto Connector Road. It was just under 15 minutes to Hopkinton.

It was quiet on West End Circle. The last neighborhood car to pull into a garage had been half an hour earlier. The driver in the Chevy Malibu parked on the street was still awake, barely. Seat reclined, he was listening to a lengthy promo announcement for The Essential Yo-Yo Ma, "coming up later here on 99.5, WCRB."

As the music resumed on The Bach Hour with Brian McCreath, headlights came around a corner behind the Chevy. The lights reflected in the rearview mirror as the car continued down the street. The driver of the Chevy didn't move. When the car passed him, he adjusted his seat forward enough to watch.

Approximately 100 feet down the street, the BMW convertible slowly eased into the driveway at 5406. The car stopped, its lights went dark and two men got out. The driver in the Chevy was now fully alert and had his seat back in the upright position. He watched as the two men went into the house.

Tapping the screen on his phone to wake it up, the driver hit 2 on his speed dial.

"Mr. Beethoven. How're we doing? Enjoying the music are we, sir?" The younger man at the other end of the call was doing a poor imitation of a BBC announcer.

"It would appear as though the prodigal son has come home," the driver replied.

"Isn't that just ducky?"

"The BMW convertible pulled up ten seconds ago. Two men, now inside."

"Well, don't touch that dial. *You* are going to have company."

The call ended and the driver of the Chevy patted his cheeks a couple times, opened his mouth wide and closed it twice, twisted his head to the left, then the right, and finally rolled his shoulders and arms twice. He was awake.

Lights had come on inside the house.

Dyson led Sal back to a rear bedroom. When he turned the light on, he was greatly relieved to see that the room appeared the same as it had the last time he'd been there the previous week.

There was no bed and no furniture in the room, save for a floor lamp and an inexpensive folding camp chair, bright red, the type you might purchase at a big box discount store. Just beyond the chair were four louvered doors for what looked to be a closet.

As Sal watched, Dyson folded the doors open. One side stuck. Dyson jerked on it and the door opened the rest of the way. Inside, tightly fitted, were four U-Haul moving boxes. It had been one of the boxes against the folding door that had caused it to stick.

Gesturing with both hands toward the boxes, Dyson turned to Sal. Neither man spoke. Sal walked toward the closet.

Sixty Four

The Advil PM that she had taken was not working. Her husband was sound asleep next to her without any aid, but Carol Fletcher was still wide awake. After lying there in bed – numb and without movement – for over an hour, she got up as quietly as possible and went downstairs.

With a glass of skim milk warmed in the microwave, she sat at the kitchen table. Slowly moving her gaze around the room, she looked at the appliances, at pots hanging on a rack, plants near the window over the sink, a calendar showing an early morning photograph of a long pier on one of the lakes. She went to the calendar and read the text beneath the photo. 'At the start of June, the sun rises in the constellation of Taurus; at the end of June, the sun rises in the constellation of Gemini.'

Carol was a Taurus. Geri was a Libra. There, the first time she caught herself thinking of 'Geri was', *not* 'Geri is.'

Why no call from Geri's husband, Richard? Had the police already been in touch with him? Was he back there in Massachusetts? Carol replayed the questions that she'd gone over with her husband a few hours earlier. When she'd told him about the police and the possibility that Geri's body had been found on a beach on Cape Cod, he'd hugged her and tried to comfort her. Told her there was nothing anyone could do until they got some official word.

None of it made sense.

She went back to the table and sat, taking another sip of the milk. She folded her arms on the table and put her head down. Closing her eyes, she tried again to hear Geri's voice, tried to replay the phone conversation from nearly a month ago, the last time they had spoken.

'We'll get through it' Geri had told her.

After moving the boxes from the bedroom closet out to the living room and next to the front door, Sal and Dyson were standing two feet apart. Sal checked his watch.

"Five minutes," he said.

"Why don't you give him a call now?" Dyson asked. Sal looked at him.

"1:30. Thirty minutes. That's what we agreed on, *that* is when I will call."

"I'm going to pack up some personal things," Dyson said, turning toward the hall.

"Make it fast. When they show up, we're gone. No fucking around."

Dyson went to another bedroom opposite the room where the boxes had been stored. Sal went to a bathroom at the end of the hall.

Now back at the Penske rental van, Donnie and Nick were preparing to leave. Inside the cab of the truck, Nick made a rolling motion with his left hand.

"Let's go. But take your time," he said.

Donnie turned the key, checked both outside mirrors, slipped the truck into gear and pulled away from the hotel. Even though there was no other traffic visible, not a car moving anywhere, Donnie put on the turn indicator before moving into the street.

Coming off the exit to Hopkinton they passed only two other cars, both going the other way toward the highway. Donnie had geared down and was travelling at 20 mph.

"Pull in up there, just past that school and the tennis courts," Nick said. He looked at his watch; 1:25.

"He'll be calling in a few minutes."

It was a repeat broadcast from earlier in the spring, edited highlights from Part Two of Johann Sebastian Bach's *St. Matthew Passion*.

Beautiful voices, full choir and soloists.

The call interrupted the performance. The driver of the Chevy Malibu lowered the volume and answered his phone.

"Your company is on the way. Maybe twenty minutes. If the BMW *leaves*, let him go. Hopkinton PD will pull him over before he gets to 495," the man at the other end said.

"As you wish. Just happy to be here, friend," the driver replied. He waited until he knew the call had ended, placed his phone back on the seat and bumped up the volume on the radio just enough.

1:30 AM, Sal placed the call to Nick. Dyson had not yet returned from the bedroom.

"We're set. Boxes ready to go," Sal said.

"No one else in the neighborhood?" Nick asked.

"We saw no one. All quiet."

"On our way," Nick said, nodding to Donnie.

The van pulled back out onto Hayden Rowe Street. The barely audible GPS voice from Donnie's phone indicating, "Turn right, onto West End Circle in one-thousand feet."

Unknown to Donnie and Nick, one street *beyond* that right turn – at the corner of Chestnut Street – a Hopkinton Police patrol car was backed in at an angle that gave a clear view of West End Circle. Only one way in and the same way out. Before the taillights of the cargo van were out of sight, its arrival was being reported.

Dyson carried a red and black duffel with a shoulder strap. It looked heavy, bulging at the sides. He moved his right shoulder around and pulled on the strap with both hands causing the bag to shift upward.

"I'm going to put this in the car," Dyson said. Sal held his arm out.

"Wait. They're on the way. Maybe put that in with the boxes, don't you think?"

Dyson wasn't sure of the implication.

"It's just clothes. And a couple pair of shoes. A few personal things," Dyson said.

"Wait," Sal repeated.

Dyson lowered the duffel and placed it on the floor next to the boxes of cash.

Sixty Five

The van slowed at 5406, stopping before backing into the driveway. Just over a hundred feet away, in the dark on the opposite side of the street, the driver in the Chevy Malibu hit the power button turning off the radio. He was on his phone immediately.

When the van stopped, both doors had opened. Two men got out, walked to the front door of the house and went inside. The door closed behind them.

Sal was leaning against the wall, Dyson was seated on a wicker bench next to the front door. Neither man spoke when Nick and Donnie came inside.

Nick looked at the boxes, then turned to look at Sal, who nodded at him. Dyson got up from the bench. Donnie stood behind Nick and said nothing.

"Let's load it up," Nick said.

As he had been not a half an hour earlier, Sal was on one side of a box carrying it out to the van, only instead of

Dyson as his helper, Donnie was on the other side lifting.

Four trips, four boxes and it did not take five minutes.

"What's this?" Nick said, pointing at the duffel.

"Clothes, shoes, my stuff," Dyson said. Nick stared at the bag.

"I can put it in the trunk with my other bag," Dyson said.

"OK. Get with it." Nick watched him heft the duffel, then followed him to the BMW. Sal and Donnie stood at the back of the truck, both rear doors still open. Nick looked inside.

"You're going to strap all of them?" Nick said, turning to Donnie but pointing at the boxes.

"Yes," Donnie said, stepping in front of Nick and up into the van. He shoved the larger boxes with his knees and wrestled them so that they were next to the banker's boxes, all of the weight at the front of the van behind the cab. On the floor were a half-dozen orange cargo straps. Donnie picked up a strap and began securing the load.

The Hopkinton patrol cruiser followed the others - two unmarked FBI units, blue lights flashing in their grill, on the dashboards and in the rear windows as well. Then a Massachusetts State Police blue and gray Ford Explorer. All four vehicles arrived at 5406 West End Circle at 1:42 AM.

Car doors opening, four men with weapons drawn were in the driveway blocking both the BMW and the yellow

Penske truck. One young State Trooper and the Detective Lieutenant riding with him bolted from the Ford, hands prepared to draw weapons. One of the FBI agents had his badge raised in the air with one hand and his gun pointing with the other.

"FBI," he shouted, the gun aimed at the men next to the truck. "Put your hands in the air. Do it *now*!"

Nick very slowly raised his hands, Sal followed. Dyson stretched his arms as though he was trying to do an imaginary pull-up. Just as another agent approached the back of the van, Donnie came out with his hands raised.

"Back away!" the agent holding the badge shouted. He flipped the case closed and put it in his back pocket, then stepped closer to the four men.

"Over here. Away from the truck," he motioned with the gun. The four men moved slowly to the lawn.

"On your knees. Right now! Hands behind your head." They did as instructed. The other agents and the two state policemen formed a circle around the men. The Hopkinton cop was out of his car, door open and standing at the edge of the driveway.

A little farther up the street, the Chevy Malibu driver got out, stretched, elbows extended like a bird's wings. He twisted from side to side, rotated his hips, then bent down to touch his toes. He held that position for five seconds, stood up slowly, looked at his watch and yawned.

Across the street from 5406, an outside light above a garage came on and the garage door began opening.

Turning the corner and coming down West End Circle was a WCVB5 TV News van. This sleepy neighborhood was about to wake up earlier than usual.

Sixty Six

Saying that Friday, June 2nd was a 'big' local news day in Massachusetts was to sell it short. Print, blogs, radio, TV – even Public Access channels, community listservs and social media – *all* were going at it, offering some take on the top stories.

Before the day ended, it would be the Hopkinton story that created most of the buzz: **Feds Find $20 Million Inside Rental Truck**.

Other stories getting attention: **Sox Streak Ends At 6 – Celtics Look To 2018 – Bruins Upbeat On Draft – Goddell Still On To Attend Pats Season Opener.**

Receiving little attention was a story of the tentative identification of a body found a week earlier.

SANDWICH, MA (AP) – Cape & Islands District Attorney Martin O'Connell announced the preliminary identification of the body discovered near Town Neck

Beach in Sandwich on May 26th. In a written statement, the district attorney said the body appears to be that of a Michigan woman. The Sandwich Police Department, working with O'Connell's staff and Massachusetts State Police detectives, with assistance from police in Michigan, have obtained photographs of the woman and are currently in the process of contacting relatives and others to make a positive ID. The woman's name has not been released.

Sandwich Police Chief Peter Whalen had no additional comments on how the woman's body had gotten to Massachusetts. Whalen referred all questions related to the investigation to O'Connell's office.

Sal Hurley was ripped. In all the years of inching his way up the ladder in the Detroit Metro area, not *once* had he had even a 'brush' with law enforcement agencies.

Reflecting on his strategic cultivation of 'The Safari Boys' and being in their good graces, not to mention all the assignments and a boatload of money he had been able to dock, he now found himself being pulled into what appeared to be a fucking serious investigation. Sal could not pretend to be completely surprised, but he certainly was pissed. And maybe a little frightened.

Since the middle of the night gathering on the front lawn of the house in Hopkinton, of the four men being detained by the FBI, it looked as though Sal was ranked at number three. At least that's what he told himself. He surmised that the front end of the questioning was being focused on Nick and Dyson, not Donnie. The four had been separated as soon as they had arrived in Boston.

Sal knew that as soon as he heard his first question, perhaps any minute, regardless of what the question might be, he would ask to call his attorney.

Donnie Richards was not particularly worried about what the feds might have on Dyson and his geek buddies. Nor did he particularly care about Nick and his connection to Dyson's uncle. He'd never laid eyes on this 'Big Joe' character.

Being able to show that he had been hired to drive a truck and had had nothing to do with this particular cargo, Donnie was comfortable with that. He would claim that he had no idea of the contents of the banker's boxes and the U Haul moving cartons.

Back home in Detroit, Donnie had saved years of documentation that would confirm his self-employment history as that of one who provided transportation and courier services. None of the considerably more lucrative, and not documented 'off the record' trips, would be an issue. Those came from Sal. And Donnie firmly believed that Sal would never give him up.

But there *were* some photos on his phone.

Idling away time waiting to be questioned, Donnie occupied his mind with a trivia game that he'd created on one of his long road trips a few years earlier. The game had been inspired by the Jefferson Starship song, *We Built This City*. As he drove through cities, he would dredge up all the different names he'd ever heard for that particular city.

Detroit was easy, he knew all of the nicknames. The Motor City; Hockeytown; Motown; Hitsville, USA; and more recently, America's Comeback City. Pittsburgh was his favorite, only 60 miles south of where he grew up, the city with radio station signals beaming into northeastern Ohio. Today, millennials called it Blitzburgh, or just the 'Burgh. In the long ago old days, it was City of Bridges, or City of Champions. But most widely recognized, going back to right after the Civil War was the name The Steel City.

This trip, that found him now in a federal holding facility at Fort Devens, had been his first real visit to Boston, the previous stop at the airport excluded. He was trying to spin up the names he knew about: The Hub; Beantown; and The Cradle of Liberty. Then there were two names that some of the sports talking heads on radio often used; Titletown, and also City of Champions.

Donnie stood up and walked to the locked door of the room where he was being held.

"Come on, guys, can we get on with this?" he said to himself. "Give me a little liberty here, huh?"

Sixty Seven

Dyson Manetas was easily motivated to cooperate with investigators. The confirmation of his earlier suspicion that *someone* had been watching his home came almost as a relief.

More than once in recent weeks he had truly believed that people he didn't know, most likely from Brazil, were going to show up at his door the middle of the night. The fear had driven him from his home in Hopkinton to his friend's apartment in the city.

How many others might be involved, in the US and elsewhere, and the names of Whiz Brain's backers in São Paulo - that was information Dyson did not have. He was simply one a few pawns who were being used to hustle US investments and, later, to find gullible customers.

The fact that a sizeable chunk of *PhoneDat Global's* slush funds happened to be stored at his home, he could and very gladly *would* explain to authorities when he got the first opportunity. Dyson thought of himself as a really smart guy. He would jump at a chance to tell his story and cut a deal.

Terrorism and drugs, Dyson knew, were 'top of the mind' for most authorities in the US. Didn't matter if the investigation was being run by the FBI, DEA, ICE or the IRS. They all worked together when it came to the various forms of money laundering and the all too frequent hiding and manipulation of other assets.

Was the money hidden in his house? Yes. Did he follow orders and act on behalf of others who devised the scam? Yes. Did he actively engage in attempts to transfer funds *out* of the US? No. He rehearsed the questions in his mind and tried to bolster his self-confidence. He was ready to show his willingness to cooperate.

One remaining *really big* challenge, Dyson knew, was keeping his uncle Joe out of it. He hadn't quite worked out how he could do that. Perhaps he'd get lucky and that hurdle would be left for Nick to clear.

From the first minute they'd been invited to get on their knees and place their hands behind their heads, it had been fairly obvious that the leader of this little squad of late-night minglers was the one identifying himself as Nick Orologas.

The FBI and the Mass State Police had expected to get Manetas. His car twice had been seen in the neighborhood, as well as being spotted in a parking garage downtown.

Officials had reason to believe that Manetas would provide information that would help in the PDG investigation. They also happened to believe that much of that information was stored at his home on West End Circle.

The $20 million though, *that* was a surprise.

Any connection with this Orologas, investigators now reasoned, was very likely to take them down an avenue previously unknown when the scam first broke. Already, in three major US cities – Atlanta, Dallas and Boston – bank accounts, automobiles, boats and real estate connected to men already charged in the scandal had been seized by authorities.

"I will not answer any questions without my attorney present," Nick said. "Tipota."

The feds were about to learn that Nick's attorney was in Detroit. How soon he would be here with his client in Boston was yet to be determined.

And how quickly any of these men were placed 'under arrest' would depend. This surprising jerk forward in the investigation were bound to shake things up. New names were likely to come into play, more specificity on names already in the mix – both in the US and abroad - as well as some tedious work pulling together a chronology of events that had occurred just here in Massachusetts.

One expanding chart would document a lengthy cast of scammers, along with all of their witting and unwitting associates at *PhoneDat Global*. On the victim side of the ledger there was this ever-growing international list of names of the thousands of individuals who had been duped over an extended period of years.

Journalists in several countries were about to jump on the story. Maybe.

Had this all been broadcast on TV as a reality show, or some ongoing series about to have its season finale, many viewers would have placed their money on Dyson as the one to blow it all up.

Sixty Eight

Late Friday afternoon, I got a phone call from Chief Peter Whalen. He was thoughtful enough to let me in on the update of what was happening with the investigation and to again thank me for the hunch on the white jumpsuit.

"It's likely we would have gotten there, eventually," he said. "The DA's office would have tracked down where it was manufactured, maybe where it was purchased. But your observation gave us a good start. Saved some time."

"You never really know," I replied. "You see stuff, you remember things. Glad this actually led somewhere."

"Yeah," he said.

"Nothing more on the van?"

"Not yet. Description and photo is all over the place. Could take a while. We'll see."

"So, I'm guessing that falls to the state police. DMV?" I said. "Not really something for the DA's office."

"Right. CPAC, the state police, has a network. It helps with video being more common just about everywhere."

"Has O'Connell put out the word to the media yet, on the woman being from Michigan?"

"Yes. Issued a statement earlier this morning," Whalen said. "AP ran with it already."

"Didn't hold a press conference?"

"Too soon. That'll happen after the official ID."

"Bet his phone's been busy since the AP story," I said.

"And mine. I'm sending all of the calls to his office. By the way, O'Connell wanted me to tell him again about how we got onto the balloon angle. Said that he would like to thank you personally."

"I don't vote down here, no sweat," I said.

"Nah, he really means it. He started out as a cop, you know?"

"In fact, I do know. Ragsdale and I talked about it."

"I'm going to his office in the morning. Let me check it out. Maybe you could stop in for just a minute. You're still going to be around, not headed back yet?"

"Going home tomorrow afternoon," I said. "Sure."

The Ragsdale's were doing the family routine for the day, as in going over to visit the John F. Kennedy Museum in Hyannis with Becky's brother and sister-in-law.

Rocco and I headed for a new spot: Lighthouse Beach in Chatham. Part of the walk took us down toward the Monomoy National Wildlife Refuge. Lovely weather, lots of shore birds, not too many people, and maybe the first time

322

in two weeks when I was beginning to feel relaxed. The conversations with Bonnie still popped up, just not quite as intense as previously. More of the warm memories rather than personal angst.

A lobster roll and large fries to go from the Chatham Pier Fish Market, some beer from a store on the way back and we would have dinner at the bunk house. The Sox were playing in Baltimore and I had the game on the radio. I turned off my phone and stretched out to read *What's the Story?* by Sydney Lea.

Police in Michigan had located Richard 'Dick' Stuart,

husband of the woman whose body had been discovered in Massachusetts.

Following preliminary questioning, Stuart agreed to give police items from their home that would likely provide both finger prints and DNA. An hour later, he was on the phone and it was clear that the man was beginning to dissolve. All on his own, he went to police headquarters, broke down emotionally minutes after he arrived there and rambled through a story of regret. And a confession.

What Stuart told the police was a plausible tale of a disintegrating marriage, alcoholism, gambling debts and very bad judgement on his part. After months of planning, he had arranged to have his wife murdered, her body removed from a motel outside Detroit and disposed of on Cape Cod.

Murdered by whom was not yet revealed, other than Stuart's offhand reference to "some guys who handle that kind of thing."

When asked about the body being transported to such a distant locale, Stuart went into a sob story of fights that he had had with his wife. He'd considered a town in upstate New York, in the Finger Lakes region, but had settled on one of two towns on Cape Cod. *Why* had yet to be disclosed. And throughout the erratic and marginally coherent statement, Stuart also made repeated references to a belief that the proceeds from his wife's life insurance would have helped him set his life straight.

With tears that appeared to be genuine, he ended the story by saying, "She never really loved me. It was all a big act. She married me for status."

The police would write up this strange confession as they had interpreted it. Just as soon as Stuart signed it, the process of shifting part of the investigation to the Michigan State Police could begin. The phone calls from Michigan *reporters* would commence in short order.

Detective Sergeant Murtaugh back at the Sandwich PD relayed the information about Stuart. He told Whalen the little that he'd been given by Michigan police and that a signed confession was anticipated shortly.

Whalen passed it along to O'Connell. They knew that before any formal charges were made, municipal and state police both in Michigan and here in Massachusetts would be involved, possibly the FBI if there was an indication that the woman had been kidnapped and transported across state lines before she was murdered.

Whalen speculated about just how soon a chunk of the investigation might shift to Michigan.

"I'm OK with that," O'Connell said. "Not like we don't have anything else to do, right?"

He was also OK with Whalen inviting the Vermont guy to come by his office on Saturday morning.

When Carol Fletcher first heard the news about Dick Stuart's confession, how he had arranged for the murder of his wife Geri, her sadness momentarily passed through disbelief before landing on anger.

"That no good son-of-a-bitch," she said, voice dripping with disgust. On the phone with her ex-husband back in Massachusetts, she quickly added, "I never liked him. But once they got married, I wouldn't tell Geri that."

The two reminisced about ballooning days, when Geri had first joined them and happier times gone by. They agreed to talk again when they knew of plans for a service for Geri.

The body was still at the Medical Examiner's lab on Joint Base Cape Cod. Pending confirmation from both the finger prints and the DNA test, the ME could then make her final report.

The search for the closest living blood relatives of Geri Stuart was underway. Police had been told by Fletcher, and had tentatively confirmed with Richard Stuart, that she had family living in northwestern Connecticut near the Mass border.

No matter the outcome of the investigation, or who did what time in prison, and where, one less unidentified victim would show up on the *NamUs* website.

Sixty Nine

Ragsdale and I met Peter Whalen at the DA's office in Barnstable at 9:30 on Saturday morning. It was a short visit, informal and to the point. O'Connell, in fact, did seem like a guy who 'really meant it.'

After a few minutes of chit chat, as Louie often calls it, we were outa there and on our way for one final breakfast at Diner Shore. Whalen was going to join us.

The family crew was in full force when we got there; Willie, cleaning up plates and mugs from the counter, with both grandsons working the booths and the kitchen. We got a booth. I looked around for my crowd assessment and counted nine other customers. Whalen came through the door, stopped to talk with Willie for a minute, then joined us, smiling and shaking his head when he sat down.

"It's never boring with him," Whalen said, with a thumb gesture back toward Willie.

"You live out here, so you must have a pretty fair perspective on the locals. Aren't you *surprised* that he doesn't piss off a few people?" I asked.

"Oh, he certainly does that. Some of the thin-skinned types who don't know how to take him and get all offended by one of his blasts," Whalen said, quickly perusing the menu before he continued. "But Willie is a decent guy. He's done a lot for the community, some things not many know about. Most people around here take him with a grain of salt. If the chips were down, there are a bunch of people who would do just about anything for him."

"I knew an old-timer in Vermont a little like him," I said. "He was also a World War II vet. Usually not the first guy to speak, but when he did, he was blunt, *not* politically correct. And usually pretty amusing," I added.

We ordered breakfast from twin grandson Brandon, aka Phil, or Don? Whalen went with the corned beef hash, Louie ordered blueberry pancakes and I decided to eat enough for the day by asking for a double order of French toast and a side of bacon.

Five of the nine other customers had finished eating and were paying their tab and leaving. As soon as Willie had cashed them out, he came to our booth, bumped Whalen's shoulder with his hip, then sat next to him.

"Nice of you to join us," Whalen said. I noticed that Willie had a tattoo of an anchor over the letters USN on his left forearm.

"Just want to be sure you're being nice to these boys," Willie said. "They don't have any places like this up there in the hills, you know."

"I'm sure not," Whalen replied.

"I've been reading about that body you found," Willie said. "I think you oughta be looking at Comey and Giuliani. That's the kind of crap they'd get up to."

I nearly choked on my coffee. Whalen was trying to suppress a smile as Louie gave me the eye roll and his smirk.

"Comey and Giuliani, huh?" Whalen said.

"You know. The two turds who were selling the illegal fish last year. Their picture was in all the papers." Whalen nodded.

"I think you look a little closer, they're doing more than selling bad fish."

"A couple of 'frequent flyers' who finally got nailed for peddling illegal catch," Whalen said to Louie and me. "Both have had many previous encounters with law enforcement up and down the Cape."

"That's not really their names," Willie said. "Just what I call 'em."

"Comey. And Giuliani. *Why* would you tag them with *those* particular nicknames?" Whalen asked.

Willie rubbed the stubble on his left cheek, then made a show of scratching his ear for a few seconds.

"Let me try the short version. I'll go slow," Willie said, "so you can keep up.

"You will remember that we had an election last year and just about everybody was buzzing about it for months and months." Whalen nodded, keeping his grin in check. Willie went on.

"Now, even young squirts like you boys know that politics can be a dirty, *nasty* business. Been going on for a long time. Lots of mud. More than a few crooks in both parties, right?" Willie looked at me, then at Louie, who gave him a nod, so he rambled on.

"But when one party's major domo hack, *himself* a grandstanding, self-promoter, along with some rogue FBI buddies, peddles a dory full of whale shit to a federal appointee, *in the Justice Department*, a man not elected by *anyone*, and then *that* shitbird starts posturing, trying to cover his ass, interfering with a campaign just ten days before the election," Willie paused for a breath, then concluded with, "that kind of spineless, chickenshit, self-serving conduct would get your ass thrown in the brig back in my day. For a *long* time. And it sure as hell isn't what most people think this country is about."

We were all silent for a minute, not sure if Willie had more. Then Whalen put a hand on his shoulder. "Could you maybe tell us how you really feel?" Willie shook his head and slowly rose from the booth.

"No sympathy from me when he got fired. No matter what kind of dirt he might have on The Trumpy," he said, laughing. "FBI Director, my ass. He could join Goodell now as a Director of Clowns."

We watched as Willie started to shuffle back toward the kitchen. He stopped, looked back at us, then added, "I apologize. I didn't mean to cast any aspersions on a noble profession. I'm sure there are some good clowns out there, still working, who are really honorable.

"And that egomaniac nitwit there in the White House is gonna need more than some half-assed neckties made in China to land a good lawyer,' Willie concluded, shaking his head as he disappeared into the kitchen.

At 11:15 AM we were in the lot outside Diner Shore and Whalen was getting ready to leave. We talked for another minute, shook hands and agreed to check in the next time we were on the Cape.

"I'll put you onto a guy up the street from me. He can take you clamming," Whalen said.

"I'd love to," I said.

"Stay safe, Chief" Louie said, giving him an informal salute.

We walked to my car and Louie reached through the window to scratch Rocco under the chin. Rocco played the 'Mister Mellow' bit, then got a whiff of the bacon I'd wrapped in napkin. He stuck his head out and I gave him the bacon.

'So, you're leaving now?" Louie asked, looking at everything packed into the back of my car.

"Yeah. Take my time. I should get home by 4 o'clock."

"Saturday afternoon. Traffic won't be too bad going through Boston."

"You're leaving tomorrow?" I already knew that was the plan they had discussed.

"We're checking out of the cottage tomorrow. May try to go to Martha's Vineyard for a night or two," he said.

"When did that plan get hatched?"

Louie did a quick flick with his fingers of his neatly trimmed beard before answering. "John's idea. He was there a long time ago. Becky and I have never been there. She's checking on places to stay. May have it all set when I get back."

"Are you gonna fish some more?" I said.

He looked at his watch. "Low tide at 2:03. Yeah, I'll go out for a couple of hours."

"OK. Thanks for suggesting the trip," I said. He held his hand out for a shake and gave me a shoulder grip.

"You're all right?"

"I'm fine. This really did help. I'm getting my head squared away."

He scratched Rocco's ears one more time.

"Becky always thought that you were a blockhead." He fist bumped the center of my chest, turned and walked to his truck.

We drove west, crossed the Sagamore Bridge 20 minutes later and headed north.

Seventy

Back in Vermont the following day, I did something that I rarely do; I went to church. It was a regular Sunday morning service at Bonnie's old church, her father in the pulpit. Hughie didn't seem surprised to see me.

A bit self-conscious and pretty sure that this was *not* the beginning of a new habit, nonetheless I was glad to be there. It had been two weeks since the memorial service in this very same building.

Reverend Hugh Clarkson Mackin began his sermon.

"Sunday, June 4th, the one-hundred-fifty-fifth day of the year. That leaves two-hundred and ten days for 2017, days when good and bad acts will occur all over the world. Thirty more weeks when some will go to prison. And some who perhaps *should* go, will not.

"More wars, more hunger and disease, more natural disasters, some in places that we've never heard of. Many wealthy people are likely to become *richer* in the weeks ahead. Many poor people? Not so much.

"Another seven months remaining in this year, not unlike preceding years and those ahead, long after many of us are gone. People of all ages will die, every day, every hour. Their absence will cause sadness. In many instances, regret. And for most of those left behind, extended periods of heartache and grief."

Hughie paused, swallowed, then went on.

"How many different people, in different places and at different times, have uttered the words, 'Life is a gift'?"

Almost everyone in the congregation was silent, save for a couple of kids squirming, and at least one deep sigh from someone seated behind me. We watched as Reverend Mackin slowly took in all the parishioners in attendance.

He walked away from the pulpit, stood for a few seconds gazing at length through a window at the bright day outside, then came back to his spot and smiled before he continued.

"As we are fortunate to have many young people in our community, not all of them here today, I might add," he said, which got some laughter, "I always find that no matter how badly my day is going and no matter how discouraged I become, that can change in an *instant*, when I look at the face of one of these children." He opened his arms, extending them out to both sides of the nave.

"So, with our hymns, and all of our prayers, and the scripture reading this morning, and the lessons our little ones had with Miss Courtney in the Sunday School class, I want to share some good fortune with all of you.

"This may be the shortest sermon that I have ever given." His smile was broader.

"Many of you know that I am not a very good singer." Some chuckles from the pews. "But I *try*." There was more laughter. "I have asked for some help here this morning. And just so you know," he placed both hands to his mouth to pretend that he was whispering, "we have practiced. Young Linda Lou, would you please come up?"

A girl of nine or ten, who had been seated with her parents, went up front to join Reverend Mackin. He took her by the hand. They stepped in front of the pulpit and he looked down at the girl, then nodded.

A capella, they began.

"Some bright morning when this life is over, I'll fly away."

Now it was just the little girl. *"To that home on God's celestial shore, I'll fly away."*

"Please join us. Turn to page 527," Hughie said. The congregation took up their hymnals, a woman at the piano began playing.

Four minutes later, when the song ended, I heard and saw a mix of tears and laughter. Hughie hugged the young girl, kissed the top of her head and she went back to join her parents. He went back to the pulpit.

"Let us conclude this morning's service with a prayer." He waited until all heads were bowed and most eyes were closed.

"Life is a gift. Our father, we ask for your guidance, your blessings and your everlasting and unconditional love. Now and forever. Amen."

AUTHOR'S NOTE: all 'media reports' and the wording of 'Press Releases' in this story were created by me and <u>not</u> attributable to the sources identified with same.

More info about this book and the New England Mystery series on the following pages.

Acknowledgements:

- *Here Comes the Sun* – The Beatles (9/69 – Apple)
- *Night Moves* – Bob Seger & The Silver Bullet Band
                                        (12/76 – Capitol)
- *Wake Up Little Susie* (9/57) – *Bird Dog* (4/58) –
  Cathy's Clown (4/60) – The Everly Brothers (Cadence)
- *Gimme Some Lovin* – The Spencer Davis Group (10/66 -
  Fontana)   Traffic (10/71 – United Artists)   The Blues
  Brothers (5/80 – Atlantic)
- *I'm So Lonesome I Could Cry* – Hank Williams (11/49 –
                                                MGM)
- *Sunshine Superman* – Donovan (7/66 – Epic)
- *Walking Shadows* – Joshua Redman (5/13 – Nonesuch)
- *Long Train Runnin* – The Doobie Brothers (4/73 – Warner)
  and *Listen To The Music* (9/72 – Warner)
- *Suite: Judy Blue Eyes* – Crosby, Stills & Nash (9/69 –
                                                Atlantic)
- *Proud Mary* – Creedence Clearwater Revival (1/69 – Fantasy)
- *We Built This City* – Starship (8/85 – Grunt)
- *I'll Fly Away* – Alfred E. Brumley (1929 Hymn)

Thank you for the music.

- Weather Underground – www.wundereground.com
- Woods Hole Oceanographic Institution – www.whoi.edu
- Wikimapia – www.wikimapia.org
- NamUs – www.identifyus.org
- AP (*The Associated Press*) – www.ap.org
- AFP (*Agence France Presse*) – www.afp.com
- WIRED – www.wired.com (see Andy Greenberg's article '*How
  Hackers Hijacked a Bank's Entire Online Operation*' 4/4/17)
- *2016 – The Best American Science and Nature Writing*
                        (Houghton Mifflin Harcourt 2016)
- *WHAT's The STORY?* – Sydney Lea
                        (*Green Writers Press* 2015)

ABOUT THE AUTHOR

The author is an award winning former broadcaster living in Vermont. He began his radio career as a news reporter covering both municipal and state government meetings, political campaigns, everyday community events and the incidents which frequently made the lead story of the day.

Many characters, conversations and real life experiences have inspired much of what you read in these books, but *the stories are fiction*.

www.nemysteries.com

Next up in the New England Mystery series:

- *A Rainy Weekend in RHODE ISLAND*
  (Fall 2018)

Preview on the next page.

Excerpts from

A Rainy Weekend in RHODE ISLAND –

"Maybe," the man said. "On average, they get less than four inches of total precipitation here in October."

About to take a seat at the bar and he was getting up to leave, I had asked him if he thought the downpour would let up anytime soon. Idle chatter about the weather, even though practically everyone had a smartphone app that could tell you the precise minute when the rain would stop.

Shrugging his shoulders, he pulled the zipper up to the collar of his jacket, started to head for the door, then stopped. He turned back and gestured at me with his travel umbrella.

"Of course, you could just hunker down right here and ask Pauly there to make up a whole pitcher of Dark 'n Stormys," he said, tipping the umbrella at the man behind the bar who was fiddling with an electric coffee maker.

"Good idea," I said. "Though I might have to call a cab to get back to my hotel."

The man smiled at me, nodded, then turned and went out into the rain.

I pulled my rain slicker off, shook it and hung it on the back of the bar stool.

"Be with you in just a second," the bartender said.

"Take your time. I'm OK," I said.

According to one eyewitness, a man with an umbrella had been walking west and had turned onto Whitaker Street. A couple of seconds later, the witness said, "Pop, pop. Sounded like firecrackers."

The reliability of the 'eyewitness' could be an issue. Known to many as a harmless old wino who spent most of his time walking the streets in this section of downtown Providence, Billy 'Quick Whistle' Woodson was also well-known to the city police.

The body being loaded into the emergency vehicle would come in as the eleventh homicide of the year. With another two months plus on the calendar, there was a possibility that the year-end total could follow a recent pattern of being *below* the five year average.

The official code 09A – Murder and Nonnegligent Manslaughter – had a weighted annual average of 16. But the stats were down now, by nearly a third, over the high of 20 recorded in 2014.

Columbus Day Weekend and we had come to check out the Rhode Island Broadcast Pioneers exhibit of classic old radios, as well as some of the restaurants.

I looked down at my phone to see if Ragsdale had

sent a text. Nope.

"What can I get you?" the bartender asked. He was tall, thin, brown hair brushed straight back, high forehead. Maybe sixty years old, but looked younger.

I thought for a second about the Dark 'n Stormy, but instead ordered a pint of Leaning Chimney Porter. A bit early in the season for a dark beer, but I liked the name and the brief description on the chalkboard behind the bar.

The driver's license identified the victim as one Clifton A. Torres of Parsippany, New Jersey, DOB 3-10-53. The license photo made the man look heavier than he now appeared there on the gurney.

The EMT had said the man had two gunshot wounds, both from the back; one below his left shoulder and another at the base of the skull.

A Rainy Weekend in RHODE ISLAND – book six in the New England Mystery series – to be published in the fall of 2018.

Visit the website – www.nemysteries.com

CONTACT:

threeriversgrouppvt@gmail.com